A Garland Series

The
Flowering of the Novel

Representative Mid-Eighteenth Century Fiction
1740-1775

A Collection of 121 Titles

A Full and Particular Account
of the Life and
Transactions of Roger Johnson

Anonymous

The Life and Adventures
of Gilbert Langley

Anonymous

A True and Impartial History
of the Life of Somebody

Anonymous

An Apology for the Life of
Mrs. Shamela Andrews

Henry Fielding

Garland Publishing, Inc., New York & London

1975

Copyright © 1975

by Garland Publishing, Inc.

All Rights Reserved

Library of Congress Cataloging in Publication Data
Main entry under title:

A Full and particular account of the life and transactions of Roger Johnson.

    (The Flowering of the novel)
    Reprint of 4 works: the 1st originally printed in
1740 for C. Cotbett, London; the 2d originally printed
in 1740 for and sold by J. Applebee, London; the 3d
originally printed in 1740 for R. Higgins, London; and
the 4th originally printed in 1741 for A. Dodd, London.
    1. English fiction--18th century. I. Series.
PZ1.F957 [PR1297]   823'.5   74-31332
ISBN 0-8240-1102-3

Printed in the United States of America

LIFE AND TRANSACTIONS
OF
ROGER JOHNSON

Bibliographical note:

this copy has been made from the facsimile in the Library of the University of Illinois (B.J686f.facsim) of the original in the British Museum

A FULL and PARTICULAR.

ACCOUNT

OF THE

Life and Notorious Transactions

O F

ROGER JOHNSON,

C O N T A I N I N G,

I. His early Inclination to
all Manner of Villanies,
the roguish Tricks he
play'd even while a Boy.
II. His getting acquaint-
ed with a Gang of Thieves
Pickpockets, &c. that at
that Time infested the
Playhouses, &c. his first
meeting with the noted
Mrs. *Jolly*, and cohabi-
ting with her.
III. His dressing himself
in the Habit of a *Parson*,
and the several Pranks he
play'd in that Disguise.

IV. His turning Smugler,
and the remarkable Bite
he put upon two Custom
House Officers.
V. His being seiz'd and
committed to *Newgate*;
his Behaviour there, and
a particular Account of
his Escape from thence
with *Fisher*.
VI. His being apprehend-
ed a second Time; His
Discharge from thence,
and living *honestly* as a
Pawnbroker to the Time
of his Death, *Aug.* 22.

L O N D O N:

Printed for C. CORBETT, Bookseller and Publisher,
at *Addison's* Head in *Fleetstreet*. MDCCXL.

(Price Six Pence.)

THE
LIFE
OF
ROGER JOHNSON.

 ATURAL Curiosity incites in us a Desire of enquiring into the Lives and Actions of those who have, in any Shape, render'd themselves famous or infamous in the World: When a JONATHAN WILD, or a MACRAY, meet the just Reward of their Villanies, tho' we approve of their Punishment, and abhor their Crimes, yet, at the same Time, it is a secret Satisfaction to hear an Account, how such Men have perpetrated those Villanies, and gull'd the Unwary, as it may, in some Measure, enable us to be upon our Guard, if any such Attempt should be made upon us.

A 2   As

As no one hath been more conspicuous in the World, for a long Series of Tricks and Impoftors, tho', notwithstanding that, he had the Luck to escape from the End that usually attends a Life so spent; yet, we believe, it will be no unprofitable, or unpleasant Thing to the Reader, to be acquainted with the Methods, which a Man hath taken, to go on successfully in Scenes of the greatest criminal Excess, and capital Offences for near Five and Forty Years together, and yet die in Plenty, and peaceably in his Bed at last, which was the Case of *Roger Johnson*. And this, we hope, will suffice as an Apology for this Relation; and further to evince that the Substance of it is true, we must beg Leave to acquaint the Public, that we had this Account from a Person, who knew him from his Cradle; and who, not only knew several of the Facts to be real, but who has had the Relation of them oftentimes from *Johnson*'s own Mouth, during his Confinement in *Newgate*, and since his Enlargement.

ROGER JOHNSON, was the Son of *William Johnson*, a Taylor, in the Parish of *St Clement's Danes*. His Father was not in any extraordinary Circumstances; for as he labour'd hard at the Needle for a small Subsistence, his Mother being a good industrious Woman kept a little Stall in *Clare Market*, and there sold Butter and Eggs, and might, in all Probability, have continu'd doing so still, had they not been led away by their unlucky Son *Roger* to their Ruin, as we shall shew hereafter.

Roger's Inclination to Villany discover'd itself in his early Age, before he could well speak plain; but being grown big enough to go to

School,

School, his Parents put him to one Mr. *Stevens,* who kept a School in St. *Clement's Lane.* He had not been there long, before he behav'd in fuch a Manner, that his Mafter declar'd, he would keep him no longer in the School : And, after repeated Trials for his Amendment finding him no better, he abfolutely refus'd to admit him into the School, upon any Account. *Roger* upon this, was taken Home, and clofely confin'd, in Order to fee, if they could do any Thing to reform him, or keep him fome Time till they could find an Opportunity of fending him to Sea ; but *Roger* (tho' he was then very young) found Means of giving his Keepers the Slip, and would run away from them for whole Days and Nights together. His ufual Haunt was in St. *Clement's* Church-Yard, which, at that Time, was a Sort of a Nurfery for all Manner of young Thieves ; and here he imbib'd his firft Principles in that *Art,* in which he was fince fo great a Proficient; for here he met with feveral loofe and diforderly Boys like himfelf, who under Pretence of affembling together to divert themfelves with harmlefs boyifh Games, would get into the more pernicious ones of Huffel Cap, Thimbles and Balls, *&c.*

Roger's natural Bent and Inclination to Mifchief, would not let him be long idle, and being a Lad of a great Spirit, and a good Deal of Cunning, it is not to be wonder'd at if he quickly furpafs'd his Companions. He knew it was cuftomary for the Children to have Half-Pence given them to buy Hot Rolls, or fomething for their Breakfafts, as they went to School on cold Mornings; but *Roger* could not bear, that they fhould be provided for, and he not ; he therefore fet his Wits to work in Order to get it

from

from them ; he provided himself with a little
Stool and a Trencher, and planted himself in
the Corner near the Pump in St. *Clement's Lane,*
and here he lay to catch several who had been his
Schoolfellows, and inveigle them to play at his
Thimbles and Balls till he had cheated them of
all their Money, and he has often declar'd, that
he had taken then as much Pleasure in sending
the Boys hungry to School, without Money as
he hath since in some of his more labour'd Artifices.

But to give a greater Proof of his daring Spirit and enterprizing Genius, even at this Age,
we shall relate the following Story. *Roger* was
weary of preying upon such small Game as Boys,
look'd out for others ; and one Day, being fixed, with his Stool and Trencher, in the Court,
near Doctor *Burgess's* Meeting House, as was
then : He sat some Time without meeting with
any Sport, was at last tir'd with his Situation,
and was going, but he spy'd a Footman coming
down the Court. He was Servant to a noted
Counsellor in *Lincoln's Inn.* His Master had
sent him with Seventeen Pounds to pay off a
Tradesman's Bill, and he like a Fool came
down the Court playing with the Money in his
Hand. *Roger* was tempted with the delicious
Morsel, and tho' he had never made so bold a
Push before, yet he resolv'd at any Rate to be
Partaker of the Cash ; by his artful Insinuations
he drew the Fellow in to play with him, and it
is reasonably to be imagin'd, that the Footman,
seeing one so young, might not expect so much
Cunning from *Roger,* and might be fill'd with
the Hopes of winning the Boy's Money : However *Roger* prov'd too hard for him in the End,
and by the artful Management of the Thimble
and

and Balls blinded the Fellow in ſuch a Manner,
that he got all the Seventeen Pounds from him,
but to ſhew the Generoſity of his Spirit, he gave
the Footman Half a Crown to drink his Health,
and went away rejoicing, leaving him to curſe
his Fortune, and go Home to his Maſter on a
ſleeveleſs Errand. But this Adventure, in the
End, prov'd of ill Conſequence to *Roger*, for he
was ſo fluſh'd with his good Succeſs, that he
could not contain himſelf, or help *flaſhing the
Cole*, as he us'd to call it. *Roger*, at that Time,
had a Brother living, but who died ſome Time
ago : *Roger*, in the Fulneſs of his Heart ſhews
him his Handfull of Money, and offer'd to let
him partake of it. The Brother, who was not
only a little older, but a little honeſter than *Roger*, was ſo far from accepting his Offer, that
he ſuſpecting, in what Manner *Roger* came by
ſo much Money, thought proper to acquaint his
Father and Mother with the Affair, *Roger* was
ſeverely ſcrutiniz'd and call'd upon by his Father
to know, how he got that Money ? *Roger* made
a lame Excuſe, and ſaid he got it of a Boy by
toſſing up, but being of an obſtinate Temper he
would confeſs nothing further, notwithſtanding
his Father us'd all Methods ; and finding good
Uſage ineffectual, after laſhing him heartily, he
bought a ſmall Chain and Lock, and faſten'd
the young Gentleman to the Bed's Poſt, and in
this Condition he remain'd ſome Time, yet he
would not confeſs in what Manner he came by
the Money. After having been thus chain'd a
conſiderable Time, his Father and Mother being
gone both Abroad, and *Roger* impriſon'd thus by
himſelf, he thought now or never was the Time
to contrive his Eſcape. Accordingly, after a
good deal of Trouble he found Means to pick
the

the Lock, and run away. His Father when he came Home was greatly surpriz'd at his being gone, and after a fruitless Search and Enquiry where he was fled to, he, with the utmost Regret, gave him over entirely for lost, and as one abandon'd to all Manner of vicious Courses.

Roger, being now quite got loose from his Friends, got in amongst a Gang of Thieves and Pickpockets that usually lurk'd about the Playhouse Doors and Passages of a Night, and being idling about *Lincoln's Inn Fields*, and gaming all Day, *Roger* lay idle upon their Hands a considerable Time, which they disliking, and the Search being pretty well over from his Friends, he ventur'd to creep out of his Covert, and put himself into Practice; accordingly he took his first Commencement in picking Pockets, &c. about the Playhouses, but he had not been long enter'd, before he became more expert than any of his Companions, and he was grown such an Artist that he was reckon'd the only Lad in *England* for *filing a Lob*, or *nailing a Tilt*, that is, in their cant Language taking a Gentleman's Snuff Box out of his Pocket, or snatching his Sword from his Side: It is needless to enumerate the several Things he got, or the Feats he perform'd, if it was possible to be done, but they were so many that he himself hath often declar'd, that he could not repeat a Hundredth Part of them; it is sufficient to say, that he was reckon'd the most expert of them all at his *Business*, and not only made a *comfortable* Subsistence thereon, but was reckon'd to be worth Money, having such a Reputation among the Professors thereof, but much more the Money he had acquir'd made him agreeable to some of the Fair Sex, who had lifted themselves in
the

the Undertaking, tho' ſetting aſide thoſe Qualifications, *Roger* had a Perſon capable of alluring
Ladies of much ſtricter Virtue than theſe uſually
profeſs, and which afterwards help'd to forward
the uncommon Succeſs he oftentimes met with,
as we ſhall ſhew preſently.

Roger was grown up to that Age, which in
thoſe of a ſoberer Caſt of Life, incites them to
Actions of Gallantry, and the inordinate gratify-
ing of their looſer Paſſions: No Wonder then,
that in one who had no Reſtriction on himſelf,
but who ſacrific'd every Thing to the Bent of
his Inclination, they broke out into greater Sal-
lies of Intemperance than in other People; or
that among ſuch as the Gang *Roger* was then in,
no Diſtinction was made: The Men were wicked, and the Women were lewd; *Roger* had a
handſome Perſon, and a conſiderable Deal of
Money; no Wonder therefore if he was Favourite to ſeveral of them. Amongſt the Reſt,
one *Madam Jolly*, the moſt conſpicuous amongſt
them, ingratiated herſelf into his Favour; ſmall
Ceremonies were requir'd in adjuſting their Affairs, and where Love is upon ſuch Terms as
theirs, their Contracts are eaſily form'd and as
eaſily broke: However, ſhe perſuaded her Huſband (as he then paſs'd for) Mr. *Johnſon*, that
picking Pockets was a little below his Character, and that as now he was capable of appearing
in a more reputable Light, ſhe thought it would
be more to his Character to be a Houſekeeper,
not only that but it might be of Service to the
Gang, by giving them a Sanction upon his Appearance ſometimes. Purſuant to her Advice,
he accordingly took an Houſe of CIVIL RE-
CREATION, in the Hundreds of *Drury*.

B   Both

Both *Johnson* and his *Wife* were so well known
that they did not long want Custom. All the
Ladies of that Order were constantly there, and
they got considerable Profits by their Business,
and they continu'd together for some Time, but
Roger being of a roving Disposition in Love as
well as in all other Affairs of Life, soon grew
uneasy of his new Spouse, and look'd out for
fresh Amours : He was a Man of a good Presence and a facetious Companion as we observ'd
before : Therefore it is not to be suppos'd that
in that Class of Life he could be long without
entering into fresh Amours. He was quite tir'd
of Mrs. *Jolly*, and to make up his Affairs and
part with her, he knew not how, but such an
Ascendancy had his lewd Inclinations got over
him, that notwithstanding all those Obstacles he
was determin'd to pursue his Resolutions.

In the Course of his keeping the Punch House
in *Drury Lane*, he became acquainted with a certain Butcher's Wife in *Clare Market* ; *Roger* behav'd in such Manner that he soon alienated her
Affections from her Husband, and in short she
left the poor Man, and cohabited with Mr.
Johnson, Mrs. *Jolly* was immediately discarded,
and *Roger* now thought himself quite happy in
his new *Wife*. But to shew, that Persons in that
unhappy Station of Life are never free from Un-
easiness, it will not be amiss to relate the following Circumstance.

Notwithstanding Mr. *Johnson*'s having commenc'd Housekeeper, it did not prevent his following his old Practice, for he still could not
forget the Sweets of the Money he got by it,
and he has often declar'd, that it piqu'd him in
some Measure to think, that as he was the greatest Proficient in his Way, he should suffer others
through

through his Indolence to creep in; so that he was continually trying a little to keep his Hand in; but this was attended with ill Consequences, for one certain Night, he had *nail'd a Gentleman of his Tilt*, that is, he had taken his Sword, and *Roger* was so closely pursu'd that he had much ado to make his Escape, but his Ingenuity assisted him, and seeing a Stand of Coaches and near them a Crowd of People gather'd together about a Ballad Singer, he crept under one of the Coaches, and getting in among the People he stood as unconcern'd as one of the Hearers; for he had given the Sword to one of his Companions, whom he always had attending him upon these Occasions; and by this Means he escaped for that Time, but however the Risque he run had made such an Impression on him, that when he began to think with himself how well he was known in that Employment, and that after such a narrow Escape as this, he should be more cautiously watch'd, and a stricter Search than ever made after him, he thought it high Time to look out for another Way of Living.

When a Man once gives himself up to bad Ways, he never can quit them, but flounders on in the Mud still deeper and deeper. And thus was it with *Roger*; but he now began to lay his Schemes more cunningly: He got acquainted with a Set of People, who come from a neighbouring Nation, and who are all *Gentlemen*, notwithstanding they live by Thieving and Tricking all Mankind; for it is reckon'd a particular Ingredient in the Qualification of a Thief, that if he is not actually one, he should at least be acquainted with an IRISHMAN. *Roger* accordingly introduc'd himself to some of them, and

be-

being a Man of a good Perfon and Appearance, and a ready Wit they agreed to admit him into their Society, and accordingly he was initiated into their Myfteries at a certain Houfe, where they have a weekly Meeting, not far from *Temple Bar.* They had feveral different *Lays* which they went upon, and fome were to fet up for Gentlemen, and to endeavour to marry fome old Woman or other with a good Fortune, which if they effected they were to pay Part of it into the Stock or Fund of the Society, as all their Expences were bore by them, and they were e-quipp'd out at the Public Charge: *Roger* was pitch'd upon to go (what they call) *Preaching the Parfon,* that is, he was to be drefs'd up like a Parfon to travel the Country, and by pre-tending that he fell fhort of Money upon the Road, except fome Broad Pieces, which he pre-ferv'd, and was going to make them a Prefent to his Daughter, or fome fuch Thing ; and fo to prevail on fome credulous Perfon or other to lend him the Worth of them 'till he could fend for them again, and then by artfully conveying falfe Pieces in the Room of the real ones, he would cheat the poor unwary Wretches who trufted him.

Roger being accordingly equipp'd in his Sacer-dotal Robes, and provided with fome large Pieces of Money ; fuch as your Five Moidore, and Five Guinea Pieces, and likewife with fome Pieces of Lead of the fame Size, a fufficient Quantity feal'd up in the fame Paper, he fet out upon his Expedition, but as he was to appear in a handfome Manner, *Roger* thought it proper to have a Footman with him, efpecially as he imagin'd, that an Accomplice in his Villany might be of Service to him ; for which Purpofe

he

he made Choice of an *Irish* Fellow, who is still
living, and reputed as cunning a Sharper as any
about Town, and having dress'd him up in a
genteel handsome Livery, he pursu'd his intended Scheme. Their Method was, they would go
to the best Inn in a Country Town, and then it
was the Footman's Business to enquire, who was
the richest Man about the Place, particularly if
there were any old Misers fond of hoarding Money. The Footman, having perform'd his Part,
was to give the Master the best Intelligence he
could, which among innocent Country People,
(who expected no Deceit, especially from the
Parson) he seldom fail'd of getting. *Roger* being let into the Circumstances of the Affair, was
to go and address himself to the Person designed to be made a Prey of, and tell him, that he
was a Clergyman in *London,* and perhaps sometime make Use of the Name of some Gentleman
of Worth and distinguish'd Character in the
Church, whom he imagin'd was not known
there, and shewing him the Pieces of Money
would tell the Old Cuff, that they were Family
Pieces, which he had a great Value for, but that
falling short of Money upon the Road, he was
oblig'd to beg the Favour of him to advance him
so much Money, and keep the Pieces till he
could send for them from *London,* .but begging
him not to part with them, which that he might
be sure of, he desir'd he might seal them up with
his own Seal, and while the Fools were telling
out the Money, or perhaps turn'd their Heads
another Way, he would convey a Piece of Paper of the same Form as the other, with the leaden Pieces in it, instead of the Gold. His Clergyman's Habit made them imagine, that so
much

much Villany could never be hid under such a Difguife.

Once as he was travelling in this Manner about the Country, he and his Footman going to a Village fomewhere towards *Norwich*, went to an Inn, and enquiring in their ufual Manner, they were inform'd of an old miferly Gentlewoman near the Place, who was very rich, but very crook'd and Deform'd; Mr. *Johnfon* and his Man adjonrn to her Houfe, and applies himfelf to the old Lady, who feeing him to be a clever likely Man, invited him and his Man to come in, *Roger* finding he could not come readily at what he wanted, accepted her Offer, and after having diverted the old Woman with feveral Romances and Stories, he pleafed the old Woman fo well that fhe made Love to *Roger*, inftead of waiting for his making Love to her. Notwithftanding which he ftaid there four or five Days before he could compleat his Defign ; One of which particularly was a *Sunday*, the old Woman was fo pleas'd with *Roger* that fhe dreffed herfelf in her beft Attire which had not feen Sun nor Moon for fome Years before, and very kindly invited *Roger* to go to Church with her, he was obliged to comply, tho' at the fame Time his Inclinations had they been known led him to a Baudy Houfe, rather than a Church, in the mean Time *Roger's* Man was induftrious in fpreading abroad, that his Mafter was a Minifter in *London*, had a good Living, and came down there on Purpofe to court the old Gentlewoman. However, they went to Church, the Congregation could not help ftaring though in the Time of Divine Service, to fee *Roger*, fuch a handfome Man making Love to an old decrepid Wretch, fitter for her Grave, than a Marriage Bed. *Roger* began to be very uneafy,
for

for fear he fhould be difcovered, before he had brought his Defign to bear ; he told the old Lady that he was under an Obligation to be in *London*, on the *Wednefday* following, and pulls out his Paper of Gold, telling her, that he was o-blig'd to pay Fourfcore Pounds in his Way to *London*, that he would leave her fome Family Pieces in the Room of the Money, that he would come down in a Week's Time, and vifit her a-gain, and return her the Money, the old Woman very readily told him he was welcome to the Money without leaving any thing but *Roger* preffed the old Woman earneftly to take the Family Pieces, fo that the old Lady at laft accepted them, *Roger* pulls out his Seal to feal them, and takes Care to fecure the golden Ones, and give her the leaden Ones. His Man, in the mean Time, had got the Horfes ready, and *Roger* having accomplifh'd the End of his Courtfhip and Addreffes mounted his Horfe, and took his Leave of the old Lady, with a Promife of being with her again foon.

Another Time, as he was riding thro' a little Village, confifting of fcattering Houfes far from any Church, a poor Woman runs out of a Houfe, and feeing *Roger* in a Clergyman's Habit, ring-ing her Hands, and crying, for God's Sake, Sir, alight off your Horfe, come in and baptize a Child that is dying, or it will go out of the World without a Name ; *Roger* was a little put to his Trumps here ; but, however, he brought himfelf off by faying, that he could not do fuch a Thing in another Man's Parifh, but that he would ride to the next Minifter, and fend him ; accordingly *Roger* rode away to the Minifter's Houfe, and knocking at the Door, who fhould come to it but the Minifter's Wife, and while he

he was relating the Story to her, the Minister
himself came down, and defir'd him to alight
and come in: *Roger* told him the Affair, and the
Minifter agreed to go and baptize the Child,
but was in fome Diftrefs becaufe his Horfe was at
Grafs, and he being old and infirm could not
walk there in any reafonable Time, *Roger* very
complaifantly faid, he would lend him his Horfe,
and would ftay there till he came back. The
Parfon very gladly accepted the Offer, but, I believe, had he known the Reafon of *Roger's* Complaifance he would not have been very eafy at it;
for *Roger* had obferv'd by the fparkling Eye of
the Parfon's Wife, that a little Love and Youth
would not be difagreeable to her; and accordingly when the Parfon was gone, he began to accoft
her in an amorous Strain; in fhort there was no
great Difficulty in the Affair, the Parfon was old
and feeble, *Roger* was young and vigorous, and
the Wife not averfe to foft Paffions; fo that
long before the Parfon return'd, they had grati-
fy'd each other's Inclinations, and *Roger* was
fufficiently fated with his Exercife, and the Parfon had good Reafon to remember the Chrift-
ning of the poor Woman's Child, for that Day
Nine Months he had one of his own to perform
the fame Office to.

His Fame, or rather Infamy, was fo fpread a-
bout, and his Face fo well known over all the
Country, that he found it abfolutely Neceffary to
find out fome new Employment; upon cafting
up his Accounts he found that he had got confiderably by thefe Practices, which made him very
loath to quit it; but as there were many Reafons
why he fhould, he accordingly came to *London*,
and bought a Sloop, or fmall trading Veffel, he
fitted her out in a very handfome Manner, and
made

made feveral Voyages to *Holland*; but not being well enough vers'd in Trade, he found but little Account in that; fo that he concluded upon turning *Smugler*, This Bufinefs he carried on for fome Time with wonderful Succefs, without Meeting with any Oppofition, tho' he narrowly efcaped feveral Times; once in particular he ferv'd two Officers of the Cuftoms in a very odd Manner; for having got a great Parcel of Run Goods on Board, he was by contrary Winds forc'd near *Dover*, where a Cuftom Houfe Sloop brought him to, made him caft Anchor, and put two Officers on Board him; *Roger* was very uneafy at this, and determin'd at all Events to get out of their Clutches: Night coming on the Wind chopp'd about favourable for him, and he confulted with his Mate, whether or no they could not cut away the Cable, and run away to *Dunkirk*; accordingly they agreed fo to do, and the better to carry on the Defign, *Roger* invited the two Officers into the Cabbin to drink a Bowl of Punch, and then fetting his Back againft the Door, with two Piftols in his Hands he ftood Sentry over them; in the mean Time the Mate cut the Cable, and got the Veffel under Sail. The Officers were very uneafy without Doubt in that Situation, expecting nothing lefs than Death, or to be flung over Board, but *Roger* affur'd 'em that if they would be quiet, no Harm fhould come to them, they would only carry them to *Dunkirk*, and put them on Board fome Veffel that fhould bring them back again: And in this he kept his Word with them; for he fet them down there without mentioning what they were, as knowing that if he had told, when he came to *Dunkirk* that they had been two Officers of the Cuftoms, the Smuglers there would certainly

C   have

have kill'd them. This was afterwards Part of the Extent which he was charg'd with in *Newgate*, and he was forc'd to compound with the Officers, and give them a Sum of Money not to profecute him.

His natural fickle Temper foon made him weary of this Way of Bufinefs, and having met with fome Loffes, infomuch that he began to be reduc'd: He was difhearten'd from following Smugling any longer, and fet his Head upon Coining. In Purfuance of this, he got acquainted with one *Stone*, a Coiner: They furnifh'd themfelves with all' neceffary Implements for Coining, and went on *Jehu* like for fome Time, *Roger* found Money come in again plentifully once more, and indulg'd himfelf in all Manner of Extravagance: He then married a Woman, one of his old Acquaintance. Nor was he content in following thefe wicked Courfes himfelf, but he drew in his Father and Mother to be concern'd with him; the old Folks being but poor, and feeing the Money come in fo eafily, and hoping to efcape without Difcovery, agreed to affift their Son and *Stone* in Coining: They went on for fome Time with uncommon Succefs, but all Villany fome Time or other is fure to be difcover'd, *Stone* in putting off fome of the Money was detected and apprehended, *Roger* reafonably concluded, that he could not long be fafe, and accordingly flew the Pit, *Stone* was tried and convicted, and executed accordingly; however, *Roger* efcap'd a little longer.

And here it is not amifs to inform the Reader, that *Roger* had befides Coining been fufpected and accus'd of feveral Robberies on the High-way, particularly for robbing one Mr. *Pitts*, of which he was acquitted; but tho' he had the
good

good Luck to efcape himfelf, yet he was fatal to his Friends, for the noted *Jonathan Wild* was firft apprehended upon a Warrant granted, on Sufpicion of taking a Bribe for letting him e-fcape, and hufhing up a Robbery which he was charg'd with, and tho' they could make nothing of that, yet he was detain'd upon that Warrant till they charg'd him with the Indictment for which he fuffer'd Execution ; Roger abfconded for fome Time, and kept himfelf conceal'd pretty well, till thinking the Search pretty well over, and that the Affair of the Coining was all at an End, when *Stone* was dead, he ventur'd to take an Alehoufe in *Chapple ftreet, Weftminfter ;* and there he did very well, and got Money, and continu'd a long Time undifcover'd, 'till unfortunately for him, one *Kelly,* who was an Evidence againft *Jonathan Wild* went to hire himfelf to *Roger* as a Servant, and as foon as he faw him knew him, *Roger* was oblig'd to take him then, for Fear he fhould betray him : Accordingly he hir'd him, and they liv'd very friendly together for fome Time, till at laft they quarrell'd, and *Kelly* to be reveng'd on his Mafter, went immediately to Juftice *Vaughn* in *Southampton-ftreet,* difcover'd *Roger,* and made an Information of the whole Matter, and upon that poor *Roger,* not imagining he was betray'd, was taken up, and committed to *Newgate,* and his Father and Mother likewife, and his Wife was fent to *New Prifon.* *Roger* could not at all brook Confinement, and from the Time he went in, thought of nothing but how to get out. He was at firft put on the Common Side, then remov'd to the Mafter's Side, and having rais'd a Sum of Money to make a Prefent to Mr. *Allen* the Keeper, he was at laft allow'd the Li-

berty

berty of the *Press Yard*. At that Time *Harry Fisher* was confin'd in *Newgate*, for murdering his Friend Mr. *Darby* in the *Temple*. Two such Persons as *Johnson* and *Fisher* could not long be confin'd together, without contracting an Intimacy: And after some Time, when they became a little better acquainted together, *Johnson* very freely open'd his Mind to him, and told him of his Intention of making his Escape; Says he, Your Case is desperate as well as mine, if we stay here, we shall be hang'd, and we do but venture our Lives in getting out; *Fisher* was of the same Way of Thinking, and they came into an Agreement of sharing each other's Fate in the Attempt. The next Thing was to consult which was the most proper Way to put the Design in Execution. As they had both the Liberty of the *Press Yard* they concluded, that the best Way would be to get up to the Top of the *Press Yard*, so over the Leads upon the Cells, and down into *Phœnix Court:* They were but single Iron'd, each of them; and after having help'd one another up, and got on the Top of the Leads. When they came to see the Place they were to leap cross, *Fisher*'s Heart fail'd him, and he told *Johnson* he thought it was impossible to do it; but *Johnson* still urg'd, that it was better to run the Risque of breaking their Necks there than to stay and be hang'd, and resolutely declar'd he would venture. Accordingly, he leap'd cross to the House on t'other Side of the Court, and *Fisher* being animated at seeing what *Johnson* had done, did the like : They got their Irons off by some Means or other, and got down into the Court, where they shook Hands, wish'd each other well, and parted different Ways, *Fisher* went beyond Sea, where he is still living, as

it

it is believ'd, having been in a Merchant's
Compting Houſe, as one of the Clerks lately at
Liſbon, from whence he was forc'd to retire in
the utmoſt Confuſion.

Roger being once again at Liberty took up his
old Trade of *Preaching the Parſon*, but without
his Footman, by himſelf alone, for Fear of being diſcover'd : for his breaking out of *Newgate*
had occaſion'd a Reward to be offer'd for apprehending him, or to any one that would diſcover him, and he was ſo well known, that it was
morally impoſſible he could be long without being taken ; however, he reign'd a conſiderable
Time, and went on in his old Way unſuſpected,
'till unlucky for him he went to *Newcaſtle upon
Tyne*, and ſtay'd there ſomething too long ; for
there he was apprehended in the moſt acciden-
tal Manner imaginable.   For *Perry* and *Jefferies*
the then Keeper of the *Poultry Compter*, were
down there upon ſome Buſineſs, not in the leaſt
thinking of ſeeing their old Friend *Roger*, as he
as little thought of being ſo abruptly accoſted
by them ; for *Perry* and *Jefferies* walking about
the Town, went into a Wine Cellar to drink,
and while they were drinking a Glaſs of Wine,
who ſhould unluckily come down into the Cellar
but *Roger* in his Clergyman's Habit dreſs'd very
ſpruce :   notwithſtanding his Diſguiſe, *Perry*
immediately knew him, and ſtarting up the Moment he enter'd the Cellar ſeiz'd him, *Roger*
was ſo ſurpriz'd at the Suddenneſs of the Motion, that he was not able to make any Reſiſt-
ance, nor was there the leaſt Probability of an
Eſcape ; for *Perry* knew his Tricks too well,
and therefore took Care to ſecure him effectually ; for they had him double iron'd, chain'd under the Horſe's Belly, and brought him to *London*,

don, where they left him with the Keepers at his old Lodging, who were very glad to receive him ; but Mr. *Johnson* met with far different Treatment this Time, from what he met with before ; for, inftead of being fuffer'd to go into the *Prefs Yard,* he was now ftrongly iron'd, and carried on the *Common Side,* and even in the very worft Part of that, the *Stone Hole,* that is a Place under the Gate Way in *Newgate,* where all the moft miferable loufy Creatures are put. When *Johnson* faw that they were going to put him there, he made grievous Complaints, and offered any Thing, if he might but go on the other Side, or be put in a better Place: *Roger* begg'd and pray'd heartily that he might; but he had ferv'd them fuch a Trick before, that Mr. *Allen* would hearken to nothing, and *Roger* was obliged to comply ; fo that accordingly he was put in the *Stone Hole,* and was very much fhock'd at his bad Lodging ; for when he went in, he was drefs'd in a very genteel Black Coat, but when he came out in the Morning, he was cover'd all over with white Lice ; for in the Morning Mr. *Allen* began to confider him, he order'd him to be taken out of that difmal Place : When he came into the Light, he was furpriz'd to fee the Vermin crawling all over him, and it griev'd him fo that he fell fick upon it. When he had continu'd fick fome Time, his Friends apply'd to Mr. *Allen,* and what with their Perfuafions, and the Help of a fmall Purfe, he was prevail'd upon to put him into a cleaner Ward. Soon after that, the Seffions came on, and he was brought down to his Trial for robbing Mr. *Pitts* on the King's Highway ; Every Body thought it would go hard with him, but *Roger rapp'd* it off, as they call it ; that is, he had got a Set of People

ple to fwear falfely in his Behalf, and by that
Means he was acquitted.   The World was very
much furpriz'd at his getting off, knowing what
a Life he led, and what a Character he bore:
However, the Government thinking him a dangerous Perfon, and not fit to be trufted with Liberty, fince he could make no better Ufe of it;
fo that he was detain'd as a Debtor at the Suit of
His Majefty, upon an Extent, iffuing out of the
Exchequer for defrauding the Revenue.   He was
then remov'd from the *Common Side,* and put on
the *Mafter Debtors Side :* *Jehnfon* having now
no Hopes, or at beft but very fmall, of being
reftor'd to his Liberty, fet himfelf to work to
contrive the beft Way he could to cheat and de-
fraud Mankind within the Gaol, fince he could
not do it without ; and accordingly, as if Fortune had favour'd his villanous Intentions, a
Tallow Chandler happen'd to be confin'd on the
Mafter Debtors Side, and he once mentioning
the making of Mold Candles in *Newgate,* Ro-
ger took the Hint, and immediately got great
with the Tallow Chandler, who inftructed him
in the Art of making Candles ; *Roger* did not
ufe to boggle at any Thing, or make any De-
lays, but immediately furnifh'd himfelf with
Molds, and all Manner of Materials for making
Candles, and accordingly fell to work.   He at
firft made but a fmall Quantity, but finding the
Profit they brought in, he increas'd his Number,
and continu'd making large Quantities by which
he got a great Deal of Money ; the poor Tallow
Chandler, who had let him into the Secret of
making them, expected that he fhould reap fome
Benefit by it, but no fooner had *Roger* got it
from him, that fo far from making any grateful
Return, he took all Opportunities of ufing him
ill.

ill. This Behaviour of *Roger's* fo nettled the
poor Man, that he refolv'd to fend Notice of
Roger's making Candles to the Commiffioners,
which finding no Civility from him, nor his ill
Ufage alter'd in the leaft, he at laft did, and
upon receiving the Meffage, the Commiffioners
immediately fent a *Poffe* of their Officers to *Newgate*, and feiz'd all *Roger's* Tools and Implements : And not only that but told him, they
would fue him for the Penalty for defrauding
the King of his Duty, *Roger* calmly replied,
*Defire the King to place it to my Account, for I shall
pay him all together.*

Being thus broke for a Candle Merchant, he
took up a new Trade, *viz.* of felling Brandy and
Rum to the Prifoners, and with this he did pretty well for fome Time, till he grew fo bad at laft
and impofed upon the Prifoners fo much that the
Keeper would let Him continue there no longer,
but made him go over to the Common Side ; but
Roger would not be ftill yet, but would play at
fmall Game, rather than ftick out ; for whilft he
was there, tho' he could not fell Brandy and
Rum, becaufe the poor Wretches there could not
reach the Price of it, yet they could may be raife
enough to purchafe a Dram of Gin, fo that *Roger* who loved to be doing fomething took up the
Trade of a Gin Merchant, and that he continued a good while, until he was made a Partner
with One of the People within Side the Gate ;
there he found his Gin turn'd but to little Account,
got togethrr fome of the wickedeft fet in the Place
and when any Body went in to fee the Prifoners
they'd get them to play at Dice, and then with
Loaded Ones trick them of their Money, or gat
a Needle Cafe, and Cheat them by that Juggle ;
after he had ftaid there a long Time what with

Friends

Friends and Money together, he obtain'd the Privilege of keeping the Tap.

We are now to behold *Roger* in his height of Ambition, for when he had got the Tap he did as it were govern the whole Goal *Roger's* Word, was a Law, and all the reſt of the Priſoners ſtood in fear of him ; he tried the Thieves (as they call it) before they were carried down to the Seſſions Houſe to be tried, that is, he ſate as Judge. The Priſoner told him the Truth of the Fact, and what he imagin'd would be ſwore againſt him, *Roger* then told him what to ſay, what Evaſions and Doubles to make, and told him whether he would come off or not : He behav'd ſo well latterly, having ſuffer'd for the contrary ſo much before, that he contributed as much as any Body to keep *Newgate* in proper Order : And whoever went to ſee any of the Priſoners, where he was, might come and go unmoleſted, and be us'd civilly while they were there, and without Danger of loſing any Thing, and that *Roger* piqu'd himſelf upon ; for a Gentleman once, who went to ſee a Smugler there, being unacquainted with the Ways of *Newgate*, was apprehenſive he ſhould loſe his Hat and Wig, or ſomething, every Step he took, and after he had been there ſome Time feeling in the wrong Pocket, and not finding his Handkerchief, cried out, that he had loſt it, ſince he came there. *D--n you, Sir,* ſays Roger, *do you come hither to abuſe us ? Do you think there are any Thieves in* Newgate *?*

But the moſt parricular Thing that he did, and which was a Sort of an Atonement for ſome of his paſt Deeds was the bringing *Sarah Malcolm* to Juſtice, which could not have been well done without his Evidence. *Sarah Malcolm* was apprehended for the Murder of Mrs. *Duncomb* in

D   the

the *Temple*, fhe was fent to *Newgate*, ftrong Circumftances of Sufpicion being found againft her, but fhe was obftinate and would confefs nothing: When fhe was come to *Newgate*, Mr. *Johnfon*, according to his ufual Cuftom, took upon him to interrogate her very narrowly relating to the Affair: She anfwer'd him very cautioufly, which gave him more Reafon to fufpect her, and hearing that Mrs. *Duncombe* was, after her Murder, robb'd of a confiderable Sum of Money, he began to examine, if fhe had any Money, and upon fearching, in the Struggle, fome Pieces of Gold fell out of her Hair; *Roger* upon this was more curious, and found that fhe had artfully conceal'd the Money in her Hair; and *Roger* upon her Trial fwore, that fhe had *planted the Cole* in her Hair. This being a very ftrong Circumftance her having that Money found upon her, and not being able to prove, how fhe came by it, and other corroborating Evidences appearing againft her, fhe was condemn'd and executed. So that we may fay, Mr. *Johnfon*, from being inftrumental in bringing fuch a Wretch to condign Punifhment, deferves to have fome of his Foibles mention'd in a Manner not fo harfh, as they would otherwife have been. And further, that from this Time he fet a Refolution to reform the Errors of his paft Life, and that if ever he got out of that Place he would no more be guilty of the Crimes he had formerly been guilty of, but take up and live a fober referv'd Life, which he manifeftly did.

As nothing material occurs during his keeping the Tap, we fhall only fay, that he got a good Deal of Money there, and liv'd more comfortably than any one can imagine to be in a Prifon, unlefs they have ever feen in what Manner

ner he did live. To paſs over that Time therefore, when the late *Smugling Act* commenc'd,
R*oger*, finding himſelf entitl'd to Mercy by a
Clauſe in that Act, applied to the Court at a
proper Time for the ſame, and it was allow'd :
So that at laſt, when he leaſt expected it, he obtain'd his long loſt *Liberty*, but he did not enjoy
it long, for what by the Gallantries and Debau-
cheries of his Youth, and his long Confinement
in Goal it brought him into a Conſumption, by
which he was reduc'd to almoſt a mere Skeleton
before it depriv'd him of Life.

Purſuant to his Intentions of living honeſtly,
and ending his Days with *Credit* and *Reputation*,
he knew it was proper to apply himſelf to ſome
Buſineſs; for tho' he had ſav'd ſome Money,
yet not ſufficient to maintain him in the Manner
he lik'd, he therefore thinking a *Pawnbroker* the
moſt ſuitable to his Inclinations, and a *reputable*
Buſineſs, he took a Houſe in *Round Court* in the
Strand, where ever ſince his Enlargement he follow'd that Trade to the Time of his Death,
which was *Aug.* 22. 1740, and after lying three
Days, he was carried in a decent Manner to be
interr'd in *Derbyſhire*, according to his own Deſire, leaving us to make this Reflection, That
Talents which wrongly apply'd are villanous in
one Claſs of Life might in another have been of
Uſe, and then we may ſay, *What an excellent
Lawyer Mr.* Johnſon *would have made!*

F I N I S.

THE LIFE AND ADVENTURES
OF
GILBERT LANGLEY

Bibliographical note:

this facsimile has been made from a copy in the
Houghton Library of Harvard University
(Soc.3002.4*)

THE
LIFE
AND
ADVENTURES
OF
GILBERT LANGLEY,

Formerly of *Serle-ſtreet* near *Lincoln's-Inn, Goldſmith.*

Containing particularly,

His Family, Education, and Accidents in his tender Years.

His being ſent into *Flanders,* to the Convent of *Engliſh* Benedictines at *Doway,* with a curious Detail of their Method in bringing up Youth.

His return to *England,* and his firſt Slips in point of Honeſty and Virtue.

His Amours with all Sorts of looſe Women, and great variety of Accidents which happened in Conſequence of them.

His meeting with a Cheat, who had Addreſs enough to bite him twice.

His Marriage, and fraudulent Arts to ſupport a broken Fortune.

His Contrivance to amaſs a vaſt Quantity of Jewels,

Watches, rich Toys, &c. to the Amount of 20,000 *l.*

His Flight to *Holland,* and ſtrange Adventures there, 'till detected by his Creditors, and beſt Part of his Effects taken from him.

His return to *England,* Voyage to the *Weſt-Indies,* Rogueries there, and miſerable Condition when he came back.

Impriſoned in the *Counter,* reduced to Want, hangs Himſelf at a Bailiffs Houſe; eſcape from thence, and a new Trip to Sea.

His Travels thro' *Spain,* Adventures in the *Canaries,* arrival in *Italy,* and return to *London.*

His laſt Exploit, which brought him within Sight of a Halter.

Written by Himſelf, in Maidſtone-Goal, *when under Condemnation, for a Robbery committed on the Highway.*

Printed and Sold by J. APPLEBEE, in *Bolt-Court, Fleet-ſtreet,* and at the Pamphlet Shops in *London* and *Weſtminſter,* 1740.
[Price One Shilling.]

TO THE
READER.

*T*HE *following Pages contain the Adventures of* Gilbert Langley, Goldsmith, *written by his own Pen.* *It is conceiv'd, that a liker Picture cannot well be drawn than that which he has given us of himself, it is publish'd chiefly for the Use of such as may resemble him in some Respects.* *Many wou'd fly from Vice if they saw her Face all at once, and in Day Light; here she is, never was she better known to any than to this Man, and he has sent her abroad in her own Cloaths.* *His Stile is the Stile of a Man of Pleasure, and was not altered, because it may be of Use to know what sort of a Stile that is.*

Some People may perhaps fancy the reading such a Life dangerous, for their Sakes this Advertisement is prefixed. *If they see young People make ill Use of it (as what in our Age will they not make ill Use of) let them set them right, let them bid these inconsiderate Folks mark the Growth and Progress*

of

To the READER.

of Vice, from abusing Education to cheating a Father; from cheating a Father, to defrauding the World, from defrauding the World to down right Robbery, and so to the Gallows; an open broad Road, and his unhappy Journey marks the Stages for others, that they may stop or ride back in Time, according to the old, approved Maxim:

Satius est recurrere quam currere male.
Better return, than in an ill Road run.

We commonly hear the young Spendthrifts of our Times, discourse exactly in Mr. Langley's Language, and Reason, or rather prevert Reason as he does: In such a Case, point out a similar Passage in this fine History of Modern Gallantry, and put him in Mind of the Conclusion; tell him, which is a certain Truth, that Greenwich Rambles lead to Maidstone Goal, that Intrigues with Prostitutes is the pleasure rather of a Goat than of a Man, and that the smallest Digressions from the Paths of Virtue, is walking for the Air in Tyburn-Road, where you run more Hazards than one of Choaking.

THE

L I F E

O F

Gilbert Langley, &c.

ILBERT Langley, Eldeſt Son of *Haldanby Langley*, an eminent *Gold-ſmith* in *London*, and Nephew to Sir *Thomas Langley*, Bart. was born *Nov.* 19, 1710. at three Years of Age he was ſent down to his Grandmother's Seat at *Yelderſley* in *Derbyſhire*, under whoſe Care he continued till he was ſeven Years of Age, when his Mother (whoſe Darling he was) growing impatient at his long Conti-nuance in the Country, came down from *London* to fetch him Home. No ſooner had he receiv'd the Vi-ſits common on ſuch Occaſions, and ſufficiently reco-ver'd himſelf from the Fatigue of his Journey, but he was put to School to Mr. *Adams* in *Red-Lyon-Street*, from whoſe prudent Inſtructions (being naturally addic-ted to Study) he in his tender Years made ſo great an Improvement, that few or none in the ſame School were thought his Equals, and his Father unwilling to curb the promiſing Genius of his Child, by the Advice and Conſent of his Maſter, remov'd him from thence to the *Charter-Houſe*, and thereby gave him a fairer Op-

portunity

portunity of exerting his natural Parts, rightly judging, that the numerous Concourse of Students, would excite his Son to a generous Emulation of Youths about his Age, in the Knowledge of such Authors as his Master thought proper to put into their Hands. Here in a short Time he began to read *Virgil, Ovid, Horace,* and *Demosthenes,* and had as great Knowledge of those sublime Authors, as his tender Years would admit of. But such is the Misfortune of some of our *English* Schools, that the Masters, either to please the Parents, or indulge the Child, hurry their Pupils from Class to Class, without consulting whether they are sufficiently grounded in the first Rudiments of Learning. Hence it is, that so many Youths who have ran thro' all the Classick Authors, for want of a full and perfect Knowledge of the Grammar Rules, the sole Basis and Foundation of all Learning, are unable to taste the Excellency of those Writers, and entirely incapable of retaining what they with so much Labour have endeavour'd to acquire; and therefore generally after a Year or two's Absence from School, are almost as far to seek as if their Parents had not expended any Thing on their Education. But as this does not immediately fall under my Cognizance, I shall drop these Remarks, and proceed.

Gilbert's Father being fully perfuaded of this almost universal Error and Corruption in our *English* Schools, resolv'd to send him over to the Benedictine Monks at *Doway,* in *Flanders,* there to have him brought up in his own Religion; but notwithstanding the great Disparity between a Foreign and *English* Education, was so fully prov'd by several of Mr. *Langley's* Friends, yet his Wife (who was passionately fond of this her Son) could not by any Arguments, be induced to a Compliance of parting with her Child, preferring rather the Presence of her Son in Ignorance, before his Absence in a Place where he was sure to have the fairest Opportunity of acquiring solid and useful Learning. Thus her fondness triumph'd over her Reason, and she could not bear the Thoughts of a Separation from her Darling, who to please her, tho' to his own Prejudice, was continu'd at Home, till Providence, as a peculiar Mark of its Favour,

vour, was pleafed to take her away, and by that fet afide the fole Obftacle to the intended Progrefs of our young Student ; for no fooner was Mamma dead, and decently interr'd, but the Father, earneftly bent on his Son's Advancement, made diligent Search for a propet Perfon, to whom he might with Safety commit the Truft of his Son; until he fhou'd arrive at *Doway*, the Place defign'd for his future Education. Upon Enquiry he found out Mr. *Sturton*, the Prior of the *Benedictine Monks*, who being come to *London* about fome particular Bufinefs, was now on returning to his Convent; with this Gentleman he agreed on an annual Sum for my Board, Learning, and all other neceffary Expences for my Journey, which was to be as foon as poffible. The Day being fixed for our Departure, we met at the *Crofs-Keys* in *Grace-Church-Street*, where my indulgent Father, with reiterated Entreaties, follicited Mr. *Sturton* to a fpecial and peculiar Care of his young Pupil, and after he had tenderly embrac'd me, with flowing Eyes, committed me to the Management of my new Tutor. For my Part, I readily confefs, that being naturally fond of Novelty, and having a roving Difpofition in me, I was rather pleafed than concerned at our Parting, and with Joy refigned myfelf to the Obedience of my new and ftrange Guardian. In fhort, we lay at the Inn that Night, and in the Morning took Coach for *Dover*, from whence (the Packet being ready to fail) we embarked for *Calais*, and in a few Hours, with a frefh and favourable Gale, we reached the wifhed-for Haven. My Tutor being intimately acquainted with Mr. *Francia*, (commonly known in *England* by the Name of *Francia* the *Jew*) we lodg'd in his Houfe, and were civilly and agreeably entertained by him for the Space of three Days.

Now all Things appear'd to me odd and uncommon, and being unable to underftand the Natives Language, Manners, or Cuftoms, I thought myfelf in a New World, asking feveral impertinent Queftions of my Guardian, who well pleafed with my Curiofity, and juvenile Obfervations, gave me fuch Anfwers as my tender Age was capable to receive and underftand. Now

after

after we had return'd Thanks to Mr. *Francia* for his kind Entertainment, we proceeded on our Journey, and the next Day arriv'd at St. *Omers*, where we spent a whole Day in viewing the Curiosities of that Town, which I shall not presume to describe, being then but in the 12th Year of my Age; yet I cannot forbear taking Notice of the Cathedral of St. *Bartin*'s, an ancient and stately Structure, adorn'd with several curious Pieces of Painting, and embellish'd with numerous Ecclesiastical Ornaments; but what struck me most with Wonder and Surprize, were the Skins of a Toad and a Crocodile, of an enormous Size, that were fix'd to one of the Columns of the Church; but since there are so many various Reports, and romantick Fables, devised by the Populace concerning the prodigious Dimensions of those Animals, and the Manner of their being discover'd, I shall omit troubling my Reader any further on that Head, since where I cannot give a full, true, and satisfactory Account, my Resolution is to be silent.

Adjoining to this noble Cathedral, is a magnificent and splendid Convent, more resembling the Palace of a grand Monarch, than the Receptacle of Persons, who under the specious Pretence and Disguise of Religion retire thither; altho' in Reality, they there more fully indulge their irregular Passions and inordinate Desires, than those who strugling in the tempestuous Ocean of the World, boldly expose themselves to all Dangers, and to the utmost of their Abilities, serve and glorify their great Creator. In this Convent are upwards of 150 Jesuits, and near upon 200 Students, who all pay the annual Salary of 25 *l.* Sterling, except twelve of them, who are upon the Pope's Foundation. My Guardian and I paid a Visit to the Prior, who entertained us in a sumptuous and elegant manner, none being so free and profuse in their Entertainments as the *Roman* Clergy are one among another. The next Morning we set out for *Doway*, where we arriv'd in the Evening, to the great Satisfaction and Comfort of the *Benedictines*, who with all possible Demonstrations of Joy, receiv'd their Superior, and (as I was afterwards inform'd) highly applauded him for he due Execution

of

of his Commiffion, and commended his Diligence and unwearied Endeavours, in encreafing the Number of the Faithful. I muft acknowledge, that fince I have been converfant in the World, upon the Perufal of *Milton*, and my ferious Reflection upon the Reception of Mr. *Sturton*, I was charm'd with the beauteous Defcription of *Lucifer's* return to his fallen Angels, which fo nearly refembled, and form'd in my Mind fuch lively Ideas of my former Guardian's firft Appearance to his cloifter'd Monks, that to my dying Day I fhall retain an indelible Remembrance of that grand and folemn Re-union. At the Expiration of three Days, which are ufually allow'd to young Sparks, to initiate and inftruct themfelves in the Forms and Precepts of the Colledge, I was examin'd by three Reverend Fathers, (for that is the Title they affume) and upon a ftrict Examination, was found capable of nothing higher than *Alvarus's* Grammar, and *Cæfar's* Commentaries, a plain Proof of the vanity of fome of our *Englifh* Schools. But fince my Readers may be curious, and willing to be inform'd of the Manners and Cuftoms of our Collegiate Life, I fhall for their Satisfaction give a brief but true Account thereof. The annual Salary is 25 *l.* Sterling for an elder Brother, and 20 Ditto for a younger ; at our firft Entrance we are divefted of our fecular Robes, and cloath'd with a Caffock and a Gown, refembling in Form thofe on the Foundation of the *Charter-Houfe*, which Drefs, according to the antient Rules of the Houfe, is allowed to each Student new every Year. The Scholars are divided according to their different Abilities and Capacities into feveral Claffes, each apart from one another, to prevent Noife and Interruption, and over each Clafs prefides a proper Mafter, whofe Bufinefs is to inftruct his Pupils in the Knowledge of fuch Authors as he thinks moft proper and fuitable to their Genius and Underftanding. We are oblig'd to continue twelve Months in the fame Study, that we may be entirely perfect therein, and during that Time, have Monthly Examinations, in which the moft perfect is for his Encouragement, to receive a Præmium from the Hands of the Prior, at the three

feveral

feveral grand Examinations, that are held before the
whole Houfe; at *Eafter*, *Michaelmafs*, and *Chriftmafs*,
all (except thofe who are in the *Accidence*) are compelled
at all Times, and upon all Occafions, under a certain Penalty, to fpeak the Latin Tongue. We have a large Dormitory, where each Student has his Bed a-part, a Calefactory, and at each end thereof, a large fire Place, tho'
but fmall allowances of Wood, having but one Faggot
and two Billets to each Fire, and that only in the Evening, which caufes fome of our young Sparks, fometimes privately, and fometimes by open Force, to break
into the Wood-houfe, that ftands in our Area or Yard.
Our Refectory or Dining-Room, is large and commo-
dious, and ferv'd with regular and due Oeconomy,
where each Scholar has the firft Choice of the Portions
of Meat, according to his Superiority in Learning. Our
Diet is Bread and Butter every Morning, at Noon
half a Pound of boil'd Meat, with a Porringer of
Broth, and at Night, the fame Allowance of Roaft with
a Sallad, except on Days of Faft; but at Meals, we have
as much Bread and Beer as we defire, altho' at all other
Times, we are debarr'd even from a Cruft of Bread, or
a Draught of Beer, which makes us frequently convey out
the fame under our Caffocks, and fometimes, like ra-
venous Wolves, make bold Incurfions into the Kitchen,
and there plunder and carry away all we can meet with;
but of this more hereafter. Over the Students, which
are never lefs than fifty or threefcore, a Prefect is appointed by the Prior, who ought to be a Perfon of great
Sagacity and Difcretion, for to his Care the Direction
of all the Scholars (when out of their refpective Schools)
is committed; he hears all Debates, fettles all Controverfies, and appeafes all Animofities that arife a-
mongft his Pupils; his Bufinefs is to call them up at five
in the Morning, as well in Winter as in Summer, he
rings the Bell to Prayers, at their Meals fays Grace, and
orders one of the Scholars in his Turn to mount the
Roftrum or Pulpit, and read the Martyrlogy, during
the Time of Repaft, whilft he himfelf ftands at the
upper End of the Refectory to keep Silence, and prevent any Confufion or Irregularities, that might otherwife

wife happen amongſt ſuch a Number of Boys. Hours of Study are from Five till half an Hour after Seven, the other half Hour being allow'd for waſhing and breakfaſt Time; at Eight we go to School, at Eleven to Prayers, at Noon to Dinner, at One to Study, at Two to School, at half an Hour after Four to Play, at Five to Study, at Six to Supper, and afterwards to Play if in the Summer Time, or in the Winter to our reſpective Seats in the Calefactory. None dares preſume to go into the Town without the Prefects Leave, we have a capacious Area or Yard, wherein is a Terras Walk, and a Place very ſuitable and proper for the Exerciſe of Hand-Ball, in which we with great Emulation, ſtrove to ſurpaſs each other. Beſides the uſual Hollidays at *Eaſter* and *Michaelmas*, we claim by Charter an ancient Priviledge of electing a King among ourſelves, to be our Sovereign, during the limitted Time granted by Patent. The Manner, and our Obſervance of thoſe antique Cuſtoms are as follows: A Month before *Chriſtmas*, the Senior Scholars aſſembled together in Council, debate on the Election of a Prince, and all proper Officers to attend his Majeſty, of which I ſhall afterwards give you a Liſt. The Reſult of this grand Council is kept inviolably ſecret, until *Chriſtmas* Eve, when the Clerk of the Auguſt Aſſembly aſcending the Pulpit, in an open an audible Voice, reads the Copy of the ancient Charter, and nominates the choſen King, and his Officers of State, in Preſence of the ſeveral Maſters of the different Schools. Hereupon his Majeſty ſends a ſolemn Embaſſy to the Grand Prior, and by it claims and demands the Annual Rights and Priviledges of his then Subjects, to be confirm'd, purſuant to the ancient Tenour of the above-mention'd Charter. To this legal Demand the Prior replies, *My Lords, we are both ready and willing to grant your preſent Sovereign, all ſuch Cuſtoms, Priviledges, and Immunities, as were wont formerly to be enjoyed by his Majeſty's Predeceſſors; providing that your Monarch will expreſly command, that all ſuch wholeſome Laws and Precepts (as were uſually obſerv'd) be ſtrictly adhered to, and kept inviolable, on Pain of ſevereſt Puniſhments, and his higheſt Diſpleaſure.* The

B 4   Am-

Ambaffadors return to his Majefty with this peremptory
Anfwer, who immediately commands them to return,
and deliver to the Grand Prior, a Copy of fuch Statutes
as he in Council hath approv'd of, and thought proper,
by folemn Edict, to make known and proclaim
throughout his Realm. As foon as the King receives
the Prior's Approbation thereof, he orders three feveral
Copies of his Royal Mandates to be affixed forthwith
in the Calefactory, Refectory, and Dormitory; and
for the due Execution of his Majefty's Pleafure, and
irrevocable Commands, thefe following Officers are
conftituted and appointed.

Imprimis, One of the moft facetious and merry
Youths, is chofen to perform the Part of a Harlequin,
and by Patent is ftiled his Majefty's Brother, *alias* the
Fool, he hath Liberty always to dine with his Majefty,
and is prefent on all Occafions, and in fome Meafures,
thwarts and controuls him, purfuant to the Character
he bears.

The next great Officer is the Lord High Conftable,
who beareth Rule over all his Majefty's Subjects, and
is fworn to maintain and defend the Peace and Order
of his prefent Kingdom, free and exempt from all publick Difturbances, Feuds and Animofities. None dare prefume to go out into the Town, without the Leave and
Permiffion of this great Lord; none are to fit up paft nine
o'Clock, without his Licence; he likewife performs the
Part of the former Prefect, reads Prayers, and fees all
the Minor Students lodged in their refpective Beds, puts
out the Candle, and then retires to divert himfelf in the
Company of his Sovereign, and all his Nobles; he alfo
is conftituted and appointed Lord Chief Juftice o'er all
his Majefty's Dominions, and hears and decides all Suits
and Controverfies, that arife amongft the inferior Subjects.

The next in Honour and Dignity is, the Lord Prefi-
dent, who prefides in the King's Honourable Privy
Council, his Office is diligently to obferve the Motions
and Behaviour of the feveral Officers, as well as Subjects, and when he finds juft Caufe and Reafon to fummon thofe of the Privy-Council, and there lay open his
Charge

(9)

Charge againſt the Delinquents, who, if found Guilty, are puniſh'd according to Law. This Truſt he privately executes, and for that Reaſon, is commonly called, the Inſpeƈtor of Manners.

The next is Lord High Chamberlain, who hath the Management and Care of all his Majeſty's Houſhold; he giveth Direƈtion for fixing the Royal Throne, and Iſſues forth his Orders, to the Inferior Officers of his Court to mundifye, and keep decent the ſeveral Apartments of the Palace Royal.

The next are the two Ambaſſadors, who are always and at all Times, immediately to execute ſuch Orders as ſhall be to them deliver'd.

Next in Order, followeth his Majeſty's Cupbearer, who is always attendant, at his ordinary Hours of Repaſt, and ſees that his Table be elegantly and ſumptuouſly furniſhed, agreeable to the Dignity of his ſacred Perſon.

The next is his Secretary of State, who hath the Care of all Records and Decrees, ſends and receives all Letters to, and from his Majeſty, and hath the ſole Management of all ſuch Affairs, as fall within the Sphere of his great Office.

And laſtly, are the Lords of the Bed-Chamber, who conſiſt of the moſt worthy of the Schollars, and are always in waiting to attend his Majeſty's Royal Pleaſure. The antient Term of our King's Reign, was originally, but twelve Days, but of late we have, by ſending a ſolemn Embaſſy, to the Prior, obtain'd a Licence for four Days more. Our Monarch's uſual Reſidence is in the Calefaƈtory, at both Ends whereof, are conſtantly kept two great Fires, and in the Middle is fixed a large and long Table, where forty or fifty Students may commodiouſly ſeat themſelves at one Time. Our uſual Diverſions are Card-playing, and other innocent Amuſements, which each Youth purſues (according to the *French* ſaying) *Chacun a ſon Gout*, Every Man in his own Taſte. Thoſe who by the Moroſeneſs, or Avarice of their Parents, are not ſupplied with Money ſufficient to defray their Charges, during the Term of this merry Licence, are for their Encouragement and Support, allow'd

low'd to either boil or roaft Apples, which they fell for one *Liar*, or *French* Farthing a-piece. On Twelfth-Night, the King fends his Ambaffadors to invite the Prior, and fome of the Grandees of the Houfe, to an elegant and coftly Supper, to which, none except the great Officers of State, are admitted ; all the reft being then in waiting, and receive as his Majefty's Bounty, what comes from his royal Table. For my Readers Satisfaction, I fhall mention an odd Accident that happened to me, whilft I had the Honour of ferving in Quality of an Ambaffador. On the Eve of the Epiphany, I received an Order, to take three of the Lords of the Bed-chamber, and go about two Miles out of Town to a Public Houfe, and there to purchafe four Gallons of Brandy for the above-mention'd Entertainment. As I could fpeak the *French* Language, I foon executed my Commiffion, at a far more reafonable and eafy Rate than I could poffibly have done in the Town, there being a large Duty on the Import of any Spiritubus Liquors, into the Garrifon, and that farm'd by a *Comee*, or Officer, that hath his Myrmidons conftantly attending at the Entrance of the Town Gate, who fearch all Comers in ; but it being cuftomary to let all the Students of different Colleges pafs and repafs, without hindrance or Examination, we thought ourfelves very fecure from any Danger that might arife on that Head ; fo after our Bottles were filled, we fat down in the Houfe, and drank a Glafs or two to refrefh ourfelves ; but as Ill-fortune would have it, a Soldier coming in to the fame Houfe, privately took notice of our Bottles that ftood on the Table, and went to the Searchers Office, and gave Information that four Students of the Benedictine-Monks, were going to convey Brandy into the Garrifon. We were entirely ignorant of the private Information that he had given, and therefore in a merry Mood, paid the Reckoning, and return'd homeward with the Liquor under our Caffocks, when to our great Surprize, as we were going in at the Gate, we were ftopp'd, the Brandy found upon us, and we fecur'd in the adjoining Office, till they had called a File of Mufqueteers to conduct us to the head *Comee's* Houfe

for

for further Examination. I had then a Piſtole in my
Pocket, and knowing the mighty Force of Gold, offered it to the Searchers for our Enlargement; but they
were inflexible, and therefore any one may judge, what
Horror and Confuſion we were in, at the approaching
Danger. In ſhort, as we marched along with the Guard
of Soldiers, the Inhabitants wondred what Crime ſuch
Youths could be guilty off, that had thus expoſed them
to public Scandal and Shame. Some pitied our Misfortune, and others condemn'd our Folly ; but by a lucky
Accident, we met with two *Iriſh Franciſcan* Fryers,
who enquiring of the Serjeant the Cauſe of this unuſual
Treatment, reprimanded him ſeverely for his Folly, in
carrying us to the Officer of the Cuſtoms, and at the
ſame Time advis'd him to conduct us to our own
College, and inform the Prior of what had happened,
it being properly his Buſineſs to account and anſwer for
the Miſdemeanors and Treſpaſſes of all Students under
his immediate Care and Direction. This ſage Advice
of the Fathers, prevail'd on the rigid Officer, who con-
veyed us ſafe to our Convent, and afterwards made his
Report to the abovemention'd Officer, who next Morning ſent to demand four hundred Florins of the Prior,
the uſual Forfeiture, or Fine impoſed for the Infringe-
ment of his Dues and Privileges. Our Prior was ſtartled
at his exorbitant Demand, and abſolutely refuſed to give
him any Satisfaction, which ſo exaſperated the *Comee*,
that he reſolved to proſecute us with the utmoſt Rigour.
Hereupon the Prior conſulting the Sages of the Law, was
by them advis'd to quiet the impending Storm, and bring
this unlucky Accident to an amicable Compoſition,
which was accordingly effected on the Payment of one
hundred Florins, and a further Promiſe, that none of his
Pupils ſhould ever be guilty of the like Offence. The
March following, another Misfortune happen'd to me
that had likely to have prov'd fatal, and of far greater
Conſequence than the former. *John Huſſey, William
Etherington, George Pigot, John Racket, William Brown,*
(*alias* the *Bull*) and I, form'd a Conſpiracy againſt the
Peace of the Common-wealth, and by a mutual and
ſolemn Engagement, were fully determin'd to make
an

an Irruption, into the Kitchen, and there plunder and carry away all that we could meet with. The Night before the Execution of our horrid Plot, we by the help of Gimletts, had secretly bore two Holes in the Kitchen-Door, that leads into the Refectory, and fixed two Pieces of Packthread, black'd on purpose to prevent their being observ'd, to the Bolts that faften'd the Door on the Inside ; this Scheme, though artfully managed, was perceived by one of the Scullions, who immediately gave Notice thereof, to the reft of the Servants, who judging our Intent, arm'd themfelves with Clubs, and refolv'd to difpute the Entrance into their Sooty Kingdom againft all Invaders. They likewife furnifh'd themfelves with a dark Lanthorn, either to defcry the Number of the Enemy, or if they fhould be worfted in Battle, perfonably to know the Affailants, and loudly complain againft fuch public Acts of Rapine and Hoftility. Nor lefs diligent were we, to execute our full Purport and Intent, and having provided ourfelves with lufty Battoons, or Cudgels, and a Chiffel to open the Refectory Door, between the Hours of Twelve and One, we began to attack the Garrifon ; firft we with little or no Noife, forc'd open the Refectory-Door, and gain'd an eafy Entrance into the Kitchen Paffage by the help of thofe Cords we had faften'd to the Bolts of the faid Door that guarded the Entrance. We now thought ourfelves fecure, and found in the faid Inlett into our intended Port, two large Barrels of Raifons, with the Heads of them open ; this unexpected Prize overjoy'd us, and we immediately fell to Plunder, and fill'd a large Sack that we had brought with us, to carry away our Booty ; but to our great Surprize, we were fuddenly faluted with repeated Blows on our Heads, Backs, and Shoulders, from different Quarters laid heavily on us, by the numerous Company of Servants, that were fully bent to retrieve their loft Reputation, and make us Prifoners of War. We ftraitways now quitted our Prize, and fell Pellmell on the Enemy, with true *Englifh* Courage and Bravery, and return'd their Blows fo brifkly, that they began to give Ground, which fo redoubled our Ardour, that we drove them out of their Fortifications, into the

open

open Garden, belonging to the Religious; where finding themfelves unable to withftand our Fury, they immediately fet up a great cry, calling out, *Laroon, Laroon,*
which is in Englifh, *Thieves, Thieves,* and the *Shoe-
maker,* who was one of the Gang, ftretching forth his
dark Lanthorn, look'd ftedfaftly on us; whereupon
Huffey knock'd it out of his Hand, though too late, for
he already knew us, and their out-cry by this Time having alarm'd the Houfe, we were oblig'd to make a precipitate Retreat, and endeavour to regain our Quarters,
before the Prefect's Arrival, which was happily effected,
and we all in our refpective Beds, pretending to be faft
afleep; but this Artifice would not pafs on him, for we
not having Time to Undrefs, our Caffocks were not as
ufual fpread o'er our Bed-cloaths, and he thereby eafily
difcovered us.

The next Morning we were fummon'd before the
Grand Prior, where the poor batter'd and bruis'd Servants made a moft pitious Complaint of their barbarous
Treatment, vowing that they would all leave the Houfe,
except they had ample Satisfaction for the Injury done
them. The Prior taking this Affair into his Confider-
ation, rightly judged that if he countenanc'd fuch open
Acts of Theft and Hoftility, that none would ever ferve
in the Convent, and that it vaftly derogated from his
Character, whofe Office was to maintain Tranquility
throughout his Jurifdiction, and therefore he pronounc'd
this harfh, though juft Sentence, that we fhould for this
horrid and unparalled Crime, be expell'd the College,
as an Example to deter others from the like enormous
Offence. We were now like Criminals under Sentence
of Death, none caring to converfe with us, leaft they
fhould be fufpected to be ling'd, or infected with our
wicked and perverfe Difpofitions. However, as Mercy
is fometimes extended to the moft abandon'd Wretches,
we all (except the Bull) by great Intereft, and the
Characters our Mafters gave of our being Youths of a
promifing Genius, were repriev'd, and once more on
promife of our future good Behaviour, admitted into
Favour. Notwithftanding this unexpected Clemency,
we could not fupprefs our Refentment, at the Expulfion
of

of our old Confederate *Brown*, but vowed to revenge the Injury and Injuſtice that we thought was done to our former Companion, in the moſt ſecret Manner that poſſibly we could; and therefore we had frequent Debates and Conſultations how to bring about our intended Project. At laſt, the following Method was unanimouſly reſolved on. In our Area ſtands the Wood-houſe, to which the Scullion (the Informer of our firſt Attack) uſually came every Day, with a Wheelbarrow to fetch Wood, between the Hours of four and five in the Afternoon, for the Uſe of the Kitchen. We therefore provided ourſelves with a Cloak belonging to one of the minor Students, to prevent Suſpicion, ready againſt his Entrance, to ſurprize him in the following Manner. Now there being (by good Fortune) a Ladder ſtanding in the Yard, we, by the help thereof, privately got in at the Window, and hid ourſelves behind the Faggots, and there with Impatience waited his coming, having in the mean Time provided ourſelves with ſmart Switches, to laſh the bare Bum of our Inveterate Enemy. No ſooner had he, (the *Frenchman*) open'd the Door, and began to load his Barrow, but the Cloak was thrown over his Head, and faſten'd with a Cord round his neck, ſo that being blinded, he was uncapable to diſcover who was the Foe, or make any Defence to prevent his intended Puniſhment. In ſhort, we firſt ſhut to the Door, to prevent his Cries being heard, then knock'd him down, let down his Breeches, and paid his bare Buttocks in turns, 'till we were all weary: Nor were his hideous Cries, or loud Invocations of his tutelar Saints, able to abate our Rage, or defend him from the ſevere Puniſhment that we thought that we were in Honour bound to inflict on this Delinquent, as a Retaliation, and Satisfaction for the Diſgrace of our former Companion. No ſooner was this bloody Flagellation, or Scourging ended, but the Bell rang to Study, and we left the poor unhappy Wretch alone to bemoan his dire Misfortune, and vainly Conjecture, who were the Perſons who had thus irreligiouſly and irreverently prophan'd the honour of his fluſhy Bum, and in a decent Manner retired to the *Muſæum*, or Study-place, where we took our reſpective

Seats

Seats, as innocently in Appearance, as if nothing had happened, though well pleas'd in our Conceits at the good Succefs, and Execution of what we had fo long and fo earneftly wifh'd for. The Scullion had no fooner freed himfelf from his Hood-wink, and recovered his loft Sight, but he ran crying out, *le Diable, le Diable,* with the utmoft Speed into the Kitchen, and there after having recovered his Breath, recounted the difmal Story to his Fellow-Servants, who were all amaz'd, and forely affrighted left the fame Devils fhould unexpectedly furprize and punifh them for the faid Offence. However, when the pannick Fear and Terrour they were in, was fomething abated, they in a whole Poffe, with the injur'd Party at their Head, went to the Prior, and loudly exclaim'd againft the Infult and barbarous Treatment of their Countryman, by thofe *Bougre de Chiens,* or *Englifh Dogs,* as they were pleafed to call us, his Students. The Prior calmly heard their juft Accufation, and faithfully promis'd them, in *Verbo Sacerdotis,* to redrefs their Grievances, and inflict condign and exemplary Punifhment, on thofe who fhould be found guilty of this villainous and unpardonable act of Barbarity. Accordingly he came into the *Mufæum,* and caft a piercing and obfervant Look o'er all the Scholars, hoping thereby to difcern by their Countenances, who were the guilty Perfons; but as the moft fagacious and cunning, are fometimes deceiv'd, fo was he. All his Artifices prov'd ineffectual, and therefore, he with Reafon good, as we were formerly prov'd guilty of a Mifdemeanour, pofitively charged us with the Fact, and call'd us one by one, into a private Room, for further Examination ; but we, who were always true to each other, abfolutely denied that we either directly or indirectly, were privy to, or knew any Thing of what we were thus charged with : And I, for my Part, to clear myfelf and Co-partners in the Crime, fwore by the Holy Crofs of Chrift, that then ftood on a Table in the Room, that we were no wife acceffary, or concern'd in the Commiffion of this horrid Villany, and in Confirmation thereof on bended Knees, kifs'd and embrac'd the fame. This folemn Proteftation had its intended Effect,
and

and the Prior being thorougly fatisfied with this frank
and unprecedented Manner of acquitting ourfelves, afterwards treated us with more than ufual Marks of his Civility and Efteem. Nor was it ever known, during my
Stay in the College, who were the Authors of the
abovemention'd Riot.

Affairs being thus happily accommodated, all Things-
feem'd to bear the chearful Air of Joy, Peace and
Tranquility, and I plyed my Studies fo diligently, that
for the two following Years, I had the Honour to receive the annual Præmiums, given for the Encouragement of the emulous and induftrious Student. Now
the Eyes of the whole Synod was fix'd on me, of whom
they had promifed themfelves great Hopes, if they could
by any Means or Arguments induce me, to relinquifh
all Thoughts of a gay and feculiar Life, and embrace
a religious Monaftical State. And to accomplifh this
their Defign, they treated me in a Manner different from
that ufed towards the reft of my Cotemporaries, and
by their artful and engaging Behaviour, eafily perfuaded me to promife that, with my Father's Confent and
Approbation I would accept of the Habit, and add one
more to the Number of the Faithful. But mark how
Providence, by an unexpected and unforefeen Accident,
fubverted and fruftrated what they with fo much Art
had endeavour'd to obtain. As by the Benevolence,
and kind Indulgence of my Father, I was conftantly
fupplied with Money, I frequently went into the Town,
partly for my Recreation, and partly to improve my
felf in the *French* Language, which I was very defirous
to become Mafter off, and therefore one *Thurfday* in
the Afternoon, which is always a Holyday with us, I
afked Leave of the Perfect for me and my Companion
Roger Meynel, to go out and walk on the Ramparts.
The Perfect being vexed at fome Difappointment or
other, was in a fullen, morofe Humour, and therefore
denied our Requeft. Exafperated at this unexpected
Denial, we determin'd *Nolens Volens* to accomplifh our
Intent, and thus refolv'd, we boldly went out at the
Convent-Gate, into the Town, and from thence to a
Tavern, where we gave a loofe to Pleafure, and revelled

at large, till we were weary and intoxicated with Liquor, and then to fober ourfelves, we ftagger'd for a-
bout an Hour on the Ramparts, not unobferved by many,
and from thence we reel'd Home, but had the Wit to
fteal privately to Bed: Now when the Bell rang to Supper, we being miffing, were enquired for; however,
Anfwer was made by fome of our Friends, that we
were taken ill and gone to Bed. This artful Excufe
pafs'd for two or three Days, till a Gentleman who
perfonally knew us, came to vifit the Prior, and informed him in what a fcandalous, foolifh Condition we
had been obferved to appear in on the publick Ramparts,
which fo highly incens'd our Governour, that after feveral Reprimands, he ordered us both to be fmartly flogg'd.
I was then in Poetry, and therefore was fo highly exafperated at this Infult, and heinous Offence offered to
the Mufes, that I refolved to lay afide all Thoughts of
any further Progrefs in my Learning, and therefore be-
took my felf to a fullen and continued Silence, which
I ftrictly obferved for near a Month, and no Perfuafions
were able to alter my perverfe Difpofition, till Father
Howard (a Gentleman of candid and engaging Behaviour) took me to tafk, and by his winning Affability,
and courteous Complaifance, prevail'd on my rigid and
fullen Temper. This Gentleman indulged me with the
free Ufe of his Chamber, where I fpent my leifure
Hours with the utmoft Pleafure in the Perufal of his
Books, and was highly delighted with his ingenious Remarks and Obfervations, on fuch Authors as beft fuited
my Genius, and heightened the natural Conceptions of
my growing Capacity. Thus having relinquifhed all
Defires of coming to *England*, I clofely followed my
Studies, and having ran through all the Clafficks, I proceeded to Philofophy, pafs'd through my Dialect or
Logick, and was juft entring upon a Courfe of Meta-
phyficks, when an Order came for my immediate return Home.

This unexpected News greatly furprized the whole
Houfe, and the Prior with my Confent, wrote to my
Father, and in moft moving Terms, urg'd the future
Advantage I fhould reap by a full Conclufion of what

C   I

I had fo happily began ; but all his Endeavours were in vain, for the old Gentleman remain'd inflexible, and once more fent a pofitive Order for my Removal, and alfo for five Guineas for my Return Home. Thus having bid adieu, and taken my laft Farewell of the Religious, and all my Fellow-Students, with Tears in my Eyes, I took Coach to St. *Omers*. We had not drove above a Mile or two out of Town, but my gloomy Melancholy was difpers'd and diffipated, by the Sprightlinefs and Alacrity of my facetious Fellow-Travellers, confifting of two *French* Officers and three Ladies. The ftudious Thoughts of a College Life, were now turned into Gaiety and Pleafure, emulous to out-fhine the Officers in Point of Complaifance and Politenefs of Behaviour to my fair female Companions. At Night we arrived at St. *Omers*, where we had an elegant Supper, and fpent the Evening, with the utmoft Mirth and Delight. The Ladies being excufed from any Part in the Reckoning, according to the Cuftom of *France*. From thence I took Poft to *Calais*, and lodged at the Sign of the *Ville des Londres* (or City of *London*) where I met with feveral Englifh Gentlemen and Ladies that were waiting a Paffage to *England*. Next Day, having a Letter of Recommendation to my old Friend Mr. *Francia*, I went and din'd with him, who generoufly offered me the free Ufe of his Houfe during my ftay at *Calais*; but pleafed with the Variety of diverting Company at my Inn, I modeftly declined his courteous Offer, whereby I had a greater freedom of indulging my juvenile Follies and Extravagancies. The Wind continuing *N. W.* for near three Weeks, no Veffel could ftir out of the Harbour, wherefore my Money being almoft exhaufted by this unexpected Delay, I was obliged to make Proof of Mr. *Francia*'s Friendfhip, who procured me a Paffage on Board the *Mary* Sloop, Capt. *Hawkins*, who quartered at the fame Inn with me and the reft of the Company, who were all his Paffengers. At laft the Wind chopping about to the Southward, we all embarqu'd, caft of from the Key, and had a pleafant Paffage to *Gravefend*, where we went afhore, and Supp'd at the *Faulcon*-Tavern and drank plentifully ; but here I

confefs

confefs I fat on Thorns, for having expended all my
Cafh, I was at a great Lofs how to difcharge my Share
of the Reckoning. At laft (true *Irifhman* like) I affumed an Air of Boldnefs, and putting my Hand into my
Pocket, afked the Gentleman that fate next me, if he
could favour me with Change of a Piftole, telling him
that I had no Englifh Coin; the Gentleman replied,
Sir, *a Crown is at your Service*. I humbly thank'd him
and readily accepted the pleafing Proffer, which was
fufficient to difchatge my Dividend of the Reckoning;
highly delighted at my good Fortune, and the generous
Treatment of a Stranger. At laft we arrived at
Tower-Stairs, and having returned many Thanks to the
abovemention'd Gentleman, and gave him Directions
where my Father liv'd, I took my Leave of the reft of
the Company, went afhore, and call'd a Coach, and
ordered him to drive to *Lincoln's-Inn-Fields*. My Father was ftanding at his Door, but fcarcely knew me.
habited like a *Frenchman*, and dreffed *Alamode de Paris*,
till at laft recovering himfelf from his Surprize, he took
me into the Parlour and there tenderly embraced me.
Numbers of the Neighbours came to compliment me
on my fafe return Home. Sometime after I had refresh-
ed myfelf from the Fatigue of my Voyage, the good
old Gentleman afked me, what Courfe of Life I was
willing to embrace, for my future Support and Main-
tenance. I propofed the Study of the Law, or Phyfic,
both which he rejected, and I at laft by his earneft Sollicitations, was bound Apprentice to him.

Mr. *Thomas Gilpin*, (my Fellow-Apprentice) having
then about one Year and a half to Serve, my Father
made ufe of this Opportunity, of giving me a further
Education, and more fuitable for the Tranfaction of
Publick Bufinefs than the former, and therefore he fent
me to Mr. *Yeate's* Academy, in *Chancery-Lane*, there
to be perfected in Arithmetick. He likewife provided
me a *French Mafter*, who daily came to inftruct me in
the Theory of that Univerfal and ufeful Language, of
which before I had nothing but the practick Part. In
the Evenings I went to a *German* Limner, in *Craven-
Buildings*, there to learn that noble and ingenious Science

of

of Drawing, so vastly beneficial in all the Stages of human Life. Thus for a considerable Time, my Thoughts were wholly intent on the Pursuit of the abovemention'd Accomplishments; till by Degrees falling into Company with some other gay Sparks, I grew weary of my habitual Exercises, and soon found that my weekly Allowance was not sufficient to furnish out and support these frequent Excursions, and Irregularities, that my unlimitted Desires urged on, and excited by lewd Company, often subjected me to, and therefore I privately began to pilfer, (though at first with an Intent to repay) from the several Quantities of old Silver, that were brought in the Shop, and was grown so expert and cunning in this my villainous Practice, that neither my Father, nor Mr. *Gilpin*, ever dreamt or suspected me to be any Ways concerned in such base wicked Practices.

One Summer's Evening being sent with a Bag of Plate to a Gentleman's House in *Grosvenor-Square*, as I cross'd *Covent-Garden*, I chanc'd to meet with a beautiful Lady, well dress'd and gay, who by her airy Appearance, seem'd to be a Woman of the Town; this Nymph, or Goddess, so struck me at the first Sight that I resolv'd at all Events, to follow her Home, which as it happen'd was not far off that Part of the Town, being the usual Residence for those of her Stamp. In short, seeing her go into a House, I thought myself secure, and went to a neighbouring Publicans, where calling for a Quartern of Brandy, by the Description of my fair Charmer, I soon found that that was the usual Place of her Residence and Abode. However, having then a Charge of Plate, and being in a Dishabile, I durst not presume to gratifie my ardent Desires with my fair *Phillis* for the present, but resolved at all Events to visit her, the *Sunday* following, and therefore I discharged my Trust and went Home. Her lovely Form, filled my Soul with extacies of future Joy, and sweet Delight, that I promised myself in the Enjoyment of my adorable Mistress, and therefore all my earnest Care and Study was, how to raise Money sufficient to indulge and gratifie my eager Wishes in the Possession of those

Charms

Charms, with which I was so passionately enamour'd.
Now Fortune, by the following unexpected Accident,
gave me an Opportunity to furnish myself with a suffi-
ciency to execute my amorous Exploit. My Father
according to Custom, being gone to smoak his Pipe after
Dinner, I was left alone in the Shop, and knowing that
he would not return in less than an Hour, I thought
this a proper Time to execute my intended Project;
then going to his Desk, to my great Joy and Surprize
I found the Key in it, and willingly embracing this favourable Opportunity, open'd the Desk, and took seven
Guineas out of three several Baggs, least that Sum, if
taken all out of one, should be miss'd, and I suspected
of the Fraud. No sooner had I put the Money in my
Pocket, but I called up the Maid to look after the Shop,
whilst I went backwards and hid the Money, least perchance I should be discovered, and the Cash found upon
me. But the old Gentleman, who never kept any
regular Account thereof, never missed it, and I the
Sunday following, having dress'd myself to the best
Advantage, put three Guineas of my stolen Treasure
into my Pocket, and about Three in the Afternoon
went to visit my lovely Goddess. Her Apartment was
up one Pair of Stairs, well furnished, her Attendant an
old superannuated Curtezan, worn out in the Wars of
Venus, who in a snuffling Tone, asked me what I would
please to have? I briskly replied, Your Lady. Sir, says
she, please to walk in, and she will be here immediately. I obeyed the old Hag's Command, and seated myself in the Dining-room, where the old Baud fatigued
me with fulsome and impertinent Discourse, concerning her former antiquated Amours, and desired me to
treat her with a Glass of Wine; I readily consented,
and flung down two Shillings for a Bottle; presently
after, in came my *Phillis,* I arose, and paying my Respects, civilly saluted her. She returned the Compliment,
and seating herself by me, with a pleasing Air of Gaiety,
and careless negligence, orders her Servant to put on the
Tea-kettle. Her Discourse was melting and amorous,
which so rais'd my youthful Vigour, that unable any
longer to oppose the mighty force of Love, with eager

haste

hafte, I conducted her to the Bed-chamber, where plung'd in an Ocean of Blifs, and ravifh'd with tranf- porting Delight, I revelled in the repeated embraces of my beauteous Charmer, till wearied and fatigued with amorous Toys, we both returned into the Dining-room, and there drank Tea; but not willing fo foon to quit the Company of my darling She, I propofed a Supper at the *Fountain*-Tavern, in *Katherine-Street*(and fhe rea- dily yielded to my Requeft. But it being Summer-time, and a fine Day, I handed her to the above-mentioned Place of Rendezvous, but was (to my Sorrow after- ward) obferved, and taken Notice of by my Father, who watched my Motions, and faw me go into the faid Tavern. Neverthelefs, for fome fecret Caufe un- known to me, he avoided my Sight; and I wholly in- tent on my amorous Dalliances of Love, never fo much as faw him, nor had the leaft Sufpicion of his being privy to my fecret Amour. In fhort, we had an elegant Supper, Arrack Punch, Gellies, and other Pro- vocations to Luft, and about Three in the Morning I difcharged the Reckoning, fatisfied my mercenary Nymph for her Attendance, and well pleafed with this my firft entrance into this new Scene of Life, went Home, little thinking how dearly I fhould pay for fo trivial and tranfi- tory a Pleafure.

The next Day my Father called me to him, and with an angry and frowning Countenance, afked me where I had been Yefterday in the Afternoon, and what induced me to keep fuch unreafonable Hours? I replied that I had been at Church, and afterwards in Company with two or three of my Companions. Mr. *Gilbert*, fays he, I know your Tricks, and therefore think my- felf in Duty bound to chaftife, and reftrain your lubidinous Excefles, by a timely and fevere Punifhment; fo taking me down into the Cellar, he made me ftrip, and there fcourg'd me very heartily with a Horfewhip, and after- wards ordered that I fhould not be admitted again to his Table, untill by my future good Behaviour, I had amply atton'd for my former paft Offence. But this harfh Treatment had not the defired Effect; for being banifhed from my Father's Table, I din'd below with the Maid, and

and having already tafted the fweets of Love, my Defires daily waxed more fierce and ardent; wherefore to
appeafe the Rage and Torrent of Luft, I made a vigorous Attack on the Servant, who neither arm'd with the
Shield of Modefty or Virtue, made but a faint Refiftance,
and foon render'd herfelf a Victim to my fond and
eager Embraces. Nor was I wanting in Generofity to
my new Miftrefs, for I daily prefented her with fome
Thing new and pretty. I cannot omit to tell you,
that one Day having bought a Pair of Gold laced Shoes
for my *Chloe*, (my Father being out) I call'd her up into
the Parlour, and fhut the Shop Door. *Madam*, faid I
faluting her, *pleafe to accept of this Trifle, and with it
the Heart of your Admirer. This, I prefume, is a Proof
of your being fole Miftrefs of my Efteem and Affections,
which I fhall always maintain fixed and unalterable.*
Chloe well pleafed with the Prefent, fondly careffed me,
which fo fann'd the amorous Flame, that notwithftanding my Father's expected immediate return, or any one's
coming about Bufinefs, I haften'd to enjoy the beauteous Fair-one. But as the Devil would have it (whilft
in the height of Blifs) my Father knock'd at the Door,
at which Confufion and Shame o'erfpread my Countenance. However, *Chloe* had the good Fortune to get
off unperceived by him, who feeing the lac'd Shoes ftanding on the Table, faid, Pray whofe are thefe? methinks
they are very gay. I replied, Sir, *a Lady of whom I
bought fome Silver Lace, defir'd fhe might leave them here
till her return.* This Anfwer as I plainly perceived
was not fatisfactory to the old Gentleman, who ever
after kept a ftricter Eye both on my Conduct in Point
of Honefty, and Behaviour towards the Maid; wherefore I grew more cautious and artful in tricking him of
Cafh, and more vigilant and circumfpect in the Purfuit
of my Amours, till having by Hypocrify, and a well
diffembled good Behaviour, reinftated my felf in the
Love and Efteem of my Father,

I was again admitted to his Table, and all former
Flights of Youth buried in Oblivion, till one *Sunday*
Night coming Home drunk, and finding no body there,
but the Maid, I out of a Frolick, toyed with her on the

Kitcnen

Kitchen Floor, but by ill Fortune was again furprlz'd by my Father, who contrary to Cuftom, opening the Shutters of the Kitchen Window, faw me engaged in the amorous Combat.

The Wench and I were both ignorant of this unexpected Difcovery, and he for that Night took no Notice thereof; but the next Morning he call'd up the Maid, whom he immediately difcharged, and feverely reprimanded me, vowing by all that was good and facred, that if I ever was guilty of the like Impudence, he wou'd totally difcard, and turn me like a Vagabond out of Doors; and furthermore, to prevent fuch diforders in his Houfe, he hir'd a grave, fedate Matron, and who (as he thought) was paft the Follies and Dalliances of Love; but as there can be no Reafon affigned for that bewitching Paffion, fo neither the wrinkl'd Furrows of her aged Face, nor the Vigilancy of my Father, were able to reftrain my curious and ardent Defires of enjoying that living Sepulchre; but as Youth and Age are as oppofite as Fire and Water, fo the cold and feeble Embraces of this antiquated Dame, ferv'd only to allay and quench my luftful Ardour, which reillumin'd by the various and pleafing Objects of the Town, caufed me to naufeate and abhor the falfe deluding Phantoms of Delight, that center'd in the faplefs Poffeffion of fuch a living Monument of Antiquity; and therefore in the Bloom of vigorous Youth, I purfued the willing Fair ones, who tho' like the Apples of *Gomorrah*, they appear beauteous and alluring without, yet are their Infides both rotten and peftilential.

I foon grew tainted by their poifonous Infection, for the Cure of which, I fecretly apply'd myfelf to an able, *Surgeon*, who religioufly kept my Secret, and faithfully difcharged his Truft with Honour and Integrity.

One Evening being in Liquor, as I croffed *Drury-Lane*, I was faluted by a Female, who in a foft and engaging Voice faid, *Come my Dear, won't you give me a Pint of Wine*, and as *Bacchus* is the conftant Companion of Love, I replied, *Yes, my Angel*; fo in I carry'd her to the *Feathers* Tavern, up Stairs we went, and I call'd for a Bottle of Wine, when as foon as we had

drank

drank a Glafs or two a-piece, I grew paffionately fond
of my new Prize, which fhe obferving, and feeing me
difguifed in Liquor, refolv'd to make her Market, and
therefore infifted on Half-a-Crown before Hand; I con-
defcended, and foolifhly gave it her, but was then no
nearer the Point I aim'd at than before: *Well*, faid fhe,
*Give me the other two Shillings and Six-Pence, and you
fhall be feafted with Delight*, which I had no fooner
parted with, and was preparing for the wanton Engagement, but upon a Stamp that fhe gave with her Foot,
in rufh'd four more bold Viragoes, who feizing me,
held my Hands, and rifl'd my Pockets, fwearing that if
I offer'd to make a Noife, or cry out, that they would
charge me with a Conftable, for attempting to abufe
them. At the Word Conftable I was forely affrighted,
fearing I fhould be expofed, and my Father become acquainted therewith; wherefore I feemingly condefcend-
ed to what I could by no Means prevent.

When they had robb'd me of every Thing valuable
except my Cloaths, they fwore they wou'd ftrip me,
if I did not call for a Bottle of Arrack, wherefore to
prevent this impending Ruin, that would have prov'd
my total Overthow, I readily fubmitted to their Impofition, and ringing the Bell, order'd the Drawer to
bring in my Forfeit, (for that was the Term they order'd me to make ufe of); no fooner was the Bottle out,
but the She Devils difappeared, and left me alone to
bemoan my unfortunate Difappointment.

In fhort, I went to the Bar, and loudly complained
of the ill Treatment I had met with, but it availed nothing, for the Landlady infifted on her Reckoning, and
faid, *Sir, I know nothing of the Women, they came in
in with you, had you applied to me for a Lady, I fhou'd have
provided you one, and been accountable for her Civility and
good Behaviour*; at length, finding it in vain to difpute,
I left my Waiftcoat to fatisfy her Demands, and went
Home much fober'd by the Fright and Surprize that I
had been in.

. Sometime after this, ftanding alone at the Shop
Door, an old Woman came and gave me a Letter
fealed with a Thimble, a Mark peculiar to fallen Women)

men) I open'd it, and found by the Scrawl, that it
came from the Servant whom my Father had formerly difcharg'd on my Account ; the Contents were, that
fhe was big with Child, and expected in a Fortnight or
three Weeks to be brought to Bed ; and therefore if I
was willing to skreen myfelf from publick Shame and
Difgrace, I muft take Care, purfuant to the Directions
in the Letter, either to come and fee her, or elfe fend
a conftant Supply during her Lying-in ; but that if I
fail'd to comply with this her Requeft, that fhe fhou'd
thro' Neceffity be forc'd to expofe me. I was not a
little ftartled at this fudden, and (as I thought) unreafonable Demand ; however I gave the Bearer Half-a-Crown
for her Ufe, and Six-pence for her own Trouble in
bringing the unwelcome Letter, with a Promife fhortly
to vifit my *Molly*, and eafe her under her Misfortunes ;
but as the old Saying is, *Out of Sight, out of Mind*, I
forgot my Promife, but fhe ftrictly obferv'd hers, for
in lefs than three Weeks fhe fwore the Baftard to me, and
I was taken into Cuftody for the fame. Hereupon I
immediately wrote to my Father, who came and paffed
his Word to fee the Affair compounded, which he in
three Days Time, upon the Payment of 15 *l*. with the
utmoft Secrecy effected.

This was a ftanding Memorial of my Folly, and
therefore to blot out the Remembrance of it, I feem'd
vaftly uneafy and chagrin'd, infomuch, that my Father
took great Notice thereof, and kindly compaffionating
my anxious Troubles, and Difquietude of Mind, generoufly forgave the Offence, and promifed never to reflect on thefe my former Flights of Youth. Having
thus freed myfelf from this fcandalous Reflection, I
purfued my former Pleafures, and being now in high
Efteem and Credit with my Father, I by artfully al-
tering the Figures of the current Cafh Book, amaffed
together a confiderable Sum, which I hid in the Cellar,
making Ufe thereof as my Extravagancy required.
My reigning Favourites were *Molly St. George*, *Phœbe
Player*, and *Sally King*, with whom I indulg'd myfelf
in all lubidinous Exceffes, as often as Time or Opportunity wou'd permit.

Being

Being now almoſt grown to Man's Eſtate, my Father was taken very ill, and oblig'd to keep his Bed, and therefore the whole Charge of the Buſineſs lay on my Hands, and to do myſelf Juſtice, (during the Time of his Sickneſs) I faithfully diſcharg'd the great Truſt repoſed in me; Honour, Gratitude, and filial Duty, gaining the Aſcendant o'er the baſe Allurements of a depraved Nature. Now the good old Gentleman dying, left me a large Fortune, and a Shop well ſtock'd with abundance of Plate, Jewels, and other valuable Effeƈts, as alſo a Set of worthy Gentlemen for my Cuſtomers, who (to their Honour and Credit be it ſpoken) diſcharg'd their Debts due to the Deceaſed, and continu'd their Favours to me his unworthy Son. My Father nominated three Executors, *viz. Francis Canning*, Eſq; Mr. *Richard Lacon*, and Mr. *Thomas Gilpin*, who all unanimouſly agreed, that I, altho' under Age, ſhou'd carry on the Buſineſs, and Mr. **** as an Overſeer and Obſerver of my Behaviour in this new Scene of Life, boarded with me in the Houſe.

Now the Goddeſs of Fortune ſeem'd to ſhower down her Favours on me, and my Trade daily encreaſing, I found it abſolutely neceſſary to hire a Journeyman, and a Boy to run on Errands. I now totally relinquiſh'd all Thoughts of Extravagancy, abhorr'd and deteſted my former vicious Courſe of Life, and therefore for my Inſtruƈtion and Amuſement, I furniſh'd myſelf with a ſeleƈt Library of Books, and was ſo conſtant and diligent in my Buſineſs, that it was the receiv'd and general Opinion of the Town, that young *Langley* would in a few Years gain a plentiful Eſtate ; and had I been ſo happy as to have maintain'd the prudent and diſcreet Oeconomy that I obſerv'd at my firſt launching out into the World, I had certainly verified thoſe candid Conceptions that the Town in general had conceiv'd of me ; for in the firſt Year that I follow'd Buſineſs, upon the Ballance of Accounts, I found myſelf 700 *l.* gainer by my Trade, and that more likely to encreaſe than diminiſh, if I trod thoſe Paths in which I had ſo wiſely began. But alaſs! what is ſo prevalent

on

on Youth as bad Example, difguifed under the falfe
Pretext of paternal Care, and inviolable Friendfhip.

Mr. **** (whom I mention'd before) was the only
acting Executor, wherefore to pleafe him was all my
earneft Care and Study; now this Gentleman having
imprudently entrufted me with my Brother's Fortunes,
which were a 1000 *l.* on the Payment of 5 *l. per Cent.*
I naturally grew fond of his Company, and made him
a Prefent of a Gold Watch and Chain, thinking thereby more firmly to rivet myfelf in his Affections, and
wholly engage him to my Intereft; and by my artful
and engaging Behaviour, I won fo infenfibly upon him,
that (laying afide the Refpect and Awe due to a Guardian) he not only repofed an entire Confidence in me,
and never examin'd into the State of my Affairs, but
chofe, nay, even infifted on my being his Companion,
and Partner in his frequent Debauches, which by their
continual Repetitions, fo vitiated my former Principles,
that the young *Goldfmith* was foon metamorphofed into
the profufe and prodigal Spendthrift.

Thus having none to awe and reftrain my boundlefs
and unlimited Defires, I foon became a profeft Rake
and Whoremafter; I cannot forget that one Night being in Company with ****, and having drank very plentifully, I propofed to conduct him to the Appartment of
one of my favourite Ladies; he feem'd highly pleafed
with the Proffer, and we took Coach and drove to
Madam's Lodgings, who being a well bred Women,
entertained us in a courteous and obliging Manner : The
old Gentleman was foon captivated with her Charms,
and burn'd for Enjoyment, which I obferving, call'd
her afide, and faid, *Madam, the Gentleman is my Uncle, and therefore I defire you wou'd oblige him and me
alfo in the Requeft I am now going to make you ;* fhe with
a Smile confented, whereupon I order'd her, whilft the
Fumbler was in the vain Purfuit of Delight, to pick his
Pocket of fome Notes that I knew he had about him.
She faithfully perform'd her Promife, and afterwards
gave them into my Hands.

Shortly after this, fhe and he (after feveral Attempts
to do, what in Reality he could not effect) return'd in-

to

to the Dining-Room, little thinking of the merry Trick that had been put upon him. To be brief, we ſtaid till about Three in the Morning, then calling a Coach, went Home.

The next Day, he recollecting himſelf where he had been, and miſſing his Bills, call'd for me, and acquainted me with his Loſs, and that he ſuſpected that, that damn'd painted Whore had ſtolen them from him. I ſeem'd to be in a Paſſion, and ſwore, that I believ'd ſhe wou'd ſcorn ſo baſe an Action, but that for his Satisfaction, I would go and enquire into the Matter, and at the ſame Time let him know, that if ſhe had them, ſhe would inſiſt on a handſome Preſent on the Delivery of the ſame ; *Damn her*, ſays he, *Give her two Guineas, and place them to my Account.* Thus the old Gentleman paid the Forfeit due to his Folly, and Mrs. *Morris* and I revell'd the enſuing Night at his Coſt and Charges. This Impoſition gave the old Fool ſuch a Diſtaſte and Abhorrence to the Female Proſtitutes, that after I had return'd him his Notes, he ſolemnly vow'd never to converſe with any of them for the future.

Sometime after, (as the Biter is bit at laſt) a Gentleman well dreſſed ſtopt at my Door in a Coach, and coming into the Shop, complimented me on my Fathers Deceaſe, and expreſſed the great Value and Eſteem he had for him, and that upon his Account he was willing to continue his Favours, for the Encouragement of me his Son. I humbly thank'd him for his Civility, and told him, I ſhould ſtrenuouſly endeavour to maintain the good Repute, and fair Character of my deceaſed Father, by a ſtrict Adherence to his Principles of inviolable Honour and Integrity. He full fraught with Deceit, ſeem'd highly pleaſed with my Reply, and therefore, as a ſeeming Promiſe of his Friendſhip, beſpoke 150 *l.* worth of Plate, and after he had given me the Impreſſion of his Coat of Arms, from a Seal that hung to his Gold Watch, ſaid, *He ſhould be glad to take a Glaſs of Wine with me.* I was proud of the Honour, and we went to a neighbouring Tavern, where drinking plentifully, he took the Opportunity, whilſt I was elevated with Liquor, to propoſe a Lady to me in Marriage,

Marriage, who (altho' deform'd) he faid, had 30,000 n
Fortune; and further more he added, that fhe was under his Tuition, and Direction of his Spoufe; and that
if I pleafed to come down to his Country Seat, he
would engage to gain her Confent, and bring her to a
fpeedy Compliance.

This artful Bait had its defir'd Effect, for I now not
only look'd on him as a good Cuftomer, but as a worthy Friend, and therefore I invited him to Dinner with
me the next Day, and he in return engaged me to fup
with him the next Evening, at his Lodgings in *Tavi-
ftock-ftreet*, where an elegant Entertainment was provided. The Chambers were richly furnifh'd, and il-
luminated with Wax Candles, in Silver Candlefticks,
and Sconces in the fame Metal; two Footmen in lac'd
Liveries waited at Supper, and every Thing augmented
the Opinion I had already received of his being a Gentleman of a large and plentiful Eftate. About Twelve
I took my Leave of him, and the next Day gave Orders
for getting ready his Plate as foon as poffible, which being done, he in about a Weeks Time came to me; I
fhew'd him the Plate, with which he was extreamly
pleafed, and highly commended the curious Workman-
fhip thereof, and faid, *Sir, Come let's take a Bottle before we part, for To-Morrow Morning I muft go to my
Country Seat.* I with Pleafure yielded to his Requeft,
and whilft we were in the Tavern, he pull'd out his
Pocket-Book, and gave me a Note on a *Vintner* in
Bartholomew-Clofe, for 150 *l.* payable in three Weeks,
faying, *Sir, This I prefume is the fame to you as ready
Cafh; but pleafe for your own Satisfaction, to fend immediately and enquire into the Character of the Man.* I
readily obey'd his Order, and finding by the Account I
receiv'd from my Servant, that the *Vintner* was a Perfon of a fair Character; upon his Endorfement of the
Note I accepted it in full Payment for my Goods, and
fent the Plate pack'd up to the *Gun-*Tavern at *Billingfgate*, purfuant to his Order; neither did I forget to
take a Direction where he liv'd in the Country, but
promifed as foon as poffible to vifit my intended wealthy
Bride.

In

In ſhort, we parted, and I went Home quite blown
up with the aſpiring Thoughts of raiſing my Fortune
at once, and making a ſplendid and gay Appearance in
the World; but as I lay one Night in my Bed, ruminating on the imaginary Poſſeſſion of the Nymph, who
(like the Goddeſs of Riches) was to load me with her
Favours, a ſudden Thought eclipſed my Joys, perhaps
(ſays I to myſelf) I am deceiv'd, and this great Fortune
like Fairy Land, as ſoon as ſeen may vaniſh and diſap-
pear, wherefore I reſolv'd to ſend my Neighbour
***** (a cunning and artful Man, whoſe Veracity and
Integrity I had often experienced) the next Day down
to the Gentleman's Seat, with Orders to make a private
Enquiry in the Neighbourhood, of the Truth and Reality of what my ſeeming Friend had given me ſo fair
an Expeꝗance of. Accordingly I gave him two Guineas, and loaded with Inſtruꝗions he departed.

I was now rack'd with alternate Hope and Fear till
his Return, which was in three Days Time, when he
ingeniouſly told me, that after the utmoſt Search, and
ſtricteſt Scrutiny it was poſſible for Man to make, he
could not find out, or even hear of any ſuch Gentleman or Lady that ever lived or reſided in that Country.
This was ſhocking News to me, and I reaſonably con-
jeꝗured, that ſince I was deceiv'd in my Miſtreſs, there
was alſo ſome Fallacy in the Note he had given me in
Payment for my Goods; but ſince I had accepted the
ſame, I knew no other Remedy but to wait with Patience, 'till Time ſhould bring to Light the Fraud, and
diſcover the whole Villainy. As I judg'd, ſo it happened, for on ſending my Servant with the Note, after
three Days Grace, to demand the Money, the *Vintner*
was gone, and his Houſe ſhut up. Highly incens'd at
this baſe and ſcandalous Trick. I vow'd Revenge on the
pretended Gentleman, and reſolved if poſſible, at all
Events, to lay him by the Heels, and make an Example of him, to deter others from the like Falſehood and
Treachery.

About a Fortnight afterwards a Gentlewoman came
to my Shop, and deſired to ſpeak with me in private;
I led her into the Parlour, where ſhe immediately burſt
out

cut into Tears, and for some Time could not utter a Word, till being recover'd from her Diforder, she said, *Sir, I am ruin'd and undone for ever, that Villain* **** *has impofed on my Husband's Credulity, and under a Pretence of raifing him* 450 *l. by the Difcount of his Notes, to keep his Payments good with the Wine-Merchant, has obtain'd three Notes of Hand of him for* 150 *l. each, which he has paid away, and applied the Money to his own Ufe.*

This (I confefs) at firft ftartled me, but upon a further enquiry, I found that her Husband was the fame Perfon on whom I had the above-mention'd Note, endors'd to me by the faid *Anthony G****, the fham Gentleman, and my pretended Friend ; fo commiferating her deplorable Circumftances, I not only promis'd not to trouble her Husband, but alfo to ufe my Intereft and Endeavour with the other Gentlemen (my Fellow-fufferers in the Fraud) to. engage them to a Compiyance, in granting Mr. *M****, her Husband, a Letter of Licence for three Years. Highly fatisfied with this generous Proffer, and a farther Affurance of my refenting the Injury and Injuftice done both to myfelf and her by Mr. *G****, fhe humbly thank'd me and departed, leaving Directions with me where to find her Husband.

Next Day according to my Promife, I went to the Gentlemen, who being of tender and human Difpofitions, were eafily brought to an Accommodation, wherefore fending for *M****, and an Attorney, we agreed on Terms to the Satisfaction of all Parties. But one Day walking along *Fleet-Street*, as I pafs'd St. *Dunftan's*, a ftrange Gentleman came up to me, 'and ask'd me, whither my Name was not *Langley*? I replied, Yes. Sir, fays he, have you not a Demand on one *Anthony G****? Yes, Sir, quoth I, well then, faid he, we'll ftep into the *Bull-Head*, and there I'll inform you further of the Matter. So in we went, where he told me, that he had *G**** Dead-fet, and that if I would give him one Guinea, he would engage to have him in clofe Quarters in lefs than an Hour. Overjoyed at this News, I freely granted his Demand, and told him that I would wait there till his return ; but had I been

as

as good as my Word, I fhould have ftayed there till
now, for I never after fet Eyes on him. This fecond
Bite exafperated me more than the former, and I refolved if ever I caught *G*****, to make him pay for all.
Wherefore I employed a brifk and expert Attorney to
hunt him out, and promifed to be accountable for all
Charges in the Execution thereof. At laft I took the
Villain, and clapt him into the *Marſhalſea-Priſon*, where
he obliged me to Sue him to an Execution, and there
he remain'd during the whole Time that I continu'd in
Trade.

Sometime after this, I became acquainted with a noted *Vintner*, near *Gray's-Inn-Gate*, in *Holborn*, with
whom I contracted fuch an Intimacy and Friendſhip,
that every Evening I paid him a Vifit, and he (altho'
in the decline of Life) was foolifhly fond of Horfe-
Racing, Cock-Fighting, Hunting, and the like expen-
five and coftly Paftimes, and Diverfions, and being a
conftant Attendant at *Newmarket* Seafons, kept a good
Gelding for that Purpofe. Being (as I have faid before)
daily at his Houfe, he often follicited me to accompany him thither, and greatly enlarg'd on the Grandeur
of the Affembly, and the variety of Recreations and
Amufements that prefented themfelves, for the Entertainment and Delight of the curious Spectators. At
laft I yielded to his Requeft, and furnifh'd myfelf with
a good Saddle-Horfe, and other Jockey-like Accoutre-
ments, fuitable to the Humour and Tafte of fuch vain
and giddy Fools, who neglecting their proper Employ-
ments, endeavour to fhine in a Sphere of Life, that juftly renders them the Scorn and Contempt of Men of
Fortune.

Newmarket is feated in a Bottom, and hath nothing
to recommend it, but the extravagant Impofition of the
Inn-keepers, occafion'd by the numerous Concourfe of
hair brain'd Fellows, that fwarm like Ants in a Mole-
hill, with precipitate Hafte, ftriving to ruin both themfelves and their Families; whilft the rafcally Grooms,
under Pretence of letting them into the Secret, pick
their Pockets, and run away with their Money.

In

In the high Street, or middle of the Town, is a Coffee-Houfe, a common Receptacle for N*** and Sharpers, Thieves, and common Tradefmen, who pafs the Evening at *Hazard*, where the Nobleman loofes his Eftate, the Tradefman his Cafh and Credit, whilft the others laugh at their Stupidity, and enrich themfelves by their Downfall. Early in the Morning, the *Heath* fwarms with Horfes and Dogs, as the Land of *Egypt* did formerly with Locufts, where each one purfues the Bent of his Inclinations, generally comprifed under the three following Clafles; fome Hunt, fome Courfe, and the reft ftand gaping (like peeping *Tom* of *Coventry*) at the Race Horfes, taking their Morning Sweats, who are fo fwaddled up, that were they not a diftinct Part of the Creation, any reafonable Man wou'd take them for fo many *Egyptian* Mummies raifed from the Dead, to fcamper upon the grafly Turff, for the Benefit of the Morning Air.

As for Hunting, I am apt to believe, that it was firft invented by fome *Popifh* Prieft, fince it requires fo much implicit Faith, for there a Man muft ride hard five or fix Hours, and venture his Neck for a Thing of which (if he perchance happens to fee it in the Chace) he has but an imperfect Glympfe, and when gotten is not worth his Acceptance. About Twelve each Troop haftens to its Barracks, like Oxen to *Smithfield* on a Market Day, where the mercenary Grooms are looking out fharp for new Faces, to wheedle themfelves into a good Dinner, and a hearty Booze, and ftriving to outdo each other in lying, pretending to give you as true a Genealogy of the Race Horfes, as an Antiquarian of *Wales*, and of *Owen Tudor*'s Family. About Three in the Afternoon, the Horfes are led upon the Courfe, where the whole Company affembles at the *Devil's-Ditch*, and there till Four, they are as noify and bufy as fo many Stock-jobbers, or *Jewifh* Brokers in *Exchange-Alley*, a little before the drawing of a State Lottery. A little after Four, at the folemn Beat of Drum, the Horfes ftart, and the whole Hoft, like a Company of wild *Arabs*, in a confufed and promifcuous Rout, fcoure after them, without Rhime or Reafon, and at

the

the Turn of the Lands, fet up as hideous an Out-cry
as a Parcel of naked Wenches difcover'd bathing themfelves in a River; fome damning the Riders, and others
the Horfes for loofing the Heat, whilft the Winners
laugh in their Sleeves, and pay as much Reverence and
Homage to the Victor, who is led in Triumph into
the Town, as the *Indians* do at prefent to any of their
moft celebrated *Pagods*, or a zealous *Roman* to the con-
fecrated Water. Here it was that I firft caught the ruinous Itch of Gaming, which was ever after fo prevalent, that I cou'd not fee a Box and Dice, but I was
as fond of the new Gewgaw as a Child is of a Rattle,
and at firft (as the old Saying is, *the Devil is kind to a
young Gamefter*) I won upwards of 700 *l.* and had the
Wit and Difcretion to carry it off; but this was but as a
lively Similitude of the feint glimmering of Life, that
vainly buoys up the departing Patient, before the fatal
Approach of horrid Death; for in lefs than fix Months,
I doubl'd the Lofs of my former Gain, and by my too
frequent Extravagancies, now found my Circumftances
in a melancholy Pofture, and my Subftance vaftly im-
paired; however, I play'd my Cards fo artfully, that
none of my Creditors ever dreamt or fufpected me guilty of fo much Imprudence and Folly.

One Day being at my Friend the *Vintner's* Houfe,
he called me afide, and defir'd the Favour of me to
take his Niece into my Service; I readily condefcend-
ed, and giving my old Servant a Month's Warning,
prepared for the Reception of the new one, whom, on
her Uncle's Account, I always ufed with the utmoft
Civility and good Manners. In fhort, after fhe had
been with me a Month, I difcover'd fomething fo *Je
ne fcay Quoi*, in her innocent and modeft Behaviour,
that fo infenfibly ftole upon me, that in defpight of my
vicious and inordinate Defires, her Virtue fo awed and
reftrained my villainous Intentions, that for fome Time
I durft not approach her, but with the utmoft Refpect
and Modefty; till one fatal Night to her, coming Home
a little elate with Liquor, I call'd for a Bottle of Wine,
and defired her Company to partake of it; fhe with a
Blufh modeftly excufed herfelf, which rather heighten'd

D 2   than

than diminifh'd my ardent Paffion, and therefore I infifted on her Compliance with my friendly Requeft;
fhe confented, and I took this favourable Opportunity
to acquaint her with my fincere Love and Efteem; then
turning the Difcourfe to an amorous Scene of the fweet
Delights of Love, gave her to underftand, by a double
Entendre, the meaning of my foul Intent. Whether
her amorous Star had then the Afcendant, or the God
of Love prefided in the melting languifh of her Eyes,
I foon read her approaching Deftiny, who was then upon
the point of being ruined by me, without any Regard to
my former Efteem for her, or the Friendfhip I had long
profeffed to her Uncle; fuch is the Worth of a Man
given up to Luft, and of fuch Value his Friendfhip.

My own Houfe, which before feem'd to me a Prifon, was now chang'd into a perfect *Elyfium*, and I
neither knew, nor wifhed for any greater Blifs, than
the Pleafure of my never to be forgotten *Clarinda's* in-
eftimable Society, and unparelled Generofity, in exuberant Love; for fhe (diftant as the Centre from the Pole)
difdain'd all mercenary Ends, and was far more deferving of being the legal Partner of a facred Connubial
Bed, than Miftrefs of a lawlefs Love, that fometime or
other wou'd inevitably prove her Ruin.

In fhort, had I been fo happy and prudent, as to
have made her my Wife, I am well affured, that the
Union of the facred Knot, wou'd have exempted me
from thofe various and unheard of Inconveniencics, that
deteftable Poverty and horrid Want in the Sequel expofed me to. During the Heat of my Amour, I had
feveral advantageous Offers of Marriage propofed to
me, which I declined for the following Reafon, *viz.*
That the Parents or Friends of fuch young Ladies that
were actually in a Capacity to Portion them with large
Fortunes, infifted on proper Settlements for their Daughters, and alfo an exact Scrutiny into my Affairs, which
altho' by my artful and deceitful Conduct, appear'd to
be in a flourifhing Condition, yet if nicely examin'd
into, there was nothing to be found, but the Ruins and
poor Remains of a fhatter'd Fortune; for by this Time
I had obtain'd a confiderable Credit from feveral Merchants

chants in Jewels, and by the punctual Payment of my Bills, my Notes paſſed as current as thoſe of the *Bank*, and I conſequently was reputed a great and eminent Trader, particularly in that moſt advantageous and profitable Part of Buſineſs; but alas, to my Sorrow, I only fulfilled the old *Engliſh* Proverb, *Robbing* Peter *to pay* Paul; for under the ſpecious Pretence of diſpoſing of the above-mention'd Goods to Perſons of Quality, I ſecretly pawn'd them to thoſe, who out of a ſordid Lucre of Gain, and an avaritious Deſire of more than legal Intereſt, ſupply'd me with what Caſh I requir'd, and by their Indiſcretion and Folly, in relying on my Integrity, ſuffer'd themſelves to be greatly impoſed on by me, who frequently borrow'd larger Sums on thoſe Goods, than what I had contracted to pay for them.

By this Means I had always a large Quantity of Money at my Command, and thinking this Artifice wou'd always paſs undiſcover'd, I liv'd more like an Heir apparent to a great Eſtate, than a wary and induſtrious Tradeſman; Aſſemblies, Operas, Maſquerades, Plays, and Country Journeys, were now my only Delight, and my ſole favourite Companions, ſuch young Gentlemen, who were either in the full Poſſeſſion of large Eſtates, or in a fair Expectation of the ſame.

I can't omit to inform my Readers, that two of theſe young Sparks and I, having made an Agreement to paſs a Fortnight or three Weeks at *Greenwich*, for the Benefit of the Air in the Summer Seaſon, we quarter'd at the *Greyhound* Inn there; when one Evening o'er a merry Bottle, a Propoſal was made to patrole thro' the Town in queſt of Ladies of Pleaſure, which was readily agreed too by all Parties; but finding none there either handſome enough, well rigg'd, or fitting for our Purpoſes; I immediately propoſed to return to *London*, and bring down three of the beſt of that Stamp, that I cou'd find were willing to indulge themſelves with the rural Diverſions of a Country Life. My Companions highly applauded my Deſign, and I took a pair of Oars, who preſently wafted me to *Temple-Stairs*, where as ſoon as I landed, I went in Purſuit of my Game, and being well known to the Porter at the *Roſe* in *Covent-Garden*,

to

to him I apply'd for the Execution of my Defign. The Porter went directly out, whilft I call'd for a Pint of Wine, to wait for his Return, who in about half an Hour's Time brought three wanton Laffes well dreffed, and not difagreeable; I arofe, and faluting them faid, *Ladies, pleafe to feat yourfelves ; my Bufinefs is to acquaint you, that your Company is defired for a Fortnight or three Weeks at* Greenwich, *where you may be affur'd to be treated in the moft courteous and polite manner ; for the Perfons that you will have to do with, are Gentlemen of Honour, and therefore if you approve of my Propofal, pleafe to provide yourfelves with fuch Linnen and Apparel as you fhall think proper for your Ufe, during our Refidence in the Country, I'll remain here an Hour longer, fo Ladies, if ye are willing, go and prepare yourfelves for the Journey.* They unanimoufly confented, and dropping a Curtfie at their going out of the Room, return'd with their Baggage according to the Time appointed. I call'd a Coach and drove to the *Temple-Stairs,* where I took a Pair of Oars, and landed at *Greenwich,* but not without the repeated Infults of opprobrious Language, commonly ufed by the Vulgar on the *Thames ;* however, my Female Companions verified the *Latin* Adage, *Nemo me impune laceffit,* and return'd their Scurrility, with as fmart and Satyrical Repartees, as if they had ferv'd a feven Years Aprenticefhip to any of the moft celebrated Fifhwomen at *Billingfgate.*

I look'd upon myfelf now as an *Eaftern* Monarch, bearing as abfolute Sway in my floating Seraglio, as the *Grand Seignior* ever did in his fumptuous Edifice at *Conftantinople.* In fhort, I conducted the Ladies to the *Greyhound-Inn,* where my Companions were, with impatience waiting for my Return. Upon our Entrance into the Room, they civilly complimented the Women, and we all being feated, I faid, *Gentlemen, I prefume I've anfwered your Expectations, and honourably difcharg'd my Truft, pleafe therefore to take the firft Choice, and the Nymph that hath not the Honour to pleafe either of you, fhall be the Co-partner of my Bed, and be taken under my immediate Care and Protection.* This generous Offer augmented their Delight. and each *Pyramis*
chofe

chofe his favourite *Thisbe.* Now nothing was to be feen but a perfect Harmony, and an uninterrupted Scene of Joys, the Gods of Love and Wine, by alternate Poffeffion refided in our Hearts, nor were the Sylvan Deities exempt from participating the mutual and tranf- porting Pleafures that we fully poffeffed, in the fhady Retirements of the adjacent Park ; but thofe foft and endearing Careffes of our amorous Goddeffes, by reite- rated Repetitions, grew dull and infipid, and we cloy'd and wearied with the continual Performance of daily Sacrifice to the *Cyprian* Dame, refolv'd to put a merry Trick upon the Ladies, and leave them in the Lurch.

One Day after we had din'd, we defir'd them to go and walk in the Park, and we wou'd follow immedi- ately, and order the Tea-kettle, and other Neceffaries to be brought up with us thither. They feem'd well pleafed with our Requeft, and readily obey'd, where- upon we call'd our Landlord, and paid him his Bill, and then croffed the Water to the *Ifle of Dogs,* where we fpent the remainder of the Day in Mirth and Jollity, highly diverted that we had bilk'd the Proftitutes of their expected Fare. They (as I fuppofed) walk'd in the Park a long Time, and feeing no Appearance of us, or the Servant of the Houfe, return'd to the Inn, and on Enquiry, finding that we were gone, (as the Land- lord told them by our Order) to *London,* they quarrel- led with each other for their Folly, in complying with our Requeft, before they had had Satisfaction for their Ware ; but finding it in vain to trifle away their Time in fcolding and railing to no Purpofe, they hir'd a Pair of Oars for *London,* and as ill Fortune wou'd have it, our Boats both met over-againft *Cuckolds-Point* ; they immediately fet up a Cry, that both alarm'd and fur- priz'd us, the female *Virago's* were for boarding, but we fheered off as faft as we cou'd, and encouraging our Watermen to make Way, we in fpite of our Adverfaries kept about four Boats length a Head of them, but were forc'd to bear the Lafh of their Tongues, till we got within three or four Yards of the Landing Place of the *Temple,* and then we jump'd afhore, making the beft of our Way to one of the Gentleman's Chambers, to

D 4   prevent

prevent the Scandal and Difturbance that wou'd have enfued, had they come up with us.

Sometime after this, a married Gentleman of my Acquaintance, defir'd me to accompany him and his Spoufe to *Greenwich*, to which I readily affented, being glad of this favourable Opportunity to make known my Affections to Mifs *Jenny*, their Chamber-maid ; we ftopt at the *Gun-Tavern* at *Billingfgate*, and put three Bottles of Wine into the Boat, to animate our Spirits, and excite Mirth and Gaiety, in our Paffage to the intended Port. The Gentleman afked me, if I cou'd recommend him to an Inn ? Yes, Sir, I reply'd, and the beft in Town, where I have been often very civilly entertain'd, the Landlord knows me perfectly well, and I'll engage that you and your Lady fhall be accommodated to the utmoft of your Defires ; and as for Mifs *Jenny*, fays I, in a jocofe manner, I'll recommend her to a brifk young Fellow, that's worth Money, altho' he ferves as a Drawer in the Houfe ; *Jenny* blufh'd, the Lady laugh'd, and my Friend drank a Bumper to the good Succefs of this new Amour.

In an Hour's Time we landed, and I led the Way to my old Inn the *Greyhound*, where the Landlord exprefs'd a great Satisfaction in feeing me, and return'd me many Thanks for the Favour I did him, in recommending fuch worthy Guefts to his Houfe ; here we order'd a Supper, and I took an Opportunity, whilft *Jenny* was in the Kitchen, to let her know how paffionately I lov'd her, and by a ftedfaft obfervance of her Eyes, found that my Propofals were not difagreeable ; wherefore I boldly urg'd her to a Compliance that Night. She was eafily perfuaded to yield to my Embraces, provided it cou'd be manag'd with Secrecy ; whereupon I faithfully promifed to contrive the Matter with fo much Privacy and Cunning, that none in the Houfe (except my old Particular, the Chambermaid of the Inn) fhou'd have the leaft Occafion to dream or fufpect any Thing of our Amour. With this folemn Affurance of Secrecy, confirm'd with a Volley of Oaths and Imprecations, *Jenny* confented, and the only Difficulty now remaining was, to engage the Chambermaid

to be faithful to her Truft ; wherefore I immediately took
her afide, and fliding Half a Guinea into her Hand, im-
parted my Defign to her, who (well pleafed with the
Bribe) engaged to perform her Part to my Satisfaction.
At Supper we were very merry, and I was highly pleafed
at the Conceit of the approaching Enjoyment of my new
Favourite, when we ogled each other as odly as *Adam*
and *Eve* in an old Suit of Hangings.

The hour of Repofe drawing nigh, my Friend called
to the Chambermaid to fhew him a Room with two
Beds in it, one for himfelf and his Spoufe, and the other
for Mifs *Jenny*, who (the Lady being big with Child)
was defired might lie in the fame Chamber with them;
but it was all in vain, for the artful Huffey, well vers'd
in Intreagues, with an hypocritical Cant and Smile, declared, that would the Gentleman give her Fifty Pounds,
fhe could not oblige him with that Favour, for all the
Rooms (except thofe referv'd for our Lodgings) were
taken up and engag'd. The Gentleman being an eafy
and credulous Perfon, believ'd what fhe faid was true,
fo ordering her and *Jenny* to light them to bed, took
his Leave of me for that Night. As foon as they were
gone up Stairs, I called for a Bottle of Wine, and fat
fmoaking my Pipe with Impatience, waiting the Return
of my Miftrefs, who as foon as fhe had undrefs'd her
Lady, and put her bed, came and fate down by me,
and prefently after in came my true and faithful Confidant, whom I defired to fit down and bear us Company.
When the Bottle was out, I defired her to fhew us to
our Room, and bring a Cool-tankard with her up Stairs;
right, Sir, faid fhe, for the Weather is hot, and your
Tafk is hard, for there are many Hours between this,
and the Morning. The Chamber we lay in was up
two Pair of Stairs backwards, and commodioufly contrived for the like Intreagues, for there were two Doors
to it, and a private Pair of Stairs, unknown to any but
us, and the People of the Inn ; fo that fuppofing the
Gentleman had had any Sufpicion, and fhould have attempted (if he had known my Apartment) to furprize
us in the midft of our lawlefs Pleafures, it was morally
impoffible that he fhould fucceed in his Defign, for as

I

I lock'd the Door fronting the great Stair-cafe, before we went to bed, ſo I could eaſily have conceal'd my Doxy, by turning her out at the private Stairs ; but poor Gentleman, he, I ſuppoſe had ſomething elſe to think on, for although *Jenny* and I lay together during our whole Stay there, neither he or his Spouſe ever imagin'd any thing of the Matter. In about ten Days, we return'd to *London*, where I viſited him as uſual, and by private Billets appointed my Charmer to meet me at the *Blue-Poſts*, without *Temple-Bar* ; ſhe was truly obſervant to my Aſſignations, and manag'd her growing Burthen ſo artfully, that although ſhe lay with the other Maid, yet neither ſhe, nor her Lady for a conſiderable Time, obſerved that ſhe was with Child, till at laſt, unable to conceal her publick Shame any longer, ſhe quitted her Service, and took private Lodgings, from whence, ſhe daily plagued me with Letters ſtuffed with Nonſence and Love, with which (being now pretty well cloy'd) the remembrance of her former Embraces was grown not only grating, but loathſome. However, rather than to ſuffer her to lay the Child to me, I appointed her a Meeting, at the *Anchor* and *Baptiſt's-Head* in *Chancery-Lane*, where to acquit myſelf with Honour, I gave her a Purſe of Guineas, and there took my final Leave of her, neither have I ever heard of her ſince, nor would the Gentleman or his Lady have ever been acquainted with this our Amour, had I not now publiſh'd it to the World. But notwithſtanding theſe libidinous Exceſſes and Digreſſions, *Clarinda*, by Merit, claim'd the greateſt Share of my Affections, was privy and acquainted with all my Follies and Extravagances, ſhe often with an engaging and perſuaſive Air, repreſented the diſmal State of horrid Want, and griping Penury, which ſhe clearly foreſaw muſt be the future Iſſue of my profuſe and licentious Manner of Life ; and as often with repeated Aſſurances of real Love and ſincere Friendſhip, warmly preſſed me to deſiſt and leave my vicious Courſes ; but all her Tears and amicable Admonitions prov'd abortive, and unable to curb and reſtrain me in the full Career of my lawleſs Paſſions, that blindly hurried me on to my utter Ruin. However

ever to do her Juſtice, although ſhe knew the Parties
of whom I had borrow'd conſiderable Sums of Money,
and doubtleſs might by a Diſcovery of my Affairs, been
amply rewarded by them, yet ſo extenſive was the Generoſity of her Soul, that ſhe diſdain'd ſo vile and ſordid
a Practice, deteſted and abhorred ſuch mean and mercenary Vices.

Sometime after this, I went to *Windſor*, with my
particular and worthy Friend Capt. *L*****, his Spouſe,
and a young Lady a Relation of his. We were very
merry in our Journey, and during our Reſidence there,
we enjoyed all the Diverſions of a rural Life, for having
a Coach and four at Command, we took the Benefit
of the Morning Air in the Park, and her Grace the
Dutcheſs of *Marlborough*, being then in *London*, we
frequently viſited her Lodge, ſo celebrated for its curious
and inimitable Pieces of Painting, and in the Afternoons
drove to the antient Colledge of *Eaton*, ſo fam'd for
Learning, and ſo eminent in the Numbers of bright and
ingenious Gentlemen, that are deſervedly deem'd the Pride
and Glory of their Country; Nor was the Caſtle un-
obſerv d, that noble and magnificent Structure, ſo
much honoured with the Preſence of our ancient
Monarchs, and ſo greatly ornamented and embelliſh'd
by various and bizarre Figures, form'd in different Shapes,
from Numberleſs Arms, by the ingenious and artful
Contrivers. Here is alſo a beauteous Terras, command-
ing a delightful Proſpect of all the adjacent Country,
and from whence the curious Spectators are gratifyed with
a View of the ſtately Cathedral of St. *Paul's*, in *London*.
Love and Gallantry were now the ſole Topicks of our
Converſation, and the young Lady being ſingle, I made
honourable Propoſals of Love to her, with which neither
the, nor the Captain or his Lady, were in the leaſt
diſpleaſed. In a Fortnight's Time we returned to Town,
and ſtopped at the St. *Alban's* Tavern in St. *Alban's-*
Street, where we ordered a Supper, and the Footman to
bring the Arms that we carried in the Country for our
ſafe-guard and defence up into our Room. After Supper,
we drank plentifully, and Wine growing more potent
than Reaſon, the Captain (for variety Sake) would kiſs

my

my fair Companion, whereby I thinking my Property
infring'd, oppofed his Intent, upon which Words arofe,
and the Piftols lying on a Marble Slab in the Room, we
each of us haftily fnatched up one of them, and prefenting, attempted to give Fire, ; but were providentially
difappointed in our Defign, by the diligence and care of
the Footman, who had unloaded them, well knowing
the capricious Temper of his Mafter, when difguis'd in
Liquor. The Ladies were forely affrighted at this fur-
prizing Rencountre, and fkream'd out, at which the
Landlord and his drawers came in upon us, and feeing
us (for we had thrown down our Arms) hard at it with
our Fifts, parted us, and calling two Coaches, fent us
home to our refpective Habitations. Next Morning
when I awak'd, I was ignorant of what had happened,
and about Eleven the Captain came to fee me, then
we went to take our Morning's Draught, when, upon
faying what News, Sir, News, quoth he, my Wife
tells me, that you and I were going to murther one a-
nother laft Night, on Mifs B****'s Account, but I de-
clare upon Honour, that I knew nothing of it, and fince
it was a mad Frolick, I'll engage the young Lady to
be at my Houfe this Evening, and fhall expect your
Company there likewife. I punctually obey'd his Orders,
and we fpent the Evening very agreeably, all Strife and
Contention gave Place to Mirth and Gaiety : We afk'd
the Ladies Pardon for putting them in a Fright, which
they readily granted, and Mifs B****, with a pleafing
and jocofe Air, added, that fhe had conceiv'd a much
better Opinion of her felf than fhe ever had before, fince
two fuch Gentlemen, at the hazard of their Lives, had
contended for her Favours; whereupon bowing, we returned the Compliment, and it now growing late, I waited
on Mifs Home. All Night I was reftlefs and uneafie,
her lovely Form and perfect Modefty, adorn'd with Virgin Innocence, had fo captivated my roving Heart, that
I was no more Mafter of my own Perfon, but paffed
the tedious Night rack'd with alternate Hope and Fear.
The next Evening, I fent for the Captain to the *Queen's-
Head*-Tavern, in *Holborn*, and there (to eafe my Tor-
ment) difclos'd my ardent Paffion; he Gentleman-like,
in an open and free Manner, told me that her Fortune
was

was but fmall, and that too, in the Hands of thofe who he feared would not without Difficulty, furrender it. However, faid he, if you are upon honourable Terms, I'll ufe my Intereft to bring Mifs to a Compliance. Sir, fays I, I fhould think myfelf undeferving of that Friend-fhip you always profeffed for me, fhould I even prefume to entertain the leaft Glympfe of a difhonourable Thought for a young Lady any ways related to your worthy Fa-mily. Hereupon the Captain well pleafed with my ge-nerous Reply, told me where her Uncle lived, and in a friendly Manner advifed me to apply to him, who being a Gentleman of Fortune, if he approved of my Propofal, would inevitably compell her Guardians to pay her Fortune upon the marriage Day. Purfuant to my Friend's good Counfel, I went to her Uncle, and to him opened the whole Affair, who feemed very willing for the Match, and promifed his friendly Affift-ance for the recovery of her Fortune.

Nothing now remained, but the ufual Ceremony of a few Days Courtfhip, and therefore I with the free Confent and Permiffion of her Friends, vifited her daily ; but as the old Saying is, many Things happen between the Cup and the Lip, for this young Lady had a younger Sifter, who for the firft two or three Days that I went to the Houfe, treated me with an Air of Indifferency, even little Inferior to that of Ill-manners. However, I took no Notice of it, but continuing my Courtfhip as ufual, I foon faw the Scene was changed, for fhe it feems at my firft coming, being ignorant of my Intent, refolved to refent the Affront, which fhe thought was offered her, in preferring her Sifter's Com-pany to hers, when we went the abovementioned Journey. Being apprized hereof, I communicated it to the Captain, and defired him to ufe his Endeavours to repair the Breach, and appeafe the young Lady's feem-ing Indignation. He at firft feemed to flight the Affair, as merely trivial and frivolous, till feeing me very urgent and importunate, he then promifed his friendly Affiftance to accommodate the feeming Difference, and therefore gave the two Sifters and me an Invitation to fup at his Houfe. After Supper, he very genteely, and with fo much Prudence, excufed both himfelf and me, in the

Choice

Choice of our fair Companion to *Windfor*, that they
were both highly pleafed, and were extreme good Company, particularly Mifs *Fanny*, who was naturally of a
more gay and airy Temper than her elder Sifter, and
although fhe had not the fineft of Faces, yet, fo grace-
ful was her Air, fo eafy and engaging her Behaviour,
and fo foft and alluring her Voice, not ftrained by Art,
but by the meer Effect of the lavifh bounty of Nature, that fhe (*Siren-like*) captivated the Hearts of all
who had the Pleafure of her Company ; upon the
Captain's Requeft, fhe favour'd us with a Tune on the
Spinnet. and to perfect the Mufick, joined fo melodious
a Voice, that tranfported with ravifhment and delight, I
thought myfelf amidft the bleffed Above.   'Twas then
that I began to repent of my Choice.   Mifs *B****'s*
Charms, once fo prevalent, now appeared as mere
Phantoms and Illufions, and *Fanny* reigned fole Miftrefs
of my Affections.

However, as I thought it was not Prudence in me,
to difclofe this fudden Change, I behaved myfelf as one
indifferent to her, and infenfible of thofe amicable Qualifications, that fhe was perfect Miftrefs of.   In fhort,
having paid our Complements to our generous Hoft and
Hoftefs, I waited on the Ladies Home.

The next Day I began ferioufly to confider, what
would be the Confequence of breaking my Affair with
the Elder, and making my Addreffes to the Younger ;
when upon mature Deliberation, it appeared to me fo
vile and fcandalous an Action, after fuch mutual and
folemn Affurances of Fidelity, that fearing (as with
juft Reafon I might) that I fhould not fucceed in my
Defign upon *Fanny*, I fully refolved of the two Evils,
to choofe the leaft, and therefore with great Difficulty
and Violence to myfelf, I broke of the Intimacy, and
ever after, was entirely regardlefs of that Love that at
firft I had fo warmly purfu'd.

Next Door to me, lived one Mr. *Elias B****, Pe-
ruke-Maker*, who had by his Marriage and Succefs in
Trade, acquired a very handfome Fortune.   This Man
had one only Daughter about fixteen Years of Age, a
likely young Girl enough, and well educated.   Upon
                                                    fome

some trivial Difference that arose in my Father's Time, between him and Mr. *B****, our Families were at Variance with each other; but upon my Father's decease, all Contention and Animosity ceas'd, so that from being in a manner Strangers to one another, we in a short Time commenc'd an Intimacy and Friendship; By his means I was admitted as a Member of the weekly Club, held at the *Golden-Lyon* Tavern in *Fleet-street* on *Thursday's*. Moreover, our Custom was every *Saturday* to dine at the *Castle* at *Kingston* upon *Thames*, where we usually drank hard, and play'd high; and Mr. *B**** finding that notwithstanding my Youth, I was Master of that valuable Art of Secrecy, placed an intire Confidence in me, and made me privy to all his Intreagues and lawless Pleasures. This Intimacy of the Father's, gave Birth to the Daughter's Love, that afterwards prov'd both her Ruin and mine. She took all Opportunities of being in my Company, and frequently staid so late at my House, without the Leave of her Father and Mother, that in a little Time it became the public Talk of the Neighbours, and almost all the whole Town ; and as Fame is generally attended with Falsehood, some there were that scrupled not to report, that I was more familiar with her, than was consistent with the Modesty of her Sex ; But this Accusation (I take God to witness) was utterly false, for upon my hearing that her Character and Reputation were so grosly injured, and that those malicious Aspersions arose from the innocent Pastimes with which we amused ourselves together, I acquainted my Neighbour *B**** with what I heard was currently reported, concerning his Daughter and me, and furthermore desired him (as he tendred the Welfare of his Child) to keep her away from my House ; he heartily thank'd me for my good Counsel, and accordingly removed her to her Cousin *H***'s*, at *Mile-End*, where she continu'd near three Months, but not without sending me a Letter or two, to let me know she should be glad to see me, at the Place appointed in the same. But I, who had then no Thoughts of making her my Wife, out of Friendship to her Father, scorn'd to take the Advantage of her Youth, nor ever answered her

Billet-

Billet-deux, or went according to her Requeſt to the Place of Aſſignation. In the mean Time, my intimate and boſom Friend *F*** F****. propoſed taking a Houſe on *Epping-Forreſt*, the Rent of which he ſaid was twenty-five Pounds *per Ann.* whereupon I promiſed to become his Tenant for one Room, and moreover to ſend down ſome Houſhold Goods to furniſh it withal. *F**** laughing, ſaid, but are you willing to have Leaſes drawn in your Name, for you know how my Affairs ſtand. Yes Sir, ſaid I, with all my Heart, provided that you'll en-engage for the Payment of the Rent, by all Means, quoth he, thus we concluded upon the hire of our Country-Seat, and over a merry Bottle, chriſtned it *Langley-Hall*. About a Week after, I ſent down the Goods according to my Promiſe, and likewiſe for my Part in the Houſe-warming, a large Ham, and two Gallons of Brandy. Soon after, my Friend *F**** and I with ſome other merry Blades, went down to our Country-ſeat, where we ſtaid three or four Days. On our Return, an Accident happened to me, that had like to have proved very fatal, but I verified the old Saying, Nought is often in Danger but never hurt; for being three Parts Mellow, and mounted on a Gelding of great Spirit and Courage, by my frequent tickling, him with the Spur, he in ſpite of all I could do, ran away with me, till I came to Hackney River, where to puniſh my Courſer for his Obſtinacy, and cool his Courage, I clapp'd Spurs to him, and plung'd him into the River, down he fell, broke his Knees, and in the Fall, pitched me clear over his Ears, where for ſome time I could not recover myſelf; but by good Fortune, at length I regain'd my Legs, and kept puffing and blowing like a Porpice, till my Companions came up, and ſeeing me in that pityful Condition, diſpatched old *Charon* to take me up, and waft me to the other Side of the Ferry, whence like a drownded Rat I went dripping along, ſtrip'd myſelf, got half a Pint of Brandy made hot, and went to bed, where I lay till my Shirt and Clothes were dried by the Fire. In the Evening I aroſe, return'd to *London*, and ad-journ'd to the old Place of Rendezvous, the *Trumpet*-Ta-vern.

in *Sheer - Lane*, where we pass'd the Evening very merrily, but I resolved for the future never to be guilty of the like Frolicks again.

Sometime after this, Mr. *B**** thinking that Absence had sufficiently abated the Warmth of his Daughter's Affections, sent for her Home, and I out of good Manners went to compliment Miss on her return ; but alas! her Absence had only served to smother the amorous Flame, which by frequent Interviews (no ways to be avoided, since our Houses were contiguous) soon broke out, and burnt with fiercer Rage. In fine, one Morning the old Gentlwoman sent for me to Breakfast, and there propofed very advantageous Terms of Marriage with her Daughter, and urged me to a Compliance thereto with great Warmth and Zeal. Furthermore to corroborate her Argument, down came Miss *N****, with her Hair dishevel'd, her Eyes flowing with Tears, and her Dress carelefs and negligent. See, fays the Mother, in a canting Tone, in what a Pickle poor *N**** is, how can you be fo cruel and hard hearted as not to return her Love? Come, come, Neighbour *Langley*, I'll engage yo'ill have no Occasion to repent of your Bargain, Mr. *B**** and I shall never have any more Children, and when we die, you'll come in for ALL. At the Word ALL, which had a far greater Impression on me, than what she said before, I prick'd up my Ears, and seemed to hearken to her with Pleafure, and *N**** who was before cruelly in the Dumps, now began to revive, and put on an Air of Joy. In short, I told Mrs. *B****, that fince it was an Affair of such great Confequence, I must defire a Months time to confider of it, and that then I would give her my final Anfwer. Upon this, she was well Satisfied, and I took my leave of them for the present.

Now I began ferioufly to confider the State of my Affairs, and finding by the private Accounts that I kept in my Pocket-Book, that the Payment of thofe feveral large Sums borrowed on Jewels of a confiderable lefs Value, than what I had artfully pledged them for, was within three Months of its Expiration : I thought my

Cir-

Circumstances in a very melancholy Posture, and my
Case almost desperate, for if I should not redeem those
Pledges pursuant to contract, my Credit and Reputation
wou'd by that failure, be entirely lost, and on the contrary, if Honour and Honesty should have the Ascen-
dant over Fraud and Villainy, that then I should be a
great Sufferer thereby, wherefore I resolved, that since I
had began to play the villainous Part, that I wou'd, at
all Events compleat it. Thus determin'd, there nothing
now remained, but the Manner of effectually executing
what I so fully intended, and was so stedfastly resolv'd
upon. Marriage I consider'd with myself, would not
only furnish me with a pretty Sum of ready Cash, but
would likewise corroborate my Credit, and strengthen
my Interest. For as the greatest Villainies are carried on,
and supported by the specious Pretext of Sanctity and
Dissimulation, so I thought it was but a reasonable Sup-
position, that the Town now generally acquainted with
my frequent Debauches, wou'd upon my Entrance into
the Connubial State, judge me thereby reclaimed and
metamorphis'd into a sedate and sober Man. For this
Reason, sometime before and after my Marriage, I gave
due Attendance to the *Romish* Chapel in *Lincoln's-Inn-
Fields*, and in about three Weeks Time I invited Mrs.
B*** and her Daughter to Supper, where I told her
that upon a mature Deliberation of her Proposals, I was
willing to acquiesce and condescend thereunto, on the
following Terms, *viz.* That Mr. *B**** should be at
the Expence of the Wedding-Cloths, and pay the stipu-
lated Sum on the Morning of the Wedding-Day. She
readily agreed and promis'd her Husband's punctual
Compliance with my Demands. Furthermore, as a Surety
to bind the Bargain, I gave the old Gentlewoman a Ring
set with Rose Diamonds in Form of a Coronet. *N**** was
now all Life and Gaiety, and by her Parents Consent and
Approbation, as well as mine, acted the Part of a Mistress
in my House, with the same Freedom and Authority before, as she did after the Ceremony was perform'd.
But alas! poor Girl, she little thought how short her
Reign wou'd prove, and how all the Sunshine of her
Pride

Pride and Glory wou'd fpeedily be darken'd and eclips'd by black impending Clouds that threatned fure, though not immediate Deftruction and endlefs Woe. But not-withftanding this Engagement, and folemn Contract with *N****, I continued my lawlefs Embraces with *Clarinda*, whom I made my Counfellor and Confidant in the moft fecret Tranfactions of my Life, and there-fore although to fatisfy my intended Spoufe, and pleafe her Parents, I turn'd her away foon after Marriage; yet I frequently kept Company with her afterwards, and made her feveral confiderable Prefents. Mrs. *B**** im-mediately purchafed all Things fuitable for the future Wedding, and alfo was fo Kind and Indulgent, as to bring the feveral Patterns of Silks and Laces, defign'd for *N****'s Paraphanalia, to me for my Approbation thereof: This Courtefy, and the richnefs of the Drefs, fo pleaf-ed me, that I made her Daughter a Prefent of a Gold Watch and Chain, and likewife a brilliant Diamond round about Ring, that fhe might appear in the Fafhion of other married Ladies; and now the Licence being taken out, and all Things ready for the Confumation of our Nuptials. Mr. *B**** defired me to fix the fo-lemn Day, which he faid he fhou'd choofe (if I were willing fhou'd be) on that of his Birth-day. But I de-clin'd fo fpeedy an Execution, on Account of a Tour I had promis'd to take with fome Friends, to a Gentle-man's Seat in *Effex*, and defired the Marriage might be deferred for three Weeks longer, which Favour was eafily granted. And now all Things being agreed on, I bethought myfelf of a Clergyman of my Acquaintance, a Gentleman void of a Living, and reduced to a low State, greatly inferior to that of his Profeffion. Never-thelefs he was a boon Companion, told a merry Tale, and fung a Song with a good Grace, and by his In-duftry had made a Shift to get a red Face in the Service of the Church; for having given my Word to this Gentlemen, that he fhould be my facred Magician, whenfoever I alter'd my prefent State of Life, I thought myfelf in honour bound to perform my Promife there-in. I therefore fent for him to the *Bull-Head*-Tavern,

in

in *Lincolns-Inn-Fields*, where, o'er a merry Bottle, I acquainted the Doctor with my Intent, and enjoin'd him
to be ready on the Day appointed, for the Performance thereof. Having thus prepared the Minister, I
went down in the Country, and after a sincere and
hearty Welcome, returned to *London* on the Evening
before our appointed Nuptials, when after having drank a
Bottle or two with the Inn-keeper, where my Horse
stood at Livery, I went to Mr. *B****'s, who had prepar'd
a very handsome Supper for my Reception, where none
were present but Capt. *H****'s Lady, and our own
Family. After Supper, Mr. *B***n* ask'd me if I was
provided with a Clergyman. Yes, Sir, said I, and
he'ill be punctual to his Appointment at *Gray's-Inn-
Chapel*, at eight in the Morning; well then, replied he,
all's right, for I have ordered a Coach and Four to be
here at Seven, and after the Ceremony, we'ill drive to
Tim. Harris's, at *Egham*. Agreed to, Sir, said I; so
taking my leave, I went Home, where according to
Custom, I lay with *Clarinda* all Night. At Six in the
Morning I arose, and went to my Neighbour *B****'s,
where they were all very busy in preparing the new Bride;
he call'd me aside, and ask'd me whether I would have
the Cash before, or after Marriage. Before Sir, said I,
by all Means; whereupon he immediately complyed
with the Contract, by Notes drawn on Sir *Francis
Child*, and likewise gave me the Writings of a House,
belonging to his Daughter, in *Charles-Court*, in the
Strand, and afterwards taking a Bottle of Rum out of
his Corner Cupboard, we drank all Health and Prosperity
to each other. Now the Bride being ready, we drove
to the Chapel, where my good Friend the Doctor, was
waiting, and perform'd his Duty as a Gentleman, worthy of his Profession. From Chapel we drove to
Egham, where an elegant Dinner was provided at Mr.
B***'s Expence, and to use the Words of the Ingenious
Mr. *Phillips*, nought but Mirth and Joy around the
Table flow'd. At Four we return'd to *London*, and I, re-
gardless of my Spouse, mounted the Coach-box, and drove
to the *Queen's-Head* Tavern, in *Holborn*, where *Clarinda*,

by

by my Direction, had ordered a fumptuous, and elegant Entertainment to be provided, at which, Mr. *L***n*, Mr. *H***d*, jun. and his Spoufe, the Hoft and Hoftefs, were all prefent. About Eleven we adjourned to my Father *B***'s*, where whilft the Men drank a Bowl of Punch, the Women out of their pious Care, difh'd out the Bride in Bed, fit for the Reception of her Hufband. To expatiate on a Topick fo generally known, and fo daily practifed, would be equally as ridiculous as impertinent, wherefore I fhall leave my Readers to purfue the Bent of their own Thoughts on that Head, and proceed to the next material Bufinefs in Hand.

I muft obferve, that we were married on a *Thurfday*, and therefore I thought if I could prevail on my Wife (who was one of the Church of *England*) to accompany me to Mafs on the *Sunday* following, that I fhould thereby gain the Applaufe and Efteem of all thofe blinded Zealots. This I confefs, I did not attempt out of a religious Motive, but from a Thought of private Gain, hoping by this well feigned Hypocrify, to infinuate myfelf further into the good Graces, and Efteem of the moft eminent and wealthy Followers of that implicit Faith, and fuperftitious Profeffion. My Spoufe to pleafure me, yielded to my Requeft, and her Condefcenfion thereunto had its defir'd Effect ; for a wealthy Merchant in *Bafinghall-Street*, fent for me the next Day, and commending the meritorious Act of making a Convert, favour'd me with nine hundred and feventy-five Pounds worth of Silver, on my Note, payable in a Months Time. This was a great Encouragement to me, and ferv'd to further and facilitate my Defign, in running away as much in Debt as poffibly I could. Wherefore I refolved to ftrike while the Iron was hot, and make as much of my Credit (whilft it was unftain'd) as Time and Occafion would permit. For the effectual Performance of which, I took up large Quantities of Jewels of feveral Merchants, under pretence of difpofing of them to Ladies, whom I had the Honour to ferve, and in three or four Days, artfully re-

E 3   turned

turn'd them again, telling the Owners, that the Ladies were not as yet come to a full Refolution for the Purchafe of them. I likewife took up a repeating Watch of one Mr. *Vernon*, in *Fleet-ftreet*, the outfide Cafe whereof, was fet with large Brilliants of the firft Water, in Form of a Mariners Compafs, betwixt the Hours and Minutes were interfpers'd fome Brilliant Sparks, with Rubies, Topazes, and various precious Stones of different Colours, refembling the beauteous Iris. The Rims of the Cafe were alfo ornamented with coftly Jewels, imitating the twelve Signs of the *Zodiack*, and on the Top of the Spring, that caufes the Movement to ftrike, was fet a large Brilliant of the firft Water. The Chain was three continued Rows of fine Diamonds, and on the Top of the Hook was a very large oval Brilliant. In fhort, it was the richeft and moft curious Performance of that Nature, that had been feen in *Europe* at that Time.

This Watch I pretended was defign'd for the Queen of *Spain*, and having the Honour to fhew it to feveral Noblemen and Ladies of the higheft Rank. I could have difpofed of it to them ; however, I thought it would turn more to my Advantage, to refufe the Sale thereof, for this Reafon, *viz.* If I fold it in *England*, the Owner would have expected Payment thereof in a fhort Time, and on the contrary, it was not reafonable to think that he would refufe to wait, for the return of foreign Bills, if (purfuant to my falfe Report) it was fuppofed to be fent to her *Catholick* Majefty. And now the Time drawing on for the Execution of my full Purport, I made it my Bufinefs to frequent *Slaughter's* Coffee-Houfe, in St. *Martin's-Lane*, where I foon got acquainted with a fet of Foreigners, of whom, I enquired into the Laws and Cuftoms of thofe Countries relating to broken Tradefmen, that fled thither for their Refuge and Safety, and being affur'd by them that *Holland* was the fafeft Afylum, and fecureft Receptacle to fkreen Villainies of that Nature, I refolved to fteer my Courfe thither, and therefore went to *Bland's* on *Tower-Hill*, to enquire for a Veffel, that would be ready to fail

in

in about a Fortnight's Time. Upon Enquiry, I met with one *T***; J***s*, Commander of the *C***;* Sloop, a Gentleman obfervant of his Word, if Wind and Weather permitted; with this Captain I agreed for the Paffage of two Perfons, to have the Conveniency of his State Room, and great Cabbin, and gave him a Guinea earneft. The next Thing I did was to get a Bill of Exchange for five hundred Pounds, in the Name of *Robert Clifton*, Efq; payable to him or order, which being eafily obtain'd, I then applied myfelf to the above-mentioned Merchants for their Jewels, pretending that the Ladies were now come to a final Refolution, and would purchafe them, and now the Prices being agreed on, I gave them my promiffory Notes, three Months after Date for the fame. All Things being thus carried on with the utmoft Secrecy, I appointed *Clarinda*, with whom I ftill kept Company, (but not fo privately, but that it was fufpected by my Wife and her Mother) to meet me at the *Prince William's Head* at *Charing-Crofs*. She was punctual to my Affignation, and there after mutual Affurances of conftant Love and inviolable Friendfhip, I acquainted her with my fecret Defign, and infifted on her accompanying me in my Voyage thither, and that upon her Condefcenfion thereunto, fhe fhould be an equal Copartner and Sharer of my large and flowing Fortune, which in all human probability, was fufficient for our Maintainance, in a polite and genteel Way, during the Term of our Lives. But fhe, like a generous Girl, declin'd my bafe Propofals, and in her Defence, urg'd my being already married to a deferving young Lady, whom in Honour I cou'd not leave, and that if fhe confented to my Proffer, fhe fhou'd thereby defervedly incur the Scandal of the moft vile and abandon'd Adultrefs. In fine all the Arguments I cou'd ufe, were fruitlefs. So having engag'd her religioufly to keep my important Secret, I took my Farewell of her; and then refolv'd that fince I could not obtain her Confent, that I wou'd take my Wife over with me, which I confefs I did not fo much out of pure Love, as out of a View of Intereft, hoping that if I fhou'd be fruftrated in my De-

figu

ııgn, that her Father out of Love and Regard to her
wou'd look with a favourable Eye on me, and impute
my Misfortune, or rather ill Conduct, to the Folly of
Youth.

Wherefore as foon as I came Home, I propos'd to
my Wife a Country Journey on the *Saturday* following, and ordered her to get ready, and pack up all her
Clothes, my Intent being to ftay there for three Weeks
or a Month. In the mean Time I hir'd a Chaife and
Four for two Days, to be ready at the Time appointed, and to prevent my being feen, or taken Notice of
in paffing thro' the City, I ordered the Chaife to wait
for me on St. *Margaret's-Hill, Southwark.* I then
fealed up my Jewels, Bank-Notes, and the above-mention'd Watch, with Bills of Exchange, amounting in
all to the Value of nineteen or twenty thoufand Pounds.
in a little Trunk, and meeting the Captain at *Bland's,*
purfuant to his Appointment, on *Friday* at Four in the
Afternoon. I gave the Trunk into his Cuftody, with a
particular Charge to lock it up in his Bureau, and took
a Receipt for the fame ; being well affur'd by him that
he would fail from *Gravefend* on the *Monday* following.
In the Evening I went to my Father B***'s, and acquainted him with my pretended Journey into the
Country, with which he feem'd well pleafed, it being
the long Vacation Time. In the Morning, I gave my
Journeyman (Mr. *Blakely*) charge of the Shop, and
left all my Plate ftanding therein, leaft the removal
thereof fhould caufe a Sufpicion amongft my Creditors,
and intercept my intended Flight. I likewife ordered
him to pay off fuch trivial Sums, as were owing to my
Workmen,

And now my Spoufe and I having taken Leave of
our Parents, call'd a Coach, and drove to the above-
mentioned Place, where the Chaife and Four were waiting by my Order. Then difcharging the Coach, we
went into the *King's-Arms*, and breakfafted. From
thence we went to *Gravefend*, and put up at the *Faulcon*,
where I paid two Guineas and a Half for the Difcharge
of the Chaife according to my Agreement.

On

On *Sunday* we din'd with the Captain, and other Gentlemen and Ladies that were going Paſſengers with us. On *Monday* Morning the Captain according to his Promiſe, heav'd up his Anchor with the Wind, *S. W.* All the Paſſengers, with my Spouſe, went on Board, but I ſtaid aſhore till the Commander went off, which was nigh an Hour after, and now the Ship being adrift, lay to for his coming on board. In the mean Time as I was drinking with my Landlord, in his back Yard fronting the Water, I eſpy'd a one Eye Game Cock, which I purchaſed of him for half a Crown, for a Venture in *Holland.* Now the Captain having compleated all his Buſineſs aſhore, hurried me and my new Purchaſe on Board, we then brac'd about, fill'd our Head Sails, and ſpread all the Canvas we cou'd to the welcome Gale, that freſhing on us, waft'd our Ship the next Day to the *Bombkays* at *Rotterdam*, where we went aſhore, and by the Commander's Recommendation lodg'd at the Sign of the *Koning Van England*, (or King of *England's* Head) kept by one *John Gadbury*, on the *Vine-Haven.*

The next Day Capt. *J****came to Dinner with us, and acquitted his Charge honourably. Thus all Things ſeem'd to favour my Undertaking, and I being of a vain and aſpiring Temper, reſolv'd to paſs for the younger Son of my Lord *F*****, and to the End that I might make an Appearance ſuitable to the Dignity I had falſely aſſum'd, I order'd a *Taylor* to make me a very rich Suit of Cloaths; and as it happen'd, one Mr. *Loven*, a decay'd Gentleman, quarter'd at the ſame Inn with me, who ſpeaking the *Dutch* and *French* Languages to Perfection, with him I contracted to be my Gentleman and Interpreter, and to do him Juſtice, he faithfully executed the Truſt I repoſed in him. This Gentleman I order'd to hire three *French* Footmen, and cloath them with the utmoſt Expedition, with my Livery, which was blue Cloth turn'd up with Red, Scarlet Waiſtcoats and Breeches, trimm'd with Silver, and broad Gold lac'd Hats. As to the Coach, Mr. *Loven* inform'd me, that it was cuſtomary in *Holland* for all

Perſons

Perfons of Quality, except Foreign Minifters, to hire their Equipages, as they had Occafion for them, there being many grand and ftately ones kept for that Purpofe.

Having thus fettled my Equipage and Servants after the niceft and richeft Fancy, I refolv'd to devote myfelf to Pleafure for fome Time; altho' in the Interim I privately enquir'd for a Gentleman of Worth and Integrity, to whom I might with Safety commit the Truft of my Effects, that if Peradventure, my Creditors fhou'd come over in queft of me, that they not finding any Thing valuable in my Poffeffion, might not think it worth their while to give themfelves any further Trouble about me, but reft contented with thofe Effects that I had left in *England*.

Now I muft obferve, that upon my Return to my Quarters, I frequently found the above-mention'd Captain in Company with my Spoufe; however, I took no Notice thereof, but on the contrary, always entertain'd him with the utmoft Courtefy and good Manners; but one Night, as we were in Bed, I afk'd her the Meaning of the Captain's frequent Vifits, and whether he endeavour'd to fhew a more than lawful Love and Refpect for her. Hereupon fhe frankly told me, that fhe believ'd it was the Captain's Defign to betray her Virtue, for that he had often expreffed how paffionately he loved her; that therefore fhe had ufed all poffible Means to avoid his Company, but found it a very difficult Matter, which gave her Caufe to fufpect, that he had bribed the Landlady to acquiefce with the lawlefs Purfuit of his Amours wherefore fhe earneftly entreated me to provide frefh Lodgings, where fhe might be more retir'd, and fhun the vile Impertinence of the faid Commander; well pleafed with this open and generous Confeffion, I highly commended her Honour and Integrity, but defir'd that fhe wou'd not offer the leaft Affront to the Captain. This I artfully faid, until I could be further inform'd of the Punifhments inflicted on Perfons taken in Adultery, by the fevere Laws of the United Provinces. Upon confulting with my Gentleman, who

who was well verfed in the Statutes of that Republick, I found that the Penalty on fuch heinous Crimes, was the immediate Forfeiture of all the Delinquent's Effects, and clofe Imprifonment during Life, as a Satisfaction or Attonement to the injur'd Party, for the Difhonour thereby fuftain'd.

One Day, hearing that there was to be a Cock-fight, I order'd one of my Servants to prepare mine, who had been for fome Time in keeping, to enter the Lifts, and by my Spoufe's earneft Entreaty, I took her (tho' contrary to the ufual Cuftom of Ladies) with me, to fee the Paftime. In fhort, I backed my Cock againft all Oppofers, and he (by good Fortune) at one chance Blow kill'd his Antagonift, by whofe unexpected Death I was a Gainer of about 10 *l.* Highly pleafed with my Succefs I return'd Home, and it being Summer Time, we feated ourfelves under a fhady Tree, that fronted the Inn Door, and call'd for a Bottle of Claret, but had not been there long, before the Captain came and joined us, and being inform'd of my good Fortune, wifhed me Joy, I return'd the Compliment, and *Nancy* with an Air of Gaiety, defir'd that I wou'd favour her with my Winnings for the Purchafe of fome *Dutch* Toys ; I replied, *With all my Heart, my Dear, for this and all that I have is at your Service,* and thereupon immediately flung the Money into her Lap. Soon after this, I faw her Countenance change, and afked her what was the Matter ? But fhe made me no Anfwer, whereupon *D —— n you Madaim,* faid I, *what now, are you Dumb ?* This rafh and hafty Expreffion fo nettled her, that fhe threw the Money into the Street, which I knowing the Value of better than fhe, ran and pick'd it up, fwearing, that fince fhe had abus'd my Generofity, I wou'd give her fufficient Reafon to repent it ; but my Paffion was foon over, and by Mr. *J*****'s Mediation, I promifed to forgive and forget that filly Flight of Youth.

Hereupon the Captain propofed a Tour to the *Hague,* which was with Pleafure agreed to, and fhe next Morning fet out for that agreeable Rendezvous of Nobility, **where**

where we dined in a fumptuous and elegant Manner, at the Sign of the *Englifh Parliament*, a celebrated Houfe for polite Entertainment. From thence we returned to *Rotterdam*, where I entertained the Captain and fome other Gentlemen, with a grand Entertainment; when the Company was gone, I ufed all poffible Arguments to perfuade *N**** to yield a feeming Compliance to the Captain's lawlefs Defires, and to appoint him purfuant to my Direction, a Place proper for the Execution of his villainous Defign. Furthermore, I urg'd, the great Advantage accruing from thence, and the diligent Care and Caution I wou'd take to furprize him, blafted in the fruitlefs Expectation of fatiating his luxuriant and adulterous Paffion. But notwithftanding all my Arguments, *N**** remain'd inflexible, and could not be induced to acquiefce to this treacherous and bafe Propofal, and in her Defence urg'd, that no Lucre or fordid Gain, (tho' ever fo great) cou'd expiate, or attone for that Difhonour and Lofs of Character, that fhe muft inevitably fuftain, by condefcending to fo infamous an Act; wherefore I thought proper to drop an Argument fo difpleafing and ungrateful to her, and to proceed to an Affair far more weighty and important, *viz.* the Security of my Perfon and Effects.

For the effectual Performance of which, being well recommended to one Mr. *H******, a Man of Worth and experienc'd Fidelity, that kept a large Warehoufe on the *Bombkays*, to him I committed the Charge of my Cafh and Jewels; and now finding by his Difcourfe, that he was well verfed in the Laws of that Republick, and more in particular, in thofe relating to broken Tradefmen, that took Sanctuary in thofe Parts, him I judg'd to be the propereft Perfon to confult and communicate with about my own Affairs. Neverthelefs I was not fo rafh as to let him into the Secret of my Circumftances at the firft interview, but taking a Note of him for the Re-delivery of my Cafh and Effects on Demand, I parted with him for the prefent, and as foon as I came Home, enquir'd more ftrictly of my Landlord, into his Character and Repute. Mr. *Gadbury*, my

my Hoft, fcrupled not to expatiate largely on his un-
doubted Veracity, and unbiaffed Fidelity to his Truft,
and at the fame Time nominated feveral Gentlemen,
whofe Affairs were then in a melancholy and dangerous
Pofture, that by his Prudence and Segacity, had been
re-inftated in their priftine Glory.

Thefe Words uttered with fo much Warmth and
Ardour, eafily induced me to a Belief, that Mr. *H*****
was in Reality deferving of fo great a Character, and
therefore I engag'd him to dine with me the next Day
at the *Hague,* where without Referve I unbofom'd myfelf to him in a frank and friendly manner. Hereupon
he promifed to be ftedfaft, and true to my Intereft, and
advifed me immediately to procure a Protection from the
States-General, which he affured me, wou'd totally exempt me from the Jurifdiction of any other Foreign
Laws ; and as a farther Proof of his Sincerity, he promifed by the Affiftance of a Lawyer (his particular
Friend) to obtain what he fo heartily wifh'd, as well for
my Security as his own Satisfaction, that I were now
in Poffeffion of. Morever added he, it muft be done
with the utmoft Expedition, leaft peradventure, your
Creditors being appriz'd of your Intent, fhou'd by their
unwearied Diligence, and extenfive Intereft, undermine
your Undertakings ; wherefore you muft not regard the
Expence, for Favours of that Nature are not to be obtained but by a well timed Liberality, and fome Prefents
fuitable to the Perfons concern'd in the Management
of fo great and important an Affair ; your Protection
(which I doubt not but you will obtain) ftands good for
fix Months, both for your Perfon and Effects, and at
the Expiration of the limited Time, is eafily renew'd
for a trivial Coft.

Charm'd with his Difcourfe, that infpired me with
new Life and Vigour, and banifh'd the gloomy
Thoughts of Fear, or approaching Danger. I preffed
him to the fpeedy Execution of his Promife, and gave
him a full Commiffion to disburfe whatever he thought
proper on that Occafion ; and furthermore affured him,
that I wou'd amply recompence both him and his Friend

for

for their Trouble, and ever after gratefully acknowledge
the Favour. In the Evening we return'd to *Rotterdam*,
where we fupp'd together, and Mr. *H***** with repeated Affurances of his Sincerity, and utmoft Endeavours
to affift me in all my Defigns departed.

Four Days after this Mr. *H*****, and his Friend the
Lawyer, came to me at my Lodgings, from whence we
went to *Michael Edward's*, at the *Sun* on the *Bombkays*,
and there the Lawyer with an Air of Gaiety faid, *Sir*,
I wifh you Joy, of what replied I? *Of your fo much defired Protection, Sir, which I here prefent you with*. By
this extraordinary Difpatch, you may fee how unwearied our Endeavours have been to ferve you; the *States*
are not now fitting, but this I have by great Intereft
obtained of their Secretary for the Space of twelve Days,
at the Expiration whereof, their *High Mightineffes* will
Affemble, and grant you a further Protection for fix
Months longer. I humbly thank'd him for this fo fingular a Mark of his Efteem and Friendfhip, and order'd
Mr. *H***** to pay the Gentleman one hundred Guineas for his Trouble.

I now rambled up and down without Fear or Appre-
henfion of any Moleftation that cou'd arife from any
Quarter, and Mr. *H**** and I contracted a Partnerfhip
in Merchandife on the following Terms and Condi-
tions, *viz.* that I fhou'd lend the faid *H*——— 5000 *l.*
at common Intereft, and thereupon add 5000 *l.* more to
make up a joint Stock of 10,000 *l.* from which large
Sum, with good Succefs, we promifed ourfelves to raife
a fair Fortune. Wherefore that we might immediately proceed to Bufinefs, we went to *Amfterdam* to purchafe a Ship, and there upon Enquiry we found, that
the *Prince William Snow*, Captain *B*——— was lying
there for Sale, upon which we fent for the Commander, went on Board with him, examin'd into the Veffel,
and purchafed her for 450 *l.* Sterling, which Money
I paid on my own Account, being defirous to become
the fole Proprietor thereof. In the Interim I receiv'd
Advice, that four of my principal Creditors were came
over in Queft of me, and that they by great Intereft,
had

had engag'd the Earl of *Chefterfield* (then Ambaſſador at
the *Hague*) to intercept my promiſed Protection, and
furthermore, upon the Expiration of that which I had,
to obtain a Grant from their *High Mightineſſes* to ſeize
my Perſon and Effects. This News I confeſs, ſtruck
me with Horror and Confuſion, and judging that if I
returned to *Rotterdam*, I ſhou'd inevitably fall into their
Hands, I reſolv'd to lie perdue at the Houſe of Mr.
A — at the *Hague*, and there wait the Iſſue of their
Proceedings, and in the mean Time, to diſpatch Mr.
H — to try if poſſible, to ſubvert my Enemies Deſigns, by large Sums of perſuaſive Gold. I now laid
aſide my Equipage, and the grand Title of my Lord,
paſſed for a private Gentleman, by the Name of *Robert Clifton*, and continued at the above-mention'd Houſe
high upon a Week, without ever going out of my
Chamber. When one Morning my Landlord, who
was privy to the Affair, came into my Room, and
trembling, gave me a Letter from Mr. *H* —, which
inform'd me, that the Creditors having Intelligence
where I lay, were on the Road to ſurround the Houſe,
and take me Priſoner; that he had uſed all poſſible
Means to renew my Protection, but that all his Efforts
therein were vain and fruitleſs; that there had been publiſh'd a Reward of 400 *l.* for ſecuring my Perſon, and
likewiſe 400 *l.* more for the Diſcovery of my Effects;
that my *Taylor* had given a Deſcription of the Cloaths
that he had made, and moreover, that my Picture was
ſet up at the *Change*, and the moſt publick Places of
Amſterdam and *Rotterdam*; that the beſt Advice he was
capable to give me at preſent was, to exchange my Apparel, diſguiſe myſelf, and make into the adjacent Wood,
and there wait for his coming, which ſhould be punctually at four in the Afternoon.

Scarce had I read the Letter, before I was alarmed
with a confuſed Noiſe in the Street; whereupon my
Landlord looking out at the Window, cry'd, *Zounds,
Sir, you are taken, for my Houſe is now ſurrounded:* Be
calm, Sir, ſaid I, and ſend up one of your *Dutch* Servants to me, I'll change Habits with him; alſo let me
have

have a lighted Candle and a Cork immediately. The Landlord obey'd my Orders, I ſtript, put on *Mynheer's* Habit, black'd my Eye-brows, and paſſed out at the back Door, unobſerved by any; from thence I went into the Wood, where I lay hid until the Time appointed, when Mr. *H——* came, highly overjoy'd to find me eſcaped from the Fury of my Adverſaries. *Come Sir,* ſaid he, *you muſt now perſonate the* Dutch-man, *and we will go to* Vienna, *a protected Place, of ten Miles in Circumference, where I will obtain for you the Governor's Protection, and there you may live ſecure and free from all Moleſtations and Arreſts.* This Scheme was no ſooner propoſed than with Pleaſure agreed to, ſo from the Wood we went into the next Town, and there hired a Phaeton or Chaiſe for *Vienna.* In the Evening we arriv'd there, and the next Morning waited on the Governor, of whom for 50 Guineas I receiv'd the Favour of a Protection, with a ſtrict Charge and Caution not to exceed the Bounds of his Minute Territories.

The next Day Mr. *H——* took his Leave of me, with repeated Aſſurances of Friendſhip, and a ſolemn Promiſe not to diſcover my Effects. Here I enjoy'd all the Pleaſures, that a Place inhabited by unfortunate Perſons cou'd afford, this being nothing but a living Goal in Epitome. However, having a ſufficiency of Caſh, the Honour and Reſpect I met with there, in ſome Meaſure alleviated the Hardſhip of my Confinement. Here I became acquainted with two *Iriſh* young Fellows, of daring and bold Diſpoſitions, who had here taken Refuge and Sanctuary for Murder, no Crime being reckon'd ſufficiently black or infamous, to exclude the vile Offenders from the good Graces and Protection of his *Tartarean* Excellency. Theſe two Ruffians for want of better Society, I daily admitted to my Table, and on all Occaſions bore their Expences, and they (as the only Satisfaction that they cou'd make) faithfully promiſed at the Hazard of their Lives, to ſecure me from all Inſults and Dangers.

Hither

Hither came Mr. *H*—— purfuant to his Promiſe
Weekly, and fupplied me with what Caſh I demanded,
and aſſured me, that my Creditors began to be out of all
Hopes, and that if I patiently fubmitted to my Confinement for a ſhort Time, that they wou'd foon be
wearied out, with the large and extravagant Charges they
were at, in their vain Search and fruitleſs Purfuit.
Whereupon I charg'd him to make my Wife as eaſy
as poſſible, and to let her know, that as foon as the
Storm was blown over, I wou'd pay her a Viſit; but
at the ſame Time, caution'd him not to let her into the
Secret of my Abode, leaſt peradventure, thro' the Folly
and Indifcretion of Youth, ſhe ſhou'd inadvertently blab
it out. *Nancy*, I muſt obferve to you, had near upon
400 *l.* by her, befides her Jewels, Gold Watch, and
Snuff-box, fo that I knew ſhe cou'd not be in any Want,
and therefore made myſelf eafy on that Head.

During my Stay here, I was taken violently ill, which
prevented my intended Journey to his *Pruſſian* Majefty's Dominions, whither I had defigned to go, and by
prefenting my fo much fam'd and celebrated Watch to
his then favourite Lady, flatter'd myſelf with the Hopes
of obtaining a Commiſſion in that great Monarch's Service. Dr. *W* —— was my Phyfician, who liv'd contiguous to the Houfe where I lodg'd, and three Times
a Day vifited me, lying in a dangerous Condition in my
Bed, not able to move either Hand or Foot, but rack'd
with tormenting Pains both Night and Day. My faithful *Iriſh* Men conſtantly attended me, and for my Security brought Fire Arms into my Room, leaſt the Governor, being influenc'd by a larger Sum, or follicited
by their *High Mightineſſes*, ſhou'd cancel or fuperfeed
my Protection, and thereby expofe me to the free Arreſt
and Fury of my Adverfaries.

One Night as I lay in my Bed, two of my Creditors
came and furprized me in my Room, and infifted on
my going with them immediately, producing the Governor's Order to compel me to acquiefce to their Demands; but I excufed myſelf on Account of my Ill-
neſs

nefs for that Night, and promifed to be ready in the
Morning, to comply with their Requeft. Neverthelefs,
this Anfwer was not Satisfactory, for they infifted on
lying in the fame Room with me, as a Guard to my
Perfon. Hereupon my Comrades arm'd themfelves with
a Brace of Piftols each, and prefenting, fwore, that if
the Gentlemen did not immediately depart, that they
wou'd feverely punifh their Rafhnefs and Infolence, for
they infifted on that Room being their Property, and
that I was only there on Sufferance. Hereupon the
Creditors withdrew, but placed a Guard around the
Houfe, fwearing that they wou'd hurry me away with
them in the Morning.

Now the Fright I was in difpelled all my Anguifh and
Pain, and I, (who before cou'd not move myfelf in my
Bed) now put on my Cloaths, and walk'd haftily up
and down the Room, ruminating what Courfe to take
to extricate myfelf from this Emergency. At laft I fent
for the Doctor, who had already heard of the Affair,
and with him I agreed, that if he would leave open his
back Door, between the Hours of Twelve and One, I
would make my Efcape, and take Shelter in his Houfe.
To this Purpofe he readily confented, and promifed to
be punctual in the Execution of his Truft. Whereupon
my Companions and I call'd for Liquor very plentifully, and I feem'd to be no Ways concerned at the
Danger I was in.

Now the Time of my intended Flight drawing nigh,
we called for a large Bowl of Arrack Punch, which
whilft the Landlady, (the fole Perfon then ftirring in
the Houfe) was making, I by Favour of the Obfcuri-
ty of the Night, efcaped out at the back Door, and
flipp'd unfeen into the Doctor's Houfe, where I lay
concealed for nine or ten Days, leaving my Purfuers to
curfe their unhappy Stars, and commence a frefh Hunt
after their flown Game. At length, growing weary
of this intollerable Confinement, I refolved to venture
abroad in Difguife, and therefore borrowed a Suit of
Woman's Apparel of the Doctor's Spoufe, in return for
which

which I gave her a Diamond Girdle Buckle. The Drefs I had was *French*, and therefore I was now obliged to play the Part of the *Madam de Paris*, and for two or three Days behaved very modeftly among the Ladies, being inftructed in my Female Difcipline by the Doctor's Spoufe. At laft I fet out for *Amfterdam*, having a Gentleman of the Doctor's Recommendation to perfonate my Husband; as foon as I arrived there, I wrote to Mr. *H* , defiring him to remit me 200 Guineas, but he never complied with my Demand.

Three Days afterwards, I received a Letter from an unknown Hand, affuring me, that my Partner *H* —— had proved falfe, and betrayed his Truft to me; for that he had actually agreed to deliver up all my Effects, on the Promife of the above-mentioned Reward; that therefore the only Expedient I had left to prevent his villainous Defign was, a voluntary Surrender of myfelf. Whereupon, as the old Saying is, *Needs muft, when the Devil drives*, I determined to make the beft of my Way to *Rotterdam*, where I heard that my Creditors were affembled at Mr. *E* - —— , at the *Sun* on the *Vine-Haven*, and by a fpeedy and unexpected Precaution to fruftrate the bafe Intentions of Mr. *H* ——, hoping by a voluntary Submiffion to their Mercy and Clemency, to appeafe their juft Indignation, and thereby obtain that Reward that my Partner had by fo infamous and treacherous a Plot, endeavour'd to gain.

This Defign happily had its defired Effect, for upon my free Surrender, the Creditors not only ufed me in a generous and Gentleman-like manner, but fent for Mr. *H* ——, and abfolutely demanded all thofe Effects that I had lodged in his Hands, threat'ning upon Refufal thereof, to feize them by Authority. In fhort, he was obliged to comply, and produced all that ever I had committed to his Truft, and at the fame Time brought in a Charge againft me for Cafh drawn out of his Hands, as likewife his Bill for Attendance and Services done for me, whilft under my Misfortunes. The Gentlemen, as well as I, was greatly amazed at his exor-

bitant

bitant Demands, which were upwards of 700 *l*. but nevertheless, to avoid further Trouble and Expences, they were advised to acquiesce to his Exactions; the Laws of the united Provinces being strictly severe in compelling all Persons to satisfy the Parties by them employed, to the utmost of their Demands, tho' never so immoderate. And now as a Gratuity, the Creditors gave me the Sum of 200 *l*. enjoining me to be ready to sail with them for *England* on the first Opportunity.

Matters being thus accommodated, I went to my old Landlord's at the *King's-Head*, but to my Surprize, found that my Wife was gone from thence, at the Instigation of the above-mentioned *H——*, who had basely persuaded her to make a Tour to *Antwerp* in *Flanders*, where he said I was settled. Upon a further Enquiry about her Effects, the Landlord told me, that she had honourably discharged the House, and took her Trunk along with her. However, I made myself as easy as possible under my unfortunate Circumstances, but vowed to revenge myself on *H —* , for the Injury and Injustice he had done me, and therefore I privately bought a pair of Pocket Pistols, loaded them, and then went to his House to drink a Glass with him, under Pretence of accommodating our Differences, tho' my full and real Intent was to have shot him, as an Example to deter others from violating the sacred Tyes of Friendship, by the horrid and scandalous Breach of Trust. But he (I suppose) unable to bear the Reproaches of the Populace, was retired into the Country, by which wise Precaution, he both preserved his own Life as well as mine, which wou'd have been inevitably forfeited to the just Laws of the Republick, severely rigid against Homicide.

Soon after this, my Creditors (having authorized a proper Person to dispose of my Ship for their Use) and I return'd for *England*. On our Arrival at *London*, we went to Mr. *Barnes's* a *Goldsmith* on *Ludgate-Hill*, and one of my Principal Creditors, who was generously pleased to treat me better than I deserv'd; at this Gentleman's tleman's Houfe I lay all Night, and the next Morning was carried to the *Crown and Rolls Tavern* in *Chancery-Lane*, where the Commiffioners of the Bankruptcy were affembled ; here to my Surprize I met with my Wife and Mother-in-Law, both dreffed in Mourning, for the Death of their Relation Capt. *Holden*; when after a civil Salute, the old Gentlewoman faid, *Ah! Mr.* Langley, *this Drefs well becomes our prefent Circumftances, for we are all ruined by your Folly* ; *Mr.* Brown *raves like a Madman, and will by no Means be pacifyed, and* Nancy's Dutch *Landlord has ran away. with all her Cafh, Cloaths, and Jewels, whilft fhe was in Queft of you.* Our further Difcourfe was interrupted by an Order from the Commiffioners for me to attend them immediately ; where after a long and ftrict Examination paffed, to the Content of all Parties, I was difcharged, upon Promife of giving due Attendance to the Attorney for the Commiffion, and one of the Affignees for my Encouragement thereunto, gave me five Guineas in Hand. After this I took an Appartment for myfelf and Wife in *Devereux-Court*, near *Temple-Bar*, and daily waited on the Affignees and their Attorney, for the Execution of the then dependant Bufinefs, *viz.* to fettle my Affairs, and call in my Debts, which were large, there being upwards of 1800 *l.* in the Books, and my Plate and Houfhold Furniture were fold for upwards of 1200 *l.* more. But amongft all my Misfortunes, none fo much griev'd me as to fee the curious Library that with Pains I had puchafed for 250 *l.* difpofed of for the trivial Sum of 30 *l.* And now my Wife being taken very ill, was remov'd to her Mother's, there to be attended with all neceffary Care for a Sick Perfon ; whereupon finding that 5 *s. per* Week was too extravagant for my fallen Circumftances, 'to pay for a Room barely to fleep in, I difcharged the fame, and took another at 1 *s.* 6 *d. per* Week in *Hemlock-Court*.

During the Indifpofition of my Spoufe, I was not permitted to fee her, being ftrictly forbid the Houfe by her Father Mr. *Brown*. Wherefore having now fettl'd

the

the Book Debts, and given an Account of the respective Abodes of the different Creditors, I resolved to seek my Fortune Abroad, hoping that upon my Return, I should find my Affairs happily concluded, and myself thereby Master of a considerable Sum, arising from the Statute. Mrs. *Brown* used her utmost Endeavours to dissuade me from my Purpose, but I remain'd inflexible and deaf to all her earnest Entreaties, and therefore mustering up the Sum of 30 Guineas, I went to the *Barbadoes* Coffee-House, where I agreed with Captain *Joseph Richardson*, Commander of the *Frere* Galley, bound for the above-mentioned Island, for my Passage thither. Upon the Captain's telling me, that he should be ready to sail in a Fortnight, I prepared myself pursuant to his Directions, and having pack'd up my Cloaths and Linnen, (of which I had then a great variety) I took a final Leave of my Friends, and went down to *Blackwall*, where the Ship then lay, having giving a Letter of Attorney to my good Friend Mr. *G——*, to act for me in my Absence.

Whilst the Vessel staid at *Blackwall*, I quartered at the *White-Horse*, and being now metamorphised into a kind of a Sea Officer, with my laced Hat and speckled Shirt, I passed upon some for the Mate of a Ship. I cannot forget, that being accidentally in Company with a *Barber*, the credulous Fool forced me to accept of a handsome Tye Wig, on my Note payable on my Return, and I confess, I believe, that I cou'd then have had all the Wigs in his Shop on the same Condition.

I now went by the Name of *James Englefield*, and having purchased 20 Gallons of Alderman *Parson's* Beer, four Dozen of Wine, 100 Lemons, and a Loaf of Sugar, I went on Board, and fell down to *Gravesend*. The next Day the Captain and the rest of the Passengers arriv'd there, from whence we sailed with a fair Wind at N. W. into the *Downs*, where the Winds hanging to the Westward, we continu'd for ten Days. Here we stock'd ourselves with Brandy, at a very reasonable Rate. From the *Downs* we steered our Course to

our

our intended Port; our Company confifting of two Ladies, eight Gentlemen, and myfelf. When one Day (to
my Sorrow I fpeak it) fome of the Paffengers began to
play at *Hazard*, whereupon I, who always had a
ftrong and ungovernable Inclination to Gaming, made
one amongft them, we play'd high, and Fortune frowning on me, I foon became a broken Merchant. Upon
this Difafter, I thought myfelf the moft unhappy Man
alive, being bound to a ftrange Place, and entirely deftitute of either Money or Friends; however I amufed
myfelf with fettling the Accounts of one Mr. *Morgan*,
a yearly Trader to thofe Parts, and knowing no other
Antidote to my prefent Afflictions but Patience, I determined to bear up againft the Torrent of Adverfity,
with a chearful Alacrity, and pleafing Hopes of fome
unexpected Turn of Fortune.

On *Chriftmas* Day we went afhore, and the Ship's
Doctor invited me to Dinner with him at a Friend's
Houfe, for every one by my Apparel, judged me to be
a young Gentleman of Fortune. In the Evening I
went to Mrs. *Carmichaels*, the beft Tavern in *Charles-
Town*, where I quartered for a confiderable Time; my
good Friend Mr. *Morgan* having given me a fair Character to my Landlady, and alfo prefented me with two
Moidores, for the Service I had done him, in ballancing
his Accounts; but this ready Cafh was foon expended,
and I confiderably indebted to my kind Hoftefs, which
threw me in fo great a Dilemma how to manage my
Affairs, that I cou'd neither reft Night nor Day; full
well I knew that I could not get off from the Ifland
without giving publick Notice thereof for one and
twenty Days. Neverthelefs, as I had artfully lodged
my Cheft and Cloaths at a little Tavern adjoining to
the Water-fide, I waited in Hopes of fome favourable
Opportunity of bilking my Landlady. Accordingly,
fometime afterwards his Majefty's Ship the *Gofport* arrived in the Bay, and by good Fortune, fome of the
young Officers came to Dinner at my Quarters, where
in the Afternoon over a merry Bottle, one of the Gen-

themen

tlemen afked me, if I was not Commander of a Veffel, for fo he judged me to be by my Apparel, which
was Scarlet trimmed with Silver. Sir, faid I, my Appearance, I confefs, may fpeak me to be fuch as you
pleafe to imagine, but to tell you the real Truth, I am
the moft unfortunate young Fellow alive, for here I am
involv'd in Debt, which I am unable to difcharge, neither know I how to efcape from this accurfed Ifland.
Sir, replied he brifkly, *If that be all your Grievance, I'll
put you in a Way to redrefs it immediately; our Captain is
an honourable and good natured Gentleman, and therefore
if you apply to him for your Paffage to* Jamaica, *I doubt
not but that he will eafily grant your Requeft; he comes
afhore every Morning about Nine, and your beft Way is
to addrefs yourfelf to him on his Landing, before he is engaged in other Company; in the mean Time, be cautious
how you let any one into the Secret, and you need not fear
Succefs therein.* In fine, I heartily thanked him for his
wholefome and highly agreeable Advice, and the next
Morning met the Commander, to whom I freely and
without Referve, made known the State of my Affairs,
and he as generoufly was pleafed to promife me my Paffage on Board his Ship, and at the fame Time, as a
Signal, order'd me when I faw his Maintop-Sail Sheets
hauled Home, to come on Board, and he would receive me into his Care and Protection.

Highly pleafed with this unexpected Courtefy from a
Stranger, I was not failing in an humble and grateful
Acknowledgement of fo fingular a Favour, and elate
with Joy, return'd to my Quarters. Now my fole Bufinefs was to keep a fharp look out for my fo much defired Signal; which on the fourth Day I efpyed to my
great Joy and Comfort; whereupon I immediately
took a Canoe, put my Cheft therein, and went on
Board. Captain *Richardfon* feeing me going on Board
the Man of War, imagin'd how Affairs went, and
fent his Mate to me with three Guineas, for the Whig
which I had had of my aforefaid Friend the *Barber* at
Blackwall. From *Barbadoes* we fail'd to *Jamaica,* and
during

during the Paſſage, I had the Honour to Meſs with the
Lieutenants, who ſeemed well pleaſed at the merry ˙Re-
cital of my various Adventures. I leave my Readers
to judge of the Confuſion that my Landlady was in, at
the News of my ſudden Departure, and now proceed
to the Relation of what happen'd to me in the above-
mention'd Iſland of *Jamaica*.

I lodged at Mr. *Wade*'s, at *Port Royal*, and by my
coming there in the Man of War, paſs'd currently for
one of the Midſhip-men. Here in a ſhort Time I expended my ſmall Stock, but was happily prevented from
running in Debt, by an unexpected Accident. For one
Night being at Supper with ſome Gentlemen of the
Iſland, one of the Company gave me a kind Invitation
to come over to his Plantation, near *Salt-pan-Hill*, there
to ſpend three Weeks or a Month with him in a retired
Life. I readily embraced the Opportunity, as hoping
thereby to gain the Favour of being recommended to
ſome Employment on the Iſland. The next Day we
went to his Country Seat, far more reſembling the in-
fernal Regions, than the pleaſing Abode of a Mortal
here on Earth. His numerous Attendants, both Male
and Female, were all Black, and their young, like unto
Gallicia Swine, lay grovelin in the arid Duſt. Here the
parch'd and yawning Earth brought to my Remembrance,
how Dame *Tellus* rais'd up her then barren Head, invo-
king *Jove* to cruſh the giddy *Phaeton* in his wild and
mad Carrier, and by his deſerved Fall, to ſave her
vaſt Dominions from an univerſal Conflagration. As
this Gentleman had no *European* but myſelf to Converſe with, I ſoon became intimate and familiar with
him, who being acquainted with my Circumſtances,
promiſed to ſerve me to the utmoſt of his Capacity.
Although I here enjoyed all that the Iſland afforded, yet
a retired Life was not agreeable to my roving Diſpoſi-
tion, and therefore I reſolved to uſe ſome Stratagem to
get a little Caſh from him, and then to go on Board
the Fleet commanded by Admiral *Steward*. To
effect this, I propoſed to live with this Gentleman as
his

his Servant, or Overfeer, which Favour, after many Sollicitations, and earneft Entreaties, was granted, and my defign'd Employment was to overlook the Negroes in the Fifhery. Now as foon as Mr. *Lynch* (for that was the Gentleman's Name) and I had agreed on Terms for my Wages; I freely told him that my Cheft and Clothes lay as a Security for twenty Dollars at *Port-Royal*, and therefore I humbly entreated him to advance me Cafh for the Redemption of the fame; to which he readily confented, and ordered his Negroes to Man the Canoe, and row me over to *Port - Royal*, and there wait till I had compleated my Bufinefs.

No fooner was I landed there, but I took one of the Slaves with me to a Tavern, and there gave him a Letter to carry to his Mafter, the Contents whereof were, *That I returned him many Thanks for his kind Entertaiument, and generous Affiftance; but that Fortune had unexpectedly provided fomething for me far Superior to the Station of a Servant ; that I hop'd he would excufe my Breach of Promife, and that as to the Cafh, that he had lent me, I would repay him as foon as poffible.* Having thus difmifs'd the Negroe, I forthwith addrefs'd myfelf to the aforefaid Admiral, who generoufly compaffionating my Youth and Misfortunes, was pleafed to order me on Board the fame Ship that brought me thither, and the Commander thereof favour'd me with the Liberty of walking the Quarter Deck. In three or four Days the Fleet failed round for *Port Antonio*, fituate on the Northermoft Part of the Ifland, where we continu'd near upon four Months, all Hands being daily employed Afhore, in building a Dock for his Majefty's Service. From thence we returned to *Port-Royal*, and after a fhort ftay there, our Ship was ordered Home to *Plymouth*, and there foon after paid off. Whilft I was on Board, I had contracted an Intimacy with the Surgeon's Mate, and we two now became infeperable Companions, we both lodging at the *Three Guns* at the *Dock*. Amidft the various Company that reforted thither, was an old Gentleman (Clerk of the Dock-yard) a Man of

an

an affable and engaging Temper, with whom, as he daily frequented the Houfe, we foon became acquainted. This Gentleman had a very agreeable young Lady for his Daughter, with whom, as fhe accidentally came to call her Father Home, my Comrade, the Doctor, was fo fmitten at the firft Sight, that he could not reft, till he had engaged her Father to favour us with his, and his fair Daughter's Company, to Supper on the Evening following. Mr. *B***n*, (for that was the Gentleman's Name, readily confented, and we paffed the Hours in Mirth and Gaiety ; the young Lady, to heighten our Pleafures, diverting us with feveral Songs. Between Twelve and One we waited on our Company Home, and afterwards returned to our Quarters, where the Doctor was now more inflamed, his Thoughts and Difcourfe running continually on the Perfections of his new Miftrefs. But for my Part, I conceal'd my ardent Paffion, and refolv'd to wait a more favourable Opportunity, of difclofing my Love and Efteem, in an honourable Manner, if fo it may be called in me, who had already tyed the Conjugal Knot. In the mean Time the Doctor and I (both being flufh of Money) revelled at large, till by our repeated Extravagancies, we had almoft drain'd our Pockets, and in return to our Folly, got the *French Difeafe*.

However, one Day as we were playing at Billiards, I looking out of the Window, accidentally faw my Charmer ftanding at the Door of a Corner Shop ; whereupon giving the Game for loft, Doctor, faid I, there's *Molly*, come, let's go and drink a Difh of Tea with her ; by no means, replied he, for the People of the Houfe are Strangers, and confequently would deem it Impudence in us to force any Acquaintance with them. No matter for that, quoth I, if you won't go, I will ; fo down Stairs I ran to the Shop, and (as in a Surprize) faid, Blefs me, Madam ! what good Fortune has brought you hither, I've oftentimes promis'd my felf the Happinefs of drinking Tea with you, but never till now had the Opportunity ; fo fliping into the Shop, I told the Miftrefs

trefs thereof, that I hop'd fhe would excufe my Freedom
in defiring the Favour of her to make us a Pot of
Tea, and at the fame Time flung down half a Crown
as a Satisfaction for her Trouble. She feem'd very well
pleafed to have the Opportunity of obliging her Coufin
(as fhe called her) and me, and therefore defired us to
walk into the Parlour, whilft fhe prepared the Tea Equipage. Here I freely difclos'd my Mind to my Goddefs,
and met with a more favourable Reception than I expected; foon after, in came the old Gentleman, who
merrily faid: So, fo, Mr. *Englefield*, I fee that *Molly*
and you are got together. Yes, Sir, faid I, and fince
I've had the Pleafure of drinking Tea with Mifs, I defire the Favour that we may now go and drink a Glafs
together, for I've fomething to impart to you of great
Confequence. Agreed to, Sir, replied he, you and I
will go firft, and *Molly*, if fhe pleafes, may follow
after us. In fhort, I told the old Gentleman how paffionately I lov'd his Daughter, and that I fhould be proud
to make her my Wife; whilft we were thus difcourfing,
Molly came to us, whereupon I fhow'd all poffible
Marks of fincere Love and Efteem for her in the Prefence of her Father, who invited me to breakfaft with
him the next Morning. All this while my good Friend
the Doctor, was on Thorns, and long'd to know the
refult of our long Conferences, which I told him, was
on various Subjects, but never mentioned that I had
made the leaft proffer of Love to *Molly*, nor that I
was to go there in the Morning to Breakfaft. Wherefore I arofe early, and under a Pretence of taking a
Walk, went privately to Mr. *B***'s*, who received me
with the utmoft Civility, and left his Daughter and
me alone in the Parlour; here it was that I repeated
my Addreffes, and paffionately exprefs'd my inviolable
and conftant Love, vowing always to maintain the
fame fix'd and unalterable. At length the Nymph
confented, provided that her Father would be content
to ratifye it; whereupon, warmly faluting her, I went
out into the Garden to the old Gentleman, and there
told

told of my Succeſs and good Fortune, earneſtly defiring him to confummate our Happineſs, by his Confent; to which he generouſly replied, fince my Daughter is willing, *I am Content.* Whereupon we went in
to Breakfaſt, and all my Defires being thus happily
accompliſhed, I took my Leave for the prefent.

As foon as I came to my Lodgings, I began ſeriouſly
to reflect on my paſt Folly, in engaging myſelf in ſo
folemn and important an Affair, without any probability
of effecting what I had feemingly carried on with ſo
much Succeſs; the fole Reafon whereof was owing
to my Imprudence; for although I made a gay Appearance, yet I had but ten Shillings left in Money,
and moreover was feverely pepper'd by the Favours of
a Miſs, with whom I had Cohabits with at *Plymouth.*
Wherefore, upon mature Deliberation, of the Confequences that muſt inevitably arife from the Confumma-
tion of my intended Nuptials, I determin'd to vifit her
once more, to let her know, that I had receiv'd an
Order from my Friends to repair to *London* forthwith,
on fome urgent Affairs; but that upon the Conclufion
thereof, I would return and honourably perform my
Promife. *Molly* feem'd well enough pleas'd herewith,
but infifted on knowing how to write to me, whereupon I told her to direct to the *Gun*-Tavern at *Billingfgate.* Now there being a Sloop ready to fail that Day
for *London,* my Friend the Doctor and I, embarqu'd
therein, and landed at *Tower-Stairs.*

The firſt Thing I then did, was to fend for Mr.
G****t,* to whom I related my Adventures, and of
him enquired into the State of the Bankruptcy : Hereupon he told me that Mr. L****n,* and the Affignees,
were involv'd in Law, and that no Dividend had as yet
been made, but fays he, I've two Guineas for you, that
was left with me by your worthy Friend Mr. *Gilpin,*
which I ſhould have fent to you on board the Ship that
you went out in, had I not heard that ſhe was failed
before I could poffibly remit them to you. Mr. B***n
has fent your Wife to board in the *North* of *England,*
but

but as to the particular Place I can't inform you. I would therefore now advise you to lodge privately on *Southwark Side*, where if you send me a Direction, I will sometimes call and see you. Hereupon I took my Leave of him, and went in search of an Apartment, which by good Fortune, I soon met with, agreeable to my Taste, it being in a public House, where I had the Room *Gratis*. Near unto my Mansion liv'd a Mantua-maker and her Daughter, whom I besieged so closely, that in a little Time her Virtue began to stagger, and her Concupiscence to be a tiptoe. In short, the sole prevention of her Ruin was my being so pickled with above-mention'd Distemper. Notwithstanding this, I visited the Assignees and their Attorney, 2 or 3 times in a Week, from whom I had a costant supply of Money, though not sufficient to support my Extravagancies. Wherefore being now pretty deep in my Landlord's Debt, I resolved to make another Trip to Sea, but was happily prevented, by being one Day arrested as I was walking in *Cheapside*, at the Suit of a Person who had been Attendant on my Wife, in her Progress to *Flanders*. For this Debt *I* was clapp'd into the *Poultry-Compter*, and now thinking my self secure for sometime, I applyed to my Friend *G***e*, who generously order'd a Surgeon to attend me for my Cure. In this unhappy Place, I soon became acquainted with some of the most notorious Villains, and noted Prostitutes of the Town, from whose bewitching Conversation, I suck'd in the deadly Poison of unblushing Vice, and lost what impressions of Virtue and Honour I had yet remaining.

Here I continu'd near eleven Months, living on the Spoils of the unfortunate, whom I us'd to cheat and cozen at Cards and Dice, &c. 'till being wearied of this long and tedious Confinement, I entered into the Conspiracy with two others, to take the Opportunity, when the Turnkey brought in the unhappy Women of the Town at Night, to force our Passage out ; but this base Design was frustrated by one of the Confederates

turning

turning Informer, whereupon, I was confin'd for four Days in the strong Hold, and afterwards mov'd by a Duce to *Newgate*, where (it being the Summer-time) through the noisome and filthy Stench of the Place, I fell dangerously Ill, whereupon my Friends compassionating my Misfortunes, and to prevent the scandalous Reflection of my Death in so detestable a Place, procur'd my Enlargement, and generously paid for my Board and Lodging for three Months, hoping that in that Time, I should get into some honest and creditable Employ.

Now being pretty well recovered of my Indisposition, by propitious Fortune, I crept into the good Graces of Mr. *L***'s* Attorney, who employ'd me for a considerable Time.

One Day I chanc'd to meet *John Gadbury*, (my former Landlord in *Holland*) who had ran away with my Wife's Effects, whom I dogg'd to his Lodgings, and acquainting the Attorney for the Commission therewith, had him secur'd in the *Fleet*, from whence after seven Months Imprisonment, he made his Escape, to the great Detriment of the Warden, who was obligated thereby to satisfye our Demands. Upon the abovemention'd Attorney's going to settle in the Country, I contracted with one *K***k*, a *Buckle-maker*, in *Water-Lane*, *Fleet - Street*, to learn the Art of Carving Buckles. Our Agreement was, that I should serve him Twelve Months, and for his Trouble in instructing me in that Branch of Business, give him a promissory Note for twenty-five Pounds, payable six Months after the Expiration of my Servitude. For some time I lived very Happy with this Man, 'till by an unexpected Accident, he became jealous of me and his Wife ; the sole Reason whereof was as follows. A Relation of Mr. *K***'s*, who supplyed the Widow *A***n*, at the *Star* Musick-House, near the *Dock-head*, *Southwark*, with Wine, used annually to give an Entertainment there, to which he always invited my Master and Mistress. Now it happened that my Master was ill at the Time appointed

pointed for the Merry-making, wherefore he defired me
to accompany his Spoufe thither, to which I readily a-
greed, and the Hours paffing fwiftly away in Mirth and
Dancing, we ftaid there till four o'Clock in the Morning.
This innocent, though imprudent Action, gave Birth
to his Fears and Jealoufies, and caus'd him to imagine
that I violated the Rights of his Marriage .Bed. However, he took no Notice thereof for the prefent, but refolv'd to watch for an Opportunity to confirm. what
he already fufpected.

This Mr. *K***k*, had a Neice, a very pretty young
Girl, for whom I profefs'd a great Refpect, and ufed
always to wait on her Home, when fhe came to vifit
her Uncle. Now it fell out, that one Morning as I
was in the Kitchen, and my Mafter up Stairs, that
this young Woman came and afk'd her Aunt to take
a Walk to *Iflington*; my Miftrefs confented, and I out
of a Frolick offered my Service to accompany them to
Mr. *L***'s* there, at *the Land of Nod*, which being
readily accepted, I pretended to my Mafter, that I was
oblig'd to attend the Affignees in the Afternoon, and
therefore defir'd his Leave to make half a Holyday; he
freely complyed with my Requeft, and I according to
Agreement, met my Company at the Place appointed,
but had not been there long, before Mr. *K***k*, came
in puffing and blowing like a Porpice, and almoft as
pale as Afhes; his firft Salutation was a Blow on his
Wife's Head with a large Stick, which he would have
repeated, had I not prevented him. The Women affrighted, ran out of the Room, and he and I fat down
to drink together, where I ufed all poffible Arguments
to eradicate thofe groundlefs and jealous Whimfies that
poffefs'd his Brain. But all to no purpofe, for he remain'd inflexible, and vow'd Revenge on her. Wherefore in doing it in vain, to reconcile the Difference, and
that I fhould run in danger of my Life, if I continued
any longer in his Service, I propofed a Seperation to
prevent any farther Mifchief, which he readily agreed
to. Now being deftitute of all Bufinefs, I liv'd on the
Re-

Reverſions of a Proſtitute of the Town, till growing
weary of that ſcandalous Courſe of Life, I reſolv'd to
go to Sea, and therefore applied to my Friend *G***e*,
who was ſo kind as to obtain for me a Letter of Recommendation to Captain *Tollard*, Commander of the
Pearl Man of War, that was going on her Station to
Barbadoes. Now I might have been Happy, and recovered my loſt Reputation and Credit, had I been ſo
wiſe as to have gone on Board purſuant to Order ; but
ſo prevalent was my lewd Habit of Life, that I could
not quit the ruinous Company of my Harlot, with
whom I ſtayed in Dalliances of lawleſs Love, till the
Ship was ſailed.

By this imprudent Action I entirely diſobliged all my
Friends, and was therefore obliged to keep on in the
ſame abandon'd and deſpicable State of Life, till one
Day as I croſſed *Lincoln's-Inn-Square*, I was arreſted by
Mr. *Dod* the Officer, at the Suit of *K*——— my former Maſter. Mr. *Dod*, knowing me when I was in
Proſperity, conducted me to his Houſe, where he told
me I might remain as long as I could find Money. I
was now in the utmoſt Deſpair, and had there ended
my Days miſerably, by hanging myſelf, had not the
Rope fortunately broke.

Now Mr. *Dod*'s Wife being ill, had Lodgings in the
Country, and his Buſineſs often calling him out, I was
left in the Houſe with only two Women Servants,
which made me reſolve to take the firſt favourable Opportunity of making my Eſcape ; neither was it long
before I effected it; for one Day as *Dod* and his Fol-
lower were gone to *Kentiſh-Town*, I ſent the old Woman out for a Quart of Gin, and ply'd her ſo cloſe
with that intoxicating Liquor, that ſhe ſoon fell faſt
aſleep. As to the young one, I elevated her Spirits with
Sack and Walnuts, till by amorous Toys, and merry
waggiſh Tales, I prevailed on her to grant me the Favour of ſtanding at the Street Door for the Benefit of
the Air. In the Interim came by a Barrow of Peaches,
whereupon: Come my Dear, ſaid I, will you eat a

G   Peach!

Peach? She replying. Yes, Sir, I gave her Six-Pence to
purchafe fome of them, but did not ftay to partake of
the Repaft, for I immediately ran down to *Temple-Stairs*,
and croffed the Water, where I lay Perdue at the Houfe
of one *L———*, an Acquaintance of mine, who employed me in making Handles for Brufhes, and afterwards recommended me to Mr. *Weed*, a *Colour-Man*,
who had built a Shed in a Field remote from all Houfes,
where he boiled his Bullock's Blood, an Ingredient ufed
by them in the Compofition of Blue. This retired
Life, attended with a noifome Stench, did not long a-
gree with me, and therefore I refolved at once (for
fear of falling into the Bailiffs Hands) to fell my felf for
a four Year's Servant. Accordingly I contracted with
one *Burge*, who fent me on Board the *Spanifh Town*
Factor, Captain *Gray*, bound for *Jamaica*. In my
Paffage, I fettled the Captain's Books, who fold me for
a School-Mafter to Colonel *Sands*, at *Port-Royal*, who
having a Plantation at *Saltpan-Hill*, removed me and
his Children thither, for the better Conveniency of
their Education. Here I continued near three Months,
frequently diverting my felf in the Company of one
Quoimino, a facetious and trufty Negroe Slave, belonging to my Mafter, till growing weary of the mean and
poor Diet I met with there, I refolved at all Events to
run away; and accordingly about Four in the Morning, I went privately to *Paffage-Fort*, but had not got
into the Boat that was to carry me to *Kingfton*, before
I was purfu'd, overtaken and conducted back. Notwithftanding this, I ftill remain'd obftinate, and infifted
on going to the Colonel's at *Port-Royal*, which being
agreed to, I loudly exclaimed againft the ill Treatment
I had met with, and plainly told him, that I wou'd
ferve him no longer; which fo exafperated the Colonel,
that he threaten'd to have me whipt by his Negroes.
Enraged at this Menace, I fwore that nothing lefs than
his Life fhould expiate the grofs Affront; whereupon
he finding me fo refolute, remanded me to my former
Captain, with whom (he having buried one of his Hands)

I

I returned to *England*, and in the Downs was prefs'd by his Majefty's Ship, the *Portland*, from whence I was removed on Board the *Canterbury*, where I continu'd for ten Months, when an Order came for our being paid off at *Plymouth*. From thence I went to *Ilvercomb*, *Briftol* and *Bath*, and rambled up and down the Country with my Comrade, who was one of our Corporals on Board, till having expended all our Cafh, we made the beft of our Way to *London*, taking the Opportunity of paffing for Sea-faring Men caft away in the *Lamb*, Captain *Morgan*, bound for *Ireland*, with the Tranfport Soldiers; by which falfe Pretence we obtain'd great Relief on the Road. When we came to *London*, we lodged in St. *Giles's*, at one of thofe mean and fcandalous Houfes, that harbour Strangers for Twopence a Night. But this Life not being agreeable to either of us, I perfuaded my Companion to enter for a Soldier in the Foot-Guards, and for my Part, I fold my felf once more to go to *Penfilvania*, and continued on Board near a Week in the River; but there finding indifferent Ufage, and fearing to meet with worfe at Sea, I ftole Afhore, in Company with a *Weaver*, who was likewife going on the fame foolifh Errand. From thence we travelled to *Canterbury*, where pretending ourfelves to be *Frenchmen*, we were reliev'd by the Proteftants of that Town, and then continu'd on our Journey to *Dover*, where by good Fortune we met with Captain *Jennings*, who gave us our Paffage to *Calais*. At my Landing there, I was follicited by feveral *Irifh* Officers to enlift into the *French* Service, but wou'd by no means agree to their Propofals. My Companion now parted from me, in fearch of Bufinefs, but I entered myfelf on board a Snow, loaded with Corn, and bound for *Lifbon*. At *Calais* we ftaid feven Weeks, in which Time the Captain and all the Crew were fo involved in Debt, that we were obliged to put to Sea in the Night. When we arrived at *Lifbon*, the Commander was turn'd out of his Employ, and we all Paid off.

Now

Now the *English* Fleet lying there, I had some
thought of entring on Board thereof, but was prevented
by Meſſrs. *Abraham* and *Joſeph Gueſt*, who kept a large
Tavern at *Bull-Bay*, who agreed with me for ten
Pounds per Annum to ſerve them, in the Capacity of
a Drawer. Here I muſt confeſs, that I lived upon the
beſt that the City afforded, and each of my Maſters
keeping a ſeperate Lady of Pleaſure, I likewiſe grew
wanton, and maintain'd a Miſs for myſelf; but as this
Courſe of Life could not be ſuppoſed to have any long
Duration, my Maſters ſoon fail'd, and I thereby was
obliged to ſeek out for a freſh Service. Hereupon I
ſhipp'd my ſelf with Captain *Brook*, Commander of
the *Sarah* Galley, bound to *Sancta-Cruz*, in *Barbary*,
and from thence to *Cadiz*, and ſo home to *England*;
but the Captain and I not long agreeing together, I ran
away from her at *Cadiz*, from whence, (after I had
involved myſelf in Debt) I made the beſt of my Way
to *Malaga* by Land, all through the Province of *An-
daluzia*. In my Journey, I was greatly ſurprized at
the Poverty, and extreem Miſery of the Inhabitants,
chiefly owing to their Bigottry, they ſcarcely having
Bread to eat, whilſt the pretended Religious are pam-
pered up in the moſt exuberant Luxury.

When I arrived at *Malaga*, I lodged at one *O'Brian's*
almoſt a Month upon Credit, but finding at laſt cold
Reception, I reſolved to apply myſelf to the Clergy,
who I knew full well were the only Perſons for me to
Play upon, and having obſerved that it was cuſtomary
for ſome of them to frequent the Sea-ſide daily; I ſeated myſelf there on a Stone, and in a melancholy Poſture
waited for their coming; nor was it long before two of
the Dominican Order came, and ſeated themſelves by
me, aſking in the *Spaniſh* Tongue, what Countryman
I was? I replied in *Latin*, an *Engliſhman*; whereupon,
according to their fooliſh Notion, deeming me no
Chriſtian, and therefore incapable of Salvation, they
out of their ſeeming Piety, invited me to their Convent,
there to be inſtructed in their Faith. In ſhort, I verify'd
the

the old Proverb, *Neceſſity has no Law*; for being then almoſt ſtarved, I was glad to embrace any thing that offered for my immediate Relief, and pretending to be entirely ignorant of the *Romiſh* Principles, which to my Sorrow (I now ſincerely Confeſs I had imbib'd in my Youth) I paſs'd on them for a great Proficient therein. Here I liv'd a retir'd and indolent Life near four Months, during which Time they often preſs'd me to the Acceptance of the Habit, which I always declin'd, as having an Averſion (ever ſince I arriv'd to the Years of Diſcretion) to their Superſtitious Follies, though by them artfully contrived to impoſe on the giddy Vulgar. Theſe Fathers recommended me to the Service of a *Spaniſh* Nobleman, in Quality of Page to his Lady, with whom I liv'd eleven Months, till being unfortunately diſcovered in an Amour with his Niece, whom I had Debauched, I was forc'd to ſkreen myſelf from the Rage of the injur'd *Don*, by leaping out at the Window, and making the beſt of my Way to the Houſe of an *Iriſh* Taylor of my Acquaintance, where I lay conceal'd for a conſiderable Time, till at length meeting with a Sloop bound to *Gibraltar*, and from thence to *Ireland*, I entered on Board thereof, our Paſſage was unparalled, and hardly credible, for we were thirty-five Days before we got into the Bay at *Gibraltar*, which from *Malaga*, is but eighteen Leagues diſtant. Wherefore thinking that ſuch an uncommon and unuſual Diſappointment, portended ſomething fatal attendant on our Sloop. I there quitted her, and offered myſelf as a Soldier in the Garriſon, but was rejected, by the followers of *Mars*, on Account of my Stature, whereupon having nothing to ſubſiſt on, I was forc'd to perform the diſagreable and ſlaviſh Part of a Labourer to the *Bricklayers*, which I thought was the greateſt Hardſhip that I ever yet met with, and therefore I reſolved to quit this intollerable fatiguing Service, and ſeek out for ſome other more facile.

Accordingly I applied my ſelf to the *Tennis-Court*, and ſerved therein as a Waiter; but that likewiſe did not an-

anfwer my Expectation, for my Miftrefs, on Account of the wet Seafon, not having fo much Company as ufual, put me to fetch Water from the Fountain, and clean the Hogfties, which fervile Employs, not confifting with my Notions of Life, I quitted her Service, and then commenc'd Ufher to a School-mafter, who not living within the Bounds of his Scholiaftical Revenues, was in a little Time compelled to quit the Garrifon.

I now thought I had a fair Expectance of fucceeding him in that Occupation, but my Hopes therein prov'd Abortive, through the Malice of fome envious Perfons, who reprefented me to the then Governor (General *Sabine*) as a Perfon fent thither as a Spye, though in Difguife; whereupon his Excellency ordered me to be confin'd in the *Moore's* Caftle, in a noifome and filthy Cell, where I continued for the Space of feventeen Days; at the Expiration of which, I was releafed and turned out of the Garrifon. Whereupon I fhipp'd myfelf as *Cook* on Board a *Tartan*, commanded by one *Anthony Jenkins*, bound for *Walidea*, on the *Barbary* Shore. We went out in our Ballaft, with four *Moorifh* Merchants on Board, that were to freight our Veffel with Corn, and then return to *Gibraltar*, for the Sale thereof.

But the Mafter, either through his Ignorance, or adverfe Winds, could not gain his defired Port; but kept hufking the Sea till our Provifions were almoft expended, and we reduced to the Allowance of three Pound of *Barbary* Rufk per Week, and half a Pint of Water a Day. Thefe hardfhips, with the ill Treatment of the Mafter, made me refolve to leave him as foon as poffible, and foon after it luckily happen'd, that I had an Opportunity of Effecting what I fo much defired, for in a hard Gale of Wind we fprung our main Maft, and tore our Sails to fhatters, but at length the Storm abating, we the next Day made the *Canary Iflands,* when putting her before the Wind, under an old fpare maintop Sail, that we had on Board, we anchor'd about

bout eight at Night at the *Colerada's*, belonging to the
Ifland of *Lancerota*; our Captain being afraid to go into
the ufual Port of that Place, leaft his Hands, who had
been all barbaroufly treated by him, fhould run afhore
and leave him. Now I refolved to loofe no Time in
freeing my felf from this Slavery, and therefore about
Twelve o'Clock at Night, my two Confederates and I,
after we had taken three Pieces of Linnen, and what
elfe we could find, from the *Moors*, embark'd in the
Boat, and went afhore, making the beft of our Way
from the Sea Side, though we knew not whither it led
to. About the Dawn of Day we met with a *Spaniard*,
mounted on a *Bourico*, or Jack-Afs, who civilly bidding
us Good-Morrow, asked for an old Pipe, whereupon
I, having the Language at Command, returned the
Complement, and favour'd him with one half full of
Tabacco; whereat he exprefs'd a great Satisfaction, and
at the fame Time gave me to underftand, that he was
Mayor of that Town, which we then faw on the
Hill. I confefs that by his mean Garb, and wretched
Appearance, I had formed a defpicable Idea of the reft
of the Inhabitants, which was further augmented at the
Sight of their poor ftraggling Hutts, and miferable manner of Life; their common Diet being Greens and Oat-
meal, mixed with cold Water, which they call *Gofio*;
neither do any of the Inhabitants, except the Grandees
and Clergy (altho' the Ifland affords plenty of Corn)
ever Bake any Bread for their own Ufe.

In the Evening, by the help of our Guide, whom
we hired for two Reals of Plate, about a Shilling Value,
we reach'd the Port, where ftood ten or twelve ruined
Houfes, with only one which appear'd in tollerable good
Repair, which upon Enquiry, we found was the Manfion Seat of Seignor *Don Bernardo Trojano Cocillio de los
Efperones*, the Perfon who affumed to himfelf the Title
of the *Britifh* Conful; to this Gentleman we complain'd
of the ill Treatment that we had received from our
Commander, reprefenting him as no Chriftian, but as an
Encourager to *Mahometifm*, and to prove our Affertion,
we declared, that he had four *Moors* on Board.

In

In short, we made him appear so black in the *Spaniard*'s Eyes, that he thought him a mere Devil, often signing himself with the Cross at the mention of his Name. Whereupon he commiserated our Hardships, and entertained us very handsomely for three Days. To this Gentleman we sold our Linnen Cloth for 40 Dollars, but not thinking it secure to make any longer Stay here, least the Captain (who without Dispute would come in Search of us) shou'd on his Appearance confute our Assertions, and thereby making us appear greater Villains, than what we had represented him, obtain an Order to have us bound Neck and Heels, and carried on Board, where we cou'd expect no Mercy from him, or the injured *Moors* ; we therefore went privately in the Night to a Place called *la Villa*, the Residence of the Governor, where stood two Convents, one of *Dominican*, and the other of *Francistan* Fryars, where we took Sanctuary, my two Comrades in the latter, and I in the former Monastery.

The Priors of the respective Orders, treated us very handsomely, and promised to secure us from all Danger, if we kept in the Confines of their priviledged Territories. We had not been long here, before the Captain came up to the Governor's, and upon Complaint, that he cou'd not put to Sea without his Hands, obtained of him an Order to apprehend us, if found without the Limits of the Convents, it not being in his Power to take us out of the Pale of the Church. Hereupon the Captain endeavour'd by Flattery, to persuade us to return on Board, but all in vain, for we not only resolved to continue in our Station, but also to do him all the Prejudice we cou'd ; and therefore I drew up a Complaint to the Governor, and prevailed on the Prior to present it to his Excellency, setting forth our barbarous Usage ; and that the said Commander had *Moors* on Board, who under Pretence of Traffick, came to take a View of the Island, in order to return with greater Force, and surprise the Inhabitants. This so incensed the Governor, that he order'd a Company of Soldiers on Board,

to fearch the Veffel, and to oblige the Captain to pay
300 Dollars, as a Fine for not anchoring in the open
Port ; and furthermore, to put to Sea in ten Days time.
All which, he unable to refift their fuperior Power, was
obliged to comply with.

As foon as he was failed, we rang'd up and down the
Ifland at our Liberty, and were civilly entertain'd by the
Natives, in the beft manner they cou'd afford. My
Companions went on Board a *Genoefe* Veffel, but I
waited for the Arrival of the Father Provincial, well
knowing, that if I had the Fortune to get into his good
Graces, that it wou'd turn confiderably to my Advantage ; wherefore on his Arrival there, I play'd my
Cards with fo much Art and Cunning, that I foon obtained the Favour of waiting on his Perfon, who I
muft acknowledge treated me with the utmoft Huma-
nity, With him I went to *Sancta Cruz,* another of the
Canary Iflands, where I continu'd in the fame Poft ; but
altho' I neither wanted for the beft of Victuals, nor
Cloaths, neverthelefs feeing no Profpect of getting Money in his Service, (the Clergy of that Profeffion being
generally to much addicted to the inordinate Love thereof) I left him, and from thence proceeded to the Port
of *Oratava,* where for fome Time I was maintain'd by
the *English* Merchants; but as Courtefies of that Nature are not of any long Duration, I was foon obliged
to Ship myfelf on Board the *Charming Molly,* Captain
Patrick Mackhugh, bound to *Genoa,* where we unloaded our *Orchilea,* (a Weed ufed by the *Dyers*) and after
about a Months Continuance there, we loaded with Bale
Goods for *Cadiz.* As I now waited on the Captain,
I had an Opportunity of feeing the Directions of the feveral Letters that he brought for the numerous Merchants of that City, and amongft them I found one directed to Meffrs, *Ryan* and *Mannock* ; whereupon knowing Mr. *Mannock* to have been my old School-fellow,
and familiar Companion when in Trade, I refolv'd to
wait on him, and therefore afked the Captain Liberty
to go afhore, where I fecreted myfelf all Night in a *Ge-*
noefe

hoese House, and the next Morning waited on my worthy Friend, who receiv'd me with unusual Marks of Civility, and freely asked me, *What Service he cou'd do me?* To which generous Offer I reply'd, *Sir, please to obtain my Discharge from the Commander.* Whereupon he immediately gave me a Note to the Captain for that Purpose; yet he absolutely refused to discharge me, and the next Day sailed for St. *Lucan,* to load with Fruit for *London,* leaving me behind. Mr. *Mannock* (as my Wages were but trivial) advised me not to trouble myself about them, but ordered me to take a Lodging, and come to Dinner with him every Day, until he cou'd procure my Passage to *England,* in a Gentleman-like manner; he enabled me besides to quit my Seaman's Garb, and gave me a genteel Suit of his own, with Shirts, Hat, Wig, &c. and 20 Pistoles in my Pocket.

Now I began to taste the Pleasures of Life once more, and buried all my former Hardships in Oblivion; yet still I observed a regular and sedate Conduct, for fear of disobliging my generous Patron; till one Night in the *Carnaval* Time, I unfortunately pick'd up a *Spanish* Lady, with whom I went Home, and spent the Evening in lewd Pleasures, and as I was returning Home thro' a dark Passage, my Hat and Wig were snatch'd from off my Head, and at the same Time a Book, that I had borrow'd of my Friend was pick'd out of my Pocket. The Place was so dark and obscure, that I cou'd not discover the Villain, who fled as fast as he cou'd, and soon skreen'd himself from my fruitless Pursuit.

Stung with Remorse, not so much I confess for the Offence, as for the Loss I had sustained; I went Home greatly perplex'd, how to prevent this sad Disaster from reaching my Friend's Ear, which full well I knew I cou'd not effect, but by procuring the Book, the sole Obstacle to the Concealment of my past Folly; but Mr. *Mannock* had unfortunately heard of the Affair, by the Book being exposed to Sale; wherefore at Dinner he asked me for the same, saying, *That he highly esteemed it,*

it, *as being a Prefent from his Brother to him*. I blufh'd,
and after Dinner calling him afide, freely acknowledged
my Fault, and humbly begged Pardon for the Offence,
which he generoufly forgave ; but caution'd me to be-
ware of the like Folly for the future. I now refolv'd,
fince my Friend was acquainted with my Amour) to
make the Harlot (whom I fufpected to be an Accomplice in the Robbery) to render me ample Satisfaction
for the Injury received, and therefore I made my Complaint to the Alcade Major, or Mayor of the Town,
who order'd two Officers to go with me to the Houfe,
and to demand the Goods I had loft; and if the Profti-
tute refufed to deliver them, to feize her Effects, and
carry her to Prifon. In fhort, the Huffy to prevent the
impending Storm return'd the Things, and as an Attonement for her Crime, gave the Officers and me a
Dollar a-piece, and a handfome Treat.

Sometime after this, Mr. *Mannock* fent for me, and
told me, that he had agreed for my Paffage Home, and
that I muft go on Board in the Evening, for the Ship
wou'd fail the next Morning for *England :* Whereupon
I humbly thank'd him for all Favours, and took my
laft Farewell of him, highly overjoy'd at the Thoughts
of my returning once more to my native Land. But
as I paffed thro' the City Gates, with a full Intent to
go on Board, I unhappily met a *Courtezan,* a *quondam*
Acquaintance, with whom I ftay'd all Night; but the
next Morning when I went down to the *Mould,* I
found to my equal Sorrow and Surprize, that the Ship
was fail'd ; whereupon I was fo ehrag'd at this fatal
Difappointment, entirely occafion'd by my own Folly,
that I almoft refolved to put a Period to my wretched
Life. And now being no longer able to ftay in *Cadiz,*
for Fear of being feen by my injured Friend, I took
Boat, and went over to Port St. *Mary's,* and from
thence to St. *Lucar,* where I had heard, that one Mr.
Brown, a wealthy Merchant refided, whofe Sifter had
been married to my Uncle Sir *Roger Langley.* Here I
had the Honour to dine with this Gentleman, who
made

made me a Prefent of two Doubloons, and advifed me
to return Home. Whereupon, lodging at the Houfe
of Mr. *Smith,* who kept an Ordinary for the Mafters
of Veffels, I fortunately became acquainted with Captain *Whitaker,* bound for *Cowes* and *Hamburgh,* with
this Gentleman I came Home, landed at *Limington,*
and from thence made the beft of my Way to *London,*
where finding that my Creditors had receiv'd 10 s. in
the Pound in my long Abfence, I was in Hopes of receiving the Sum ftipulated by Parliament for Bankrupts,
and thereby reinftating myfelf in fome fettled Bufinefs
with my Wife. Mr. *Brown* her Father being dead in
my Abfence, and all Differences now feeming thereby
to be appeafed, whereupon I waited on my Mother-in-
law, and to her made Propofals of fending for my Wife
to Town, which fhe agreed to, but thro' her avaritious
Temper, refufed to affift me with Money to enable me
to recover my Right from the Statute, and to obtain
my Certificate from the Creditors. Whereupon finding
my good Defigns rend'red impracticable, I gave a Loofe
to falfe Pleafure, leading a profufe and extravagant Life,
until I had almoft exhaufted all my flender Gains, as
likewife a fmall Legacy that was left me by my Coufin
Brent. Wherefore I now refolv'd once more to range
abroad in Search of new Adventures, and accidentally
coming acquainted with one Mr. *H***,* a young Spark
of as defperate a Fortune as my own, with him I propofed to make a Tour to *Paris;* in order whereunto,
we travelled by Land to *Dover,* but on our Arrival there,
we were unhappily difappointed in our intended Progrefs,
by an Embargo laid on the Shipping in that Port.

Where on our Return Home, Money being low,
we ftopp'd *John Springate* of *Feverfham,* within Sight
of the Turnpike at *Harble-Down;* but upon riffling his
Pockets, and finding no more than three Farthings therein, not thinking fo inconfiderable a Sum worthy our
Acceptance, we return'd him the fame, and civilly dif-
miffed him.

For

For this Fact we were both taken near *Boughton*, above five Miles diftant from the Place where we committed the Robbery, and committed in *Auguft* 1739 to his Majefty's Goal for the *Eaftern Divifion* of *Kent*, from hence we were moved to the Affizes at *Rochefter*, where we both received Sentence of Death, on the 20th of *March* 1739, from Sir *John Fortefcue Aland*, who was pleafed to Reprieve us both in Order for Tranfportation.

Under this Sentence thefe Pages were written. May all young Men read them with a proper Difpofition to avoid by my Example, the miferable State I have brought myfelf to. A State too frightful to defcribe, and the very Thoughts of which ftops the Pen. Yet a State to which Numbers are running, as full of Mirth and mad Joy, as if their Fools Paradife was a real One. The Royal Mercy hath faved me from an ignominious Death, and I humbly truft in GOD, that he will give me his Grace to amend my Conduct, and by a thorough and fincere Repentance fave me from Death everlafting.

Maidftone-Goal,
July 20,
1740.

G. LANGLEY.

F I N I S.

HISTORY OF
THE LIFE OF SOMEBODY

A

True and Impartial

HISTORY

OF THE

Life and Adventures

OF

SOME-BODY.

Faithfully tranfcrib'd from a MANUSCRIPT
now in the Poffeffion of a Perfon of Quality.

Illuftrated with NOTES by the EDITOR.

LONDON:

Printed for RICHARD HIGGINS, in the *Strand*;
and fold at the Bookfellers and Pamphlet-Shops
in *London* and *Weftminfter*. MDCCXL.

[Price NINE-PENCE.]

To the **Honourable**

The Society for Encouragement of Learning.

Gentlemen,

THE Defign in publifhing this Work being to inform the World, who it is that has been the chief Manager and Tranfactor, of moft of the principal Occurrences which have happen'd in this Age; in order to prevent thofe Miftakes which Pofterity may be led into, in unriddling many dark and myfterious Paffages, and to affift fuch future Hiftorians, as fhall attempt the Hiftory of thefe Times : I think, that without Injuftice it may claim a Right to your Patronage ; to whofe Diligence the World is indebted, for retrieving fo

many

many valuable Pieces of *Antiquity*, and especially for collecting those which relate to the History of these *Kingdoms*, and publishing them at your own Expence. The Encouragement other Branches of *Polite Literature* have received from your *Society*, is too well known, to need any mention, from,

GENTLEMEN,

Your most obedient

humble Servant,

The EDITOR,

PREFACE.

IT is not long since a particular Friend of mine, was employed by the Person of Quality who is posfessed of the original Manuscript, to transcribe it. By this means, I had an Opportunity of perusing Part of it; which pleased me so well, that with some Intreaties, and a Promise not to let it go out of my Hands, I persuaded my Friend to let me have a Copy of it. He is since dead, otherwise it had not appeared in publick. Whoever the Author was, he has been very impartial; not only giving us the Virtues, but has also exposed the Vices of the Person, whose History he writes: And has entirely avoided linking himself to any Party; neither flattering the Whigs, nor applauding the Tories.

I am inclined to think the Author of these Papers, never designed their appearing publickly in the World; or he would have been more correct in his Stile, and in some Places which I have remark'd in the Notes. But I was not willing to make any Alterations, knowing that Truth unadorn'd, is more agreeable than cloathed in all the Beauties of Roman Eloquence: Or

if

if I may be permitted the Expression of a modern Philosopher, Truth is sweetest when naked.

ANNEXED to the Manuscript was a Paper wrote in a different Hand, in the Nature of a Key. If what is already published, should meet with a good Reception, that and the Remainder will soon be put to the Press; which will make a small Pocket Volume, containing the most remarkable Transactions *that have happen'd in this Age: And which others may perhaps enlarge upon, but will never be able to set in a clearer Light.*

THE

THE
HISTORY
OF THE
LIFE and ADVENTURES
OF
SOME-BODY.

T H E *Some-bodies* are a People of very great Antiquity, often mentioned both in the ſacred and profane Writings, of the earlieſt Times. The firſt Account of any of this Name, if we may allow *Moſes* to be the moſt *antient* Writer, is in *Gen.* xiv. 13.* where, in relating the Battle of the Four Kings againſt Five, fought in the Vale of *Siddim,* are theſe Words: *And there came one that had eſcaped, and told Abraham the Hebrew,*

---

* *What the Author meant by this Paſſage, I can't comprehend, unleſs it be a* Bam *upon ſome* Criticks, Tranſlators, Commentators, *&c.*

brew, concerning the taking of *Lot* his Brother's Son, his Brother's Goods, &c. which might be more properly tranflated, according to the *Englifh* Phrafeology, *And there came* Some-body *who had efcaped, and told Abraham the Hebrew.* But leaving this to be decided by the Learned, it is certain that at this time they are fpread throughout the whole Earth; but are a People of fuch uncommon Difpofition, that it remains a controverted Point, whether the World is more obliged by the good Actions which have been attributed to them, or difobliged by their bad ones.

THOSE that inhabit this Kingdom, are defcended from the *Saxons*; and are often celebrated by the *Saxon* Hiftorians, for feveral Actions wherein they fignalized themfelves, by the Name of Sumbooize. They were a confiderable People here at the time of *William* the Conqueror; and it was one of this Family who headed the Barons, at the time when they obliged King *John* to fign *Magna Charta.* The Hiftories and Chronicles, are fo full of their various Actions, that I fhall avoid repeating them, and defcend to HIM that is the Subject of this Hiftory.

SOME-BODY was born in the ‡ Year 1683; and tho' amongft thofe of this
Name,

---

‡ *Here the Author has been guilty of a great Fault, never to be forgiven by* Aftrologers *and* Figure-cafters, *in not being more punctual as to the Month, Day, and Hour of his Nativity.*

Name, as of others, there have been Wifemen
and Fools; yet if the old Adage holds good,
that *'tis a wife Child which knows its own Father*, we muft certainly reckon him one: For
he, and indeed every body elfe, knew he was
Some-body's Son ; as like his Dad as ever
he could ftare: Tho' there were fome goffip-
ing old Women in the Neighbourhood, that
gave out fome incredible Stories, of his being
brought in a Warming-pan, in the Room of
a Child which died, that the Eftate might
not want a Male Heir. But as this arofe from
their being difappointed coming in for fhare
of the groaning Cheefe, his Mother not being willing to have any, but fuch as were her
own Friends, at the Labour ; fo the Story was
not much heeded. Yet a certain impudent
Fellow that lived in the fame Town, a *Ful-
ler* by Trade, fome few Years after, had the
Affurance to talk of it publickly ; and promifed, if encouraged, to make great Difco-
veries in favour of the next Heirs to the E-
ftate : But after feveral long Examinations before a worthy Juftice of the Peace, he was
committed to *Newgate.* Nor indeed could it
ever be thought by difcerning Perfons, that a
Man of the *Father*'s Judgement, would fuffer
himfelf to be impofed on in fuch a manner:
Of whom it will be neceffary here to give a
fmall Account.——He enjoyed feveral confiderable Places in the Reign of King *Charles* I.
and the cruel Maffacre that happen'd in *Ire-*

land,

land, was always thought to be the Effect of his Management. And it is imputed to his Counfels, that the King fign'd the Warrant for taking off Lord *Strafford's* Head, as well as moſt of the Troubles which followed. But when he found the Royal Party depreſſed, and the King beheaded, he laid down all his Titles of Honour, and repreſented a Borough in the *Protector's* Parliament; aſſumed the Air of the Times, and exceeded the reſt in Canting and Hypocriſy. By theſe means he became in ſuch power with the *Fanaticks*, that on the *Protector's* Death all their Eyes were ſet on him, expecting he would fill the Vacancy; which he had certainly done, had it not been for ſome very advantageous Proffers made him by the Royaliſts, and well guaranteed; ſo now he became the firſt and moſt zealous Man for reſtoring the King, who heaped great Favours on him. He it was that ſet *Oates's* Affair on foot, and was at the bottom of it; and tho' concerned in promoting the Bill of Excluſion, yet many People fuſpected his haſtening the King's End, in order to make it up with his brother *James* II. In this Reign he exerted himſelf, by being one of the foremoſt in ordering the Declaration for Liberty of Conſcience to be read, perſuading the *King* to tower the *Biſhops* for a Libel. But indeed he prevented a great deal of Diſturbance, in diſſuading the *Queen* from ſending the Hoſt through the City, altho' it

was

was carried thro' the Park, and up *Pall-mall.*
But perceiving at what rate things went, and
that the *Jesuits* generally over-power'd him
in their Counsels, he resented it so far, that as
soon as he heard of the *Prince* of *Orange's*
landing at *Torbay,* he immediately went over
to him, and endeavour'd to ingratiate himself:
But tho' King *William* was obliged to employ
him, he having great Interest; yet the King
never confided in him; nor was he let into
the Secret of Affairs as little as possible. But
to return to the young one.

H I S Behaviour at first Appearance in the
World, was so odd and uncommon, and his
Actions so different at the time of his Sucking,
from what other Childrens usually are ; that
it raised the Admiration, and afforded Talk,
for all the gossiping old Women in the Neighbourhood. Sometimes nothing would please
the young Gentleman, but singing, dancing,
jingling his Coral Bells, and all Hoity-toity
Doings; and the next moment perhaps he
would be so grave, that the above-mention'd
would have no other effect on him than, if
used too much, to set him a squalling in so
violent a manner, that they were not able to
quiet him in some Hours; which caused the
poor Nurses often to lose their Places, *Mamma*
alledging that they did not endeavour to humour the Child. When he grew to proper
Years, he was sent to an eminent Boarding-
School, where he took his Learning exceeding

fast:

faſt : But was very arch, play'd a great many
Tricks, and never fail'd of being the foremoſt
in robbing an Orchard. But when the young
Gentleman arrived at the Age of Sixteen, he
began to have other Thoughts, and to neglect
thoſe boyiſh Pleaſures for others more ſub-
ſtantial. He had now ſuch a hankering after the Fleſh, that not a Maid-Servant in the
Houſe could be free from young Maſter *Some-
body*, continually teazing them, either by running his Hands up their Coats, tickling their
Bubbies, kiſſing, pulling, hauling, ſqueezing
them on every Opportunity. This the Girls
endured very patiently, without making any
Complaints, as he every now and then be-
ſtowed Money on them to buy Tea, Coffee,
&c. But at length one of them proving with
Child, he had dexterity enough to draw in
ſome of his Companions ; ſo that the Girl
might charge ſome other with her big Belly.
But as ſhe could not be prevailed upon to be
guilty of ſuch an Action, ſhe accepted of a
Purſe from him, and left her Service.

T h i s Accident put a Stop to young *Some-
body*'s Amours for a little while having ſo narrowly eſcaped a Scowering. Tho Nature may
be curb'd and kept under for a time, yet ſhe
never fails taking an Opportunity to get looſe
and diſplay herſelf; notwithſtanding the Rules
which ſome Philoſophers have delivered, in
order to break her, as they would a Horſe for
the *Manage*. But I am certain it would be
found

found much more difficult in the Practice, as
may appear in the following History. Not
far from this School † there was another,
kept for the educating young Ladies: Where,
as it is now the Custom to keep Girls till
they are fit for Husbands, there were some of
them pretty ripe in Years; these, young *Some-
body* had often seen at Church, and in their
Walks; these luscious Tits had often made
his Mouth water, and his Heart ake; but
he could never get an Opportunity of speaking to them, they being constantly attended
by the Mistress, or some of their Teachers.
However, as he did not want for Money, he
did not give up his hopes in time to compleat his designs, and obtain his pleasure with
some of them. To compass which, he got
acquainted at a neighbouring Shop in the
Town, by buying now and then some odd
things there, where he knew the Servants belonging to the Boarding-School bought what
they wanted. And in a short time *Master*
became so intimate here, that he went constantly after School-hours to drink Tea, or
play a Game at Cards with the Woman who
kept the Shop; where, as the Maids frequently came, and often some of the young Ladies along with them, he would kiss one,

treat

---

† *The Author has almost forfeited the Character of an Histo-
rian, in not mentioning the Town where* Some-body *was born, nor
that where this School was kept; but the latter is nearly adjus-
ted by him that wrote the* Key.—*See* Preface.

treat another, and was fo good-humour'd and engaging, that in a fhort time Mafter *Somebody* had the Hearts of all the School ; nay of the whole Houfe, except the Mafter, Miftrefs, and Teachers, who were ignorant of the Affair. The young *Ladies* were fo taken with his Company, that they could not be content with only enjoying it now and then for a Quarter of an Hour in the Shop, but were willing to have more of it ; for which they were continually entreating the Maids to admit him to come by Stealth into a part of the Houfe, where the Mafter and Miftrefs feldom came : And as they expected to be Gainers by *Mafter*'s Generofity, he eafily got Admittance. Here he ufed to fpend his Hours for fome time, enjoying as much Variety of pleafure, as the *Grand Seignior* a-midft his *Seraglio* of Beauties. The Ladies at thefe places, thro' Idlenefs and Indulgence, feldom fail of having very warm Defires at very tender Years ; which they continually improve with amorous Books, lufcious Converfations, and diverting Paftimes ; fuch as playing at Slap A—e, and many other innocent *Recreations*, equally diverting ; which ferve to provoke Nature, and makes them fit for Husbands before they are out of their Teens. And it is not unjuftly that a certain
* Philofopher allegorizes Boarding-Schools,
by

---

* *It were to be wifhed the Author had fatisfied us who this Philofopher was, whether antient or modern ; but that I fuppofe he has left to the Criticks for Decifion.*

by ſtiling them, *The Hot-beds, where the Female Plants being forced up too ſoon, grow rotten, and often wither upon the Dung-hill of the Town.* As it is not my buſineſs here to write Diſſertations, but Hiſtory, I ſhall proceed to Matters of Faɛt.

YOUNG *Some-body* here enjoyed uncontrouled, all his Heart could wiſh. Having a good Allowance of Pocket-money from the old *Gentleman,* and being very liberal of his Purſe among the Servants; he was always admitted, the ſame as if he had been one of the of the Family : His Maſter ſeldom troubling himſelf with enquiring how he ſpent his Hours after School-time, thinking him big enough to take care of himſelf : And whenever he did, young *Some-body* had always a fair Story ready at hand. Matters went on at this rate for ſome time ; and he has often declared ſince, that none of his amorous Adventures, ever gave him ſo much delight as this ; the Girls kiſſing with ſuch a *Goût,* and giving ſuch a looſe and reliſh to pleaſure, as would have moved even a Hermit, could he have ſeen them in their Embraces. At length, ſome of the young Ladies grew to be very ſick and qualmiſh after Meals; complained of frequent Dizzineſs in their Heads, and were continually puking after Breakfaſt and Dinner. Altho' theſe Symptoms were ſo plain, yet the Miſtreſs, good Woman! not having any miſtruſt of their playing at *High Gammer Cook,*

but

but taking their Illnefs to proceed from another Caufe; gave them fuch Medicines as
might have proved fatal: had not one of them,
after much Sollicitation from a Teacher, who
had feen young *Some-body* once or twice in the
Houfe, difcovered the Truth of the Affair;
and upon Examination they were all in the
fame Story, that young *Some-body* was the
Caufe of their being pregnant. Some bufy People getting Intelligence of it, it foon fpread all
over the Town; the injured Parents came crying and examining their Children; the Maids
were difcharged, Defolation and Deftruction
feem'd to threaten the whole School. To e-
vade which as much as poffible, the Mafter
and Miftrefs fummon a Jury of their Friends
and Neighbours in the Village, with the Parfon at the head of them; bring them to the
School, fhew them the Remainder of their
Scholars, (for the Parents had fetch'd fome
home) give them a handfome Entertainment,
and affure them of its being a falfe, malicious
and fcandalous Report; prevail with them to
fign a Certificate that it was fuch, which he
prints in a publick Paper, where a few Days
before had been inferted a different Account
of the Affair. The thing was thus hufh'd to
the World; but as old *Some-body* was at this
time in a confiderable-Poft, which required
his behaving with great Equity; he was oblig'd
to beftow on the unfortunate young Women
a large Sum of Money, to increafe their Fortunes,

tunes, and repair the Damage his Son had
done them.

I T was now thought full time to remove
young *Some-body* from the Boarding-School;
accordingly his Father sends him to the Uni-
verfity*, and placed him under the Care of a
famous Man, noted for his Learning and Morality ; together with a Charge to have a ſtrict
Eye upon him, and to allow him as little
time from his Studies as poſſible. It was under his Care young *Some-body* continued a few
Years, but could not refrain from his old
Tricks: If there happen'd any Quarrel between the Students and the Towns-folks, any
Whore to be reſcued from the *Bailiffs*, or indeed any other miſchief whatſoever, he was
ſure to be at the head of it. But to paſs o-
ver theſe juvenile Frolicks : When he had fi-
niſh'd his Studies, his Father ſent him to travel, with a Tutor and a handſome Allowance
for his Expences.

W H I L E he continued abroad, viewing
foreign Courts in the Day-time, lying at Bro-
thels with foreign Whores at Nights, fighting
with this *Monſieur* for cheating him at Play,
and with that *Don*, for to make him Satisfaction for lying with his Wife or Daughter,
he received the News of his Father's Death :
On which he takes Poſt, and haſtes home-

C   ward ;

---

* *Which of them, or at what College he was placed, the Author has not thought fit to let us know.*

ward; shedding a few Tears by the way, whether for Joy or Grief is uncertain : But it is
certain, that he was big with Expectation of
enjoying a large Estate ; and his Head was
full of Contrivances on what new Follies to
lavish it. But this, as the Proverb says, was
reckoning without his Host.

FOR on his Arrival he found, to his great
Surprize, that his *Father* having some time
before his Death been discharged from his
Trust, on not maintaining his Post with the
Integrity it required ; and being obliged to
spend vast Sums of Money in a Law-suit on
that Occasion, in order to justify himself, had
run so far in Debt, that his Creditors seized
on all the Effects immediately after his Decease : So that had it not been for a small
Sum of Money, the Father had in the time of
his Sickness lodged in a Friend's Hand, young
Some-body would have been destitute. But he
being used to such an extravagant Life soon lavish'd it away, and whilst it lasted, lived with
as much Grandeur, as if he was possest of an
Estate of as much *per annum*. Now being
driven to Necessity, his former Friends began
to look cold upon him ; and in a little time,
one that had formerly been his Companion,
and had shared in his Extravagance, refused
to lend him a Shilling to get a Dinner at the
Ordinary. But it happen'd, that one day
Some-body being at a Bookseller's, disposing of
a few Books he had left ; the Man of the
Shop

Shop having formerly taken a pretty deal of
his Money, taking Compaſſion on him, told
him, that it was a great pity, a Man of his
Parts and Education ſhould be reduced to
want; and that he believed it might be in his
own power to prevent it, if he would take his
Advice. As formerly he had ſeen ſome pretty Pieces of his compoſing, he might now
turn his Head that way; and what was formerly a Pleaſure, might now become profitable to him : And that he ſhould not want
for Encouragement at firſt ſetting out, he
proffers him a Room in his own Houſe, and
to ſupply him with Pen, Ink and Paper; on
Condition that he might have the Sale of his
Productions. This voluntary Encouragement,
eſpecially from a *Bookſeller*, gave him great
heart; ‡ they being a People of *univerſal
Learning*, for upon entering their Shops, and
enquiring for a Book, they'll reach it to you,
and at the ſame time deſcant as readily upon
it, and diſplay its Beauties with as much Faci-
lity, as if they had ſtudied the Author all
their Lives; no matter whether it be Hiſtory,
Divinity, Mathematicks, or any other branch
of Literature. Which Learning they acquire,
not by ſuch a ſevere Courſe of Reading, as is
practiſed by our Students at the Univerſities,
and Inns of Court, but by certain *Effluviums*
that ariſe from the *Volumes*, which fill their
C 2   Shops.

---

‡ *The Reader muſt excuſe this digreſſion, ſuch being often found
in* Burnet, Oldmixon, *and moſt other modern Hiſtorians.*

Shops. Thofe of the *Moderns* being of a damp, watry Nature, are exhaled by the Sun-beams; and them that proceed from the *Antients* on the higher Shelves, being generally of a drier, folid Nature, are put into motion by certain *Reptiles*, which in Courfe of time have taken poffeffion of thofe Works. Tho' there be fome that hold the *Metempfychofis* * of the Soul, who think them to be enliven'd by the Spirit of the deceafed Author; which finding their Works to become neglected by *Pofteri-ty*, endeavour, as much as poffible, to deprive Mankind of the Benefit of them, by continually confuming and reducing them to pow-der. And what gives this latter Account, of the Origin of thefe *Animalculæ*, the more Probability, is, that we generally find thofe Authors that are moft neglected, to be moft replete with them. But leaving this point to be difcufs'd by fuch of the *Royal Society*, as fhall hereafter think proper to proceed there-on; it is certain that the Shop being full of the abovementioned *Effluviums*, the Bookfeller can't chufe drawing them in every time he breathes vital Air; they entering by the *Na-res* †, whence afcending, they dilate them-felves throughout the *Brain*, and there fettle; being fix'd and cemented by the Weight and Preffure of certain judicious *Comments*, *Para-phrafes*, and *Expofitions*; which proceed from the Heads of the Cuftomers, and croffing the Counter, enter the Ears of the Bookfeller, and pafs

---

* *Tranfmigration.*   † *Noftrils.*

pass even to the *Glandula Pinealis* *. It is not
long since this *Hypothesis* was confirmed, by
an unhappy Instance. A certain Bookseller
who dwelt near the *Royal Exchange*, having
unfortunately placed some large Volumes of
Divinity near his Counter, and some *amorous* Authors a little too nigh the other, the
small *Particles* which proceeded from them,
jostling with one another, filled the poor
Man's Head, the Effect of which was, first
writing Concordances, *&c.* and afterwards
falling in Love; which different Passions obliged his Friends to provide an Apartment for
him, under the Care of a famous Doctor;
where he had continued till this Hour, had
he not in some of his lucid Intervals, projec-
ted means to make his Escape. And from the
foregoing *Theory*, we may justly account for
their Learning, who have large Libraries. yet
never had Patience to read an Author throughout in their Lives.

B u t to return : *Some-body* readily accepted the Proffer, takes possession of his new
Apartment, and writes a Poem; which was
universally admired, and run thro' several
Editions. This was followed by some other
Pieces, which filled the Pockets both of *Some-
body* and his Bookseller. Upon this *Some-
body* bought him new Cloaths, appeared at all
the Places of *Beau Resort*, and kept constant
Correspondence with the Wits at *Button's* †;
where

* *Where some Philosophers have placed the Seat of the Soul.*
† *A Coffee-house formerly much frequented by Wits and Poets.*

where he, and two or three more of the fame
Fraternity, enter'd into a League offenfive and
defenfive, againft all other Poets, Writers,
&c. who fhould not pay a juft Regard and
Homage to their Works. And whatever one
wrote, the other was fure to commend in his
next Piece. In this manner they monopo-
lized all the Wit of the Town. Their Works
being all fold by *Some-body*'s Friend the Bookfeller, the Man foon got an Eftate; and might
have continued getting more Money, had it
not been for an *Amour* he unluckily difcovered, between *Some-body* and his Daughter:
Who refufing to marry her, was obliged to
leave the Father's Houfe, and broke off all
Dealings between them. This *Some-body* did
not much heed, having well lin'd his Pockets;
and meeting lately with a good Run at the
Groom-Porter's, he became Mafter of a confiderable Sum of Money: Which a Friend
of his Father's advifed him to lay out in an
advantageous Purchafe, which then offer'd;
and thus he was poffeft of a pretty Eftate.
One Night being at the Play, when an Actrefs
was performing the Part of a *Harlot*, confin'd in *Bridewell*; *Some-body* became fo enamour'd with her, that nothing would content him, but he immediately takes her off
the Stage, and conveys her to private Lodgings: Thereby becoming charged with a conftant Expence for that which many before
him had enjoyed for Half a Crown, fhe being

ing no other than a Bum's Daughter. *Some-body* now began to have Thoughts of raifing himfelf in the World, and of appearing in a higher Character than he formerly had done, accordingly he takes to ftudying of *Politicks,* prints fome Pieces, which he had compofed on State Affairs, and diftributes them *gratis* in all the Corporation Towns. And to make himfelf more known on every trifling Occa-fion, hires Mobs, and heads them, continu-ally diftributing Handfuls of Silver and Half-pence amongft them ; by which means *Some-body*'s Mobs became as famous all over the Town, as formerly King *Charles*'s Regiment of Black-guards had been at *Whitehall.* This, with a conftant Attendance at a great Man's Levee, caufed him to be taken notice of by him ; and by his Intereft he got to reprefent a fmall *Borough.*

WHEN *Some-body* had thus gain'd a Seat in the Houfe, he exerted himfelf fo ftrenu-oufly on the fide of the *Miniftry,* and having a good Talent at Oratory, he was thought to be a fit Man for their purpofe ; and in a fhort time was appointed *Secretary of War.* At his Entrance upon this Poft, he behaved with great Diligence, giving a conftant Attendance at his Office; and as at that Time there was a War with *France,* it very much enlarged the Profits of his Place: But he living at his old rate, oblig'd him to have Recourfe to fome private Practices; and it being proved that he
had

had accepted a Note of 500 *l.* on account of
Forage from *Scotland,* he was tower'd, and
afterwards expelled the House. But he found
means, being an useful Person, and fit for Bu-
sinefs, so to salve up the matter as to keep his
Post, and be rechosen the following Sessions.
About this Time there came a certain *Lady* to
him, with a Petition from her Husband for a
Commission, who had attended his Levee for
a long Time before, but in vain: *Some-body*
became so fir'd with the Lady's Charms, that
had she not been a Woman of great Discretion,
she would hardly have escaped submitting to his
Embraces, even in the Office ; but she declin'd
them then, alledging the Impropernefs of
the Place, and the Hazard of her Reputation ;
but however, to give him Hopes, appointed
him a Meeting at a Chiua-house in the City,
where he was to bring her Husband's Commission with him, and to meet together as if
it were accidentally. They kept their Appointment ; *Some-body* presented her with the
Commission, and several other handsome
Presents, for which he received some Favours ; and would have made use of the present Opportunity, had not the Lady, who had
given her Husband a strict Promise not to be
unfaithful to him, intreated him to forbear,
exprefs'd her Husband's Impatience for her
Return, and appointed him another Assigna-
tion, when he was to be made happy. The
Lady being so obstinate, and he fearing if he
should

ſhould offer her any Conſtraint, ſhe might a-
larm the People of the Houſe, and ſo eſcape
entirely out of his Clutches; conſents to let
her depart, but not to be kept in Anguiſh, in-
ſiſts upon their meeting next Day : Which
ſhe agreeing to, they parted. The Lady haſtes
home to her Husband, with his long-expeſted
Commiſſion ; and aſſured him, that ſhe was
a Match for *Some-body* ; who had not obtained any thing of her in return for the Commiſſion and other Preſents. But that if he
would truſt to her Management; it would be
in their power to make a conſiderable Advantage of him ; and telling her Husband, of the
Meeting ſhe was to give him the next Day,
and the Scheme ſhe had laid, he conſented to
it, and they executed it in this manner.
Some-body met her at the Hour appointed, and
with ſmall difficulty prevails on her to go to
Bed; whither he immediately followed: The
Chamber-door was left unlock'd by deſign,
and the Husband was to have nick'd them in
an Inſtant. But 'tis thought, that the *Lady*
had deſignedly taken ſo much Compaſſion
for *Some-body*; who otherwiſe would have be-
ſtowed his Preſents for nothing, that ſhe prevented her Husband's coming before the Job
was done; and both Parties well ſatisfied.
But come he did at laſt, in a dreadful Rage,
Sword in hand : *Some-body* leaps out of Bed,
and begs his Life ; the Husband bids him
take his Sword, and defend himſelf: He
made Excuſes, and probably had exhauſted

D   his

his Spirits, fo much in the other Rencounter, that he had none left for this. However, they agreed the matter, and *Some-body* was obliged to give the Husband Five thoufand Pounds for Satisfaction ; affuring him withal, that *his Lady was untouched by him, he having gone no farther than he faw.* The Husband was very well fatisfied, they drank together, and parted Friends. *Some-body* was contented with his Purchafe ; and the Husband was as well pleafed with the Thoughts of having got a Commiffion, fuch a round Sum, and faved his Wife's Honour into the Bargain. When *Some-body* had continued in his Poft for a few Years, there happen'd fome Removals ; and he was appointed *Principal Secretary of S—te.* He now took it in his head to marry, and accordingly began to look out for fome Woman, that had Money enough to anfwer his Rank and Station in the World : Which he was not long in finding. Meeting with a *Lady,* who had been addreffed to by his *Superiors, Some-body* met with a favourable Reception from her, and in a fhort time the Match was concluded. They had feveral Children, and any one would have thought, that he fhould have relinquifhed his Gallantries ; now he was poffeft of fo agreeable a Lady, with a handfome Fortune. But on the contrary, he rather grew more profligate and abandon'd to Lewdnefs ; conftantly frequenting the moft noted *Bawdy-houfes* ; making his Pleafure to confift in Variety. Whilft

he

he continued this Courfe of *Whoring* and *Drinking*, he met with two fuch Accidents, as would have entirely ruined any one in his Poft, that had lefs good Fortune than himfelf. For going one Night as ufual, from an Apartment in the Palace where he kept his Office, to a neighbouring Houfe of Infamy, he there fpent the whole Night in Debauchery ; having Three of the handfomeft Ladies of Pleafure in the Houfe, to attend him at one time. Whom he difpofed of in the following manner : They all three went into the fame Bed, where *Some-body* enter'd ; and whilft he was careffing the middle one, faft clafped in her Arms ; each Hand was employed, in fporting with the others *Cuniculas :* And this Sport he called by the Name of —— in State. To which fometimes there were added other *Ceremonies,* too myfterious to be here revealed. When they were tired at this, they arofe ; and fpent the Night in dancing naked, playing at *Shooting London Bridge* *, a *burning Shame,* and many other fuch like Paftimes: which were firft inftituted by the Religious Society of *Adamites,* fome time fince in *Holland*; and performed in Commemoration of the Nakednefs our firft *Parents* were created in. It happen'd that when *Some-body* was at this moft elegant Retirement,

---

* *Thefe Sports being fo well known at prefent, by the Gentlemen of the Town ; it were needlefs to explain them, tho' in all probability they might be new at the time when the Author wrote.*

wallowing in the afore-mentioned Pleafures,
the Envoy * of a neighbouring Prince fent
fome Difpatches to him, to be immediately
communicated to the Crown'd Head. *Some-
body* had no Notice either of the *Envoy* or
the Difpatches. *Meffengers* were fent to all
Parts of the Town to find him out, but in
vain : The Difpatches were laid by unfealed;
Some-body thoroughly tired with the La-
bours of the Night, went to Bed to his Har-
lots, with whom he flept away the next day :
The Envoy, becoming impatient to fee himfelf thus neglected, publifh'd from his own
Copy the Contents of thofe Difpatches to the
World; and *Some-body* met with a fevere Re-
primand for his Negligence : But however had
the good Fortune to keep his Place. The o-
ther Accident which had like to have difplaced him, was caufed through the Envy of
the *Prime Minifter*; by whofe Intereft and
Favour he was raifed to fuch a high Station.
He thinking that *Some-body* did not fhew him
all the Refpect that was due to him, and fuf-
pecting withal that he was endeavouring to
undermine him, caufed him to contrive fome
means how he might get *Some-body* difplaced:
Which he durft not do openly, well knowing *Some-body's* Spirit, and the Favour that he
had crept into with a certain *Lady* that was in
great Intereft at *Court*; and to whom himfelf

felf was indebted for his Place; but conjec-
tured, that the only means to do it, muft be
to make *Some-body* become defpicable, in the
Eyes of the *Lady,* their common Friend.
Accordingly he takes the Opportunity, when
he knew *Some-body* was engaged in a Drink-
ing-bout with fome other *Debauchees;* and
waits on the Lady at her Apartment at *Ken-*
fington, where the *Court* was then kept; com-
municates to her fome Affairs of Importance;
and defires fhe would fend for *Some-body,* and
give him the neceffary Orders relating thereto.
She immediately fends to his Houfe for him,
and by the means of one of his Servants, who
had Orders, ever fince the former Accident,
where to find him, in Cafe of any Emergency,
the Meffenger foon found him out. *Some-*
body was very much intoxicated, having then
been drinking feveral Hours : However, as
he was obliged to obey the *Lady's* Command,
he orders his Chariot and Six ; and drives to
Kenfington with fuch Expedition, that he arrived nearly as foon as the Meffenger that was
fent for him. He haftes directly to the *La-*
dy's Apartment; where no fooner was he enter'd, but going to make his Obeifance, he fell
down on the Floor : She not knowing the
Caufe, and endeavouring to raife him, fell
down upon him. The Servants who were
waiting in the adjoining Rooms, hearing the
rumbling Noife of their falling, and judging
it to be fomewhat elfe, they enter'd the Room;
where

Where they found *Some-body* and their *Lady*, as proftrate as *Perfians* at Devotion : neither of them being able to raife themfelves, without Affiftance. However, by their help they were both raifed ; when, after difmiffing the Servants, fhe made fhift to give him her Orders, and he to underftand them, tho' not without much difficulty on each fide, they being both very much confufed. *Some-body*, at his departure, found means, by bribing one of her Servants, to difcover who had been lately with the *Lady* ; and immediately fmelling the Plot, was very much enraged : Meeting the Perfon next day at the C———l-Board, taxed him with it, who endeavoured to clear himfelf by fome evafive Anfwers. *Some-body* drew his Sword ; when their Friends who were. prefent interpofing, with fome difficulty brought them to a Reconciliation.

THESE Accidents did not prevent *Somebody* continuing in his old Courfe of Lewdnefs, he vifited the moft infamous Stews, and would often fpend his Nights. with *Cinderwenches*, *Rag-Girls*, and other Scum of the Town : Whereby he got a Difeafe known to the *Phyficians* by the Name of the *Pediculi Inguinales* † ; which was fo very troublefome to him, and got to fuch a height, that he was obliged to keep one of his Hands concealed

for

---

† *This is a very contagious diftemper, which by fome late* Microfcopial *Obfervations, communicated to the* Royal Society, *is caufed by the Mordication of certain* Animalculæ, *in form not unlike* Sea-crabs.——*See* Philof. Tranf.

for a confiderable Time; although he underwent the Tonfure, and other accuftomary Medicaments. This Afflidion he communi-cated to his *Wife*; and as one Misfortune feldom comes, without another attending it, not long after fhe had the *Venereal Diftemper* from him, tho' ignorantly of his fide. For when he engaged with poor paultry W——s, *Don Piego* went generally arm'd in * * * * * which fome take to be a very modern Invention, be-caufe there is no notice thereof taken in *Polydore Virgil, de Rerum Invent.* But I was inform'd by an eminent *Virtuofo*, who had been a great Traveller, that they have been in ufe, time out of mind by the *Hottentots* *; a People who inhabit near the *Cape* of *Good Hope*: And, according to our Hiftories of thofe Parts, are faid to cover themfelves with the Skins and Entrails of Beafts. From whence they were firft brought into *England* by a *Captain*, whofe Name they bear. And indeed Nature feems to have put them upon the Invention, in order to guard againft the pernicious Confequences, which attend their horrid Cuftom of ufing their Women in common. † It was from thefe People that *Mahomet*, the Founder of the *Muffulmens* Religion, firft received the Idea of his future *Paradife*:

---

* *Vide* Hift. of the Cape, in *two Vol.* † *This paffage gives me a fufpicion that the Author was either a Student or Profeffor of Divinity, efpecially as he begins the Hiftory like a Sermon, with a Text at the Head of it.*

dife : In which he promifes to reward his Votaries with * a continual Enjoyment of beautiful Women. For finding by the *Chriftian* Syftem, that they fhould neither *marry nor be given in Marriage*; and conjecturing, that they muft be created for fome other End befides the Propagation of Mankind, he places them in *Paradife*, to heighten the Happinefs of the Place, by their Charms and Enjoyment. And to make this in fome manner conformable to the Text, that it might incline the Chriftians to revoit to him;. he affirms that there fhould be a promifcuous ufe of them : Not daring, as fome modern *Divines* have done, to broach the Doctrine of Women being made only as Moulds to caft Mankind in ; and their Exiftence to ceafe with their Death.

S O M E - B O D Y was very much afflicted at this Misfortune, on account of his Lady, who proved a very virtuous Woman; and difcovering the Perfon that was the Occafion of it, refolv'd to be amply reveng'd on her: And accordingly he takes her to a famous Houfe of Refort, orders a Supper, taxes her with it, which fhe confeffed. *Some-body* orders plenty of Wine, and having made her almoft dead drunk, bids her get to Bed; where he follows, and waits till fhe was afleep, which was not long: When rifing, and uncovering the Cloaths, he turns up her S—k;

and

* *See the* Alcoran.

and having pour'd a small Quantity of *Spirit* of Wine in his Hand, with which he was provided; he gently anointed the H--r of her ————. And clapping the Candle thereto, the poor Girl, who had just been dreaming of Fire, and feeling the Smart, jumps out of Bed, and runs down Stairs; crying, Fire! Fire! which alarming the House, they run up to her Room with Water; and, to their Amazement, found *Some-body* ready to burst with Laughing: When asking if he knew whereabouts the *Fire* was, he reply'd, In the B————'s ————; for that she had burnt him at a damn'd rate. When paying the Reckoning, he departed; leaving the poor Wretch to get a Remedy for her outward Burning, as well as for that which was within.

Not long after, there was a Letter * stopt at the *Post-Office*, directed to one in the Enemy's Dominions; and in it was inclosed a Copy of another, which contain'd a Plan of the Operations that were to be in the ensuing *Campaign:* which was sent as an Instance of what Secrets they could discover, if encouraged; with a Promise of discovering more.

This Letter being happily intercepted, was sent to the *Prime Minister;* and he knowing it must come from *Some-body's* Office, upon Enquiry, found it to be wrote by an intimate Companion of *Some-body's*, whom

E   he

* *See* Burnet's *History of his own Times, Vol.* 2d.

he employed as a Clerk. He was apprehended, but would confefs nothing; only, that it
was the firft Fact, and, when brought to
Trial, upon *Some-body*'s Inftigation, pleaded
guilty, and was condemned : Thereby pre-
venting the Court's Examination into the
Affair. And being buoy'd up by *Some-body*,
with hopes of faving his Life, if he made no
difcovery ; he died without charging any one
as his Confederates, expecting a Reprieve
even at the Gallows. But this, joined with
fome other Occurrences of lefs Note, caufed
Some-body to be very much reflected upon ;
and fome of the General Officers having often before found their Defigns difcovered to
the Enemy, and prevented, refolved to quit
their Pofts, if *Some-body* was not removed :
Which being fignified to him, and finding
the Party too hot for him, he refigned; and
fo efcap'd the Difgrace they intended him :
but did not long continue out of Favour ;
for there happening a Change of Affairs, the
P———me M————r's Poft was put into
Commiffion, and he was one nominated
therein, altho' not the firft ; yet his fuperior
Genius foon prevailing over the reft, in a
fhort time he became poffeft of as much
Power, as if he had folely enjoy'd the Place ;
the others acting only according to *Some-
body*'s Orders.

He was well verfed in the Writings of the
Poets, and thought it a great misfortune he
did not live in the Times when they wor-
fhipped *Venus* in the Ifland of *Cythera* :
But

But to remedy the Inconveniency that arofe, in a Chriftian Country, of not having a *Temple* erected wherein to perform her Rites, he hired a Houfe in *P—M—*, which ftood backwards, fo as not to be ove look'd by the reft, and wherein there was a fpacious Chamber ; which *Some-body* refolved to dedicate to the Goddefs of Love. Accordingly he hires an old Woman, who had been a zealous Votary of the Goddefs in her younger Days ; and to her commits the Charge of this *facred Manfion* ; whofe Bufinefs it was, to fweep and cleanfe it free from Filth, to kindle the Fire in the holy Apartment, left *Cold*, dread Enemy to *Love*, fhould enter ; alfo to fpread the *Carpets*, whereon the Lovers were to proftrate themfelves before the Goddefs. But that this *Temple*, for thus I may call it, might be acceptable unto the Goddefs ; therein he places a *Nymph*, that with the Faireft well might vie, in Youth or Beauty's Charms ; who, at the tender Age of Fourteen Years, herfelf had offer'd at the Goddefs's Shrine, and there her Ivory Limbs extending, with melting dying Sighs, fuck'd in the balmy Blefling. Here conftant twice a Week attended *Some-body*, accompanied with other happy Lovers, three or four, like Turtles, with their Mates. Thefe, the Temple being enter'd, they firft falute with billing ; when after ufing fome fhort Prayers, to beg Afliftance from the Goddefs, they ftrip themfelves quite naked, and in amorous Combats

E 2   fiercely

fiercely engage upon the *Carpets*. The *Stair-case* was impanelled, with Plates of Look-ing Glaſs throughout ; where ſometimes they exerciſed themſelves, in running Races, that they might behold the Oddneſs of the Mo-tion which it occaſion'd unto their Parts.

SOME-BODY being raiſed to ſuch a high Poſt, began to be more nice in his *A-mours* than formerly ; and to attend Buſineſs a little cloſer than he had done : About this time he made a Peace with the Enemy, but ſuch an ignominious one, that the bad Effects of it were felt for many Years after. He was not content with getting Riches in the com-mon way, but having at the College read ſome Books of *Magick*, he laid a Scheme to get Money by Conjuration : Accordingly he draws a large ſpacious *Circle*, and gives out, that the Aſpects of the *Planets*, at that time, were ſo very auſpicious, and powerfully pro-moted by the good *Genii*, that whoever ſhould lay one Piece of Money within that Circle's Circumference, in a ſhort time would have it augmented to Ten-fold : So that Millions of *ſimple* People flock'd to depoſit their Money therein, receiving Certificates from thoſe, whom *Some-body* had ordered to attend thereon, him-.ſelf lying concealed in the South Quarter, where by the means of a Trap-door, purpoſe-ly contrived, he received the Money unſeen ; which gave an Opportunity to *them* that he had appointed to watch the *Circle* above-board, by cribing now and then a Piece for them-ſelves,

felves, to amafs vaft Sums. The firft Adven-
turers waited with fome degree of Patience, to
receive their promifed Riches; but a *few* more
wife than the reft, went and fold their Certificates to others, who could not buftle thro'
the Croud to get at the Circle: Which the
reft perceiving, followed their Example; fo
that in a few Days there were more Sellers
than Buyers, which entirely funk the Credit
of the Scheme: And thofe who had bought
Certificates, at extravagant Prices, became utterly ruin'd; while others received nearly Ten-
fold for their Money, as *Some-body* had promifed, tho' in another manner. In fine, *Some-
body's* Circle did more damage than the famous
Dragon of Wantley; fwallowing not only
Houfes and *Churches*, but even whole Towns
at a Gape.

HAVING amaffed a prodigious Sum by
this *Scheme*, he built him a noble Houfe in the
Country; and fome Years after, when he
thought the thing was pretty well buried in
Oblivion, he put another Projeſt in Execution:
For taking notice, that feveral noted *Pawn-
brokers* had acquired great Eftates, with little
or no hazard of their Fortunes, he turns
Pawn-broker; not appearing publickly in it,
but tranfaſting the Bufinefs by fome Agents,
as he had done the former. Accordingly he
opens two large Shops, and orders them to de-
fcant very pathetically on the Intention; faying
that it proceeded purely from Charity to their
Neighbours, who were welcome to join Stocks
with

with them, and partake of the Advantages. The Thing foon took, efpecially as they lent more Money upon Goods than any of the Trade, and took lefs Intereft ; fo that feveral People enter'd Partnerfhip with them. In the mean-while, *Some-body* would continually bring old rufty or damag'd *Goods, Pictures,* &c. and pledge them for double and treble their Value, in fictitious Names; which the Servants taking Example by, the Thing became blow'd upon: And when the Partners came to examine into their Affairs, they found nothing but *Lumber* left for their Money ; the *Book-keeper* and feveral of the *Servants* fled beyond Sea. *Some-body* lay fecure enough, having never appear'd publickly to be concerned in the Affair, and did his endeavour to *skreen* and protect the reft, fearing they fhould impeach him. But to return to his Amours.

SOME-BODY's Wife had an agreeable *Woman* for her *Waiting-maid,* tall and fair ; fhe foon took his Fancy, and with fome fmall difficulty he obtain'd his Pleafure with her ; and they kept a conftant Correfpondence, not altogether unknown to the poor Wife, who durft not take notice of it. At length *Some-body* having told her a Secret, which fhe divulg'd to another that was in her Graces, entirely broke off their Amity ; and the Wife taking the Opportunity, difcharged her from the Service: Where, by her Place and *Some-body*'s Prefents, fhe acquired a large Sum, built her a handfome Country-houfe, and foon got a Husband.

In

IN the Neighbourhood of *Some-body's* Country Seat, there lived a private *Gentleman*, of a small Eftate, who had married a very agreeable young Woman, and had Children by her. *Some-body* feeing her as he paft thro' the *Village*, took a great Fancy to her, fhe having fine fparkling Eyes, which fhot *Some-body* to the Heart. He was not long in finding means to come at her; he invites them to dine with him, makes the *Husband* drunk, and the mean while occupies the Wife: At length the *Husband* perceiving how matters went, thought it would be the wifeft Method to make the beft of a bad Bargain; and winking at their Embraces, perfuades his Wife to beg a Place for him at C——t, which was in *Some-body's* Difpofal. This he foon obtain'd, and by his officiating therein himfelf, was generally in Town, that his Prefence might not conftrain the Lovers. This Opportunity, together with the *Lady's* Charms and Agreeablenefs, caufed *Some-body* to forfake moft of his *Miftreffes*, and to fpend what time he could fpare, with her at his Country-houfe. But continuing there one Seafon a little longer than ordinary, the *Waters* were fo out in the Low-Countries, which he was obliged to pafs, that there was no Paffage for either Man or Beaft. Bufinefs at this time happening to be very preffing, at length he refolved to proceed at all hazards, fwimming his Horfe in fome Parts, and getting Ferry-boats in others, at laft got over; though not without being thoroughly drench'd, which, with riding hard, flung him into fuch an *Illnefs*

nefs when he came home, as had like to have coft him his Life. However, he recovered at laft; when his *Wife*, who had endured all hitherto with patience, took the Liberty of urging to him, the many Hazards and Inconveniencies that attended his Courfe of Life, to himfelf, her, and their Children. *Some-body* heard her with an unufual Patience for fome time; at length touching   much upon his Country Lady, it put him at fo violent a *Paffion*, that he gave her a K---k, and compelled her to leave the Room. Whether the *Wife* took this ill Ufage to Heart, or whatever elfe might be the Occafion, fhe foon after fell ill; and continued fo fome time, baffling all the Skill of the ableft *Phyficians*, whom *Some-body* got to attend her; he loving her very well, when his Head was free from his mad Freaks: At length they found fhe had an *Ulcer* in her *Bowels*, which by her concealing too long, thro' an ill-timed Modefty, proved mortal; and fhe died in great Mifery. *Somebody* feem'd to take on very much at firft for the Lofs of her; but foon after fends for his Country Miftrefs, kept her in his Houfe for fome time, and lavifh'd a great deal of Money on her: but at length taking fome difguft, he marries a Lady whofe *Virginity* he had purchafed of her *Father*, and had maintained her ever fince, tho' fhe did not enjoy her Happinefs for above three Months, for being with Child, and *mifcarrying*, it proved fatal to her; leaving *Some-body* again at Liberty.

F I N I S

AN APOLOGY FOR THE LIFE
OF
MRS. SHAMELA ANDREWS

Bibliographical note:

this facsimile has been made from a copy in the
Yale University Library
(Fielding 741a)

AN

APOLOGY

FOR THE

LIFE

OF

Mrs. SHAMELA ANDREWS.

(Price One Shilling and Six-Pence.)

A N

APOLOGY

FOR THE

LIFE

OF

Mrs. SHAMELA ANDREWS.

In which, the many notorious FALSHOODS and MISREPRSENTATIONS of a Book called

P A M E L A,

Are expofed and refuted; and all the matchlefs ARTS of that young Politician, fet in a true and juft Light.

Together with

A full Account of all that paffed between her and Parfon *Arthur Williams*; whofe Character is reprefented in a manner fomething different from what he bears in *PAMELA*. The whole being exaƈt Copies of authentick Papers delivered to the Editor.

Neceffary to be had in all FAMILIES.

By Mr. *CONNY KEYBER*.

LONDON:

Print_ed for A. DODD, at the *Peacock*, without *Temple-bar*.
M. DCC. XLI.

To Miſs *Fanny*, *&c.*

MADAM,

IT will be naturally expected, that when I write the
Life of *Shamela*, I ſhould
dedicate it to ſome young
Lady, whoſe Wit and Beauty
might be the proper Subject
of a Compariſon with the He-
roine of my Piece.   This,
A 3   theſe

thofe, who fee I have done it
in prefixing your Name to my
Work, will much more con-
firmedly expect me to do;
and, indeed, your Character
would enable me to run fome
Length into a Parallel, tho'
you, nor any one elfe, are at
all alike the matchlefs *Shamela*.

You fee, Madam, I have fome
Value for your Good-nature,
when in a Dedication, which is
properly a Panegyrick, I fpeak
againft, not for you; but I remember it is a Life which I
am prefenting you, and why
fhould I expofe my Vera-
city

city to any Hazard in the Front of the Work, considering what I have done in the Body. Indeed, I wish it was possible to write a Dedication, and get any thing by it, without one Word of Flattery; but since it is not, come on, and I hope to shew my Delicacy at least in the Compliments I intend to pay you.

First, then, Madam, I must tell the World, that you have tickled up and brightned many Strokes in this Work by your Pencil.

Secondly, You have intimately conversed with me, one of the greatest Wits and Scholars of my Age.

Thirdly, You keep very good Hours, and frequently spend an useful Day before others begin to enjoy it. This I will take my Oath on; for I am admitted to your Presence in a Morning before other People's Servants are up; when I have constantly found you reading in good Books; and if ever I have drawn you upon me, I have always felt you very heavy.

Fourth-

Fourthly, You have a Virtue which enables you to rife early and ftudy hard, and that is, forbearing to over-eat yourfelf, and this in fpite of all the lufcious Temptations of Puddings and Cuftards, exciting the Brute (as Dr. *Woodward* calls it) to rebel. This is a Virtue which I can greatly admire, though I much queftion whether I could imitate it.

Fifthly, A Circumftance greatly to your Honour, that by means of your extraordinary Merit and Beauty ; you was

carried

carried into the Ball-Room at the *Bath*, by the diſcerning Mr. *Naſh*; before the Age that other young Ladies gene-nerally arrived at that Ho-nour, and while your Mamma herſelf exiſted in her perfect Bloom. Here you was ob-ſerved in Dancing to balance your Body exactly, and to weigh every Motion with the exact and equal Meaſure of Time and Tune; and though you ſometimes made a falſe Step, by leaning too much to one Side; yet every body ſaid you would one Time or other, dance perfectly well, and up-rightly.

Sixthly,

Sixthly, I cannot forbear mentioning thofe pretty little Sonnets, and fprightly Compofitions, which though they came from you with fo much Eafe, might be mentioned to the Praife of a great or grave Character.

And now, Madam, I have done with you ; it only remains to pay my Acknowledgments to an Author, whofe Stile I have exactly followed in this Life, it being the propereft for Biography. The Reader, I believe, eafily guefles, I mean *Euclid's Elements* ;

ments ; it was *Euclid* who taught me to write. It is you, Madam, who pay me for Writing. Therefore I am to both,

A most Obedient, and

obliged humble Servant,

Conny Keyber.

LETTERS

TO THE

EDITOR.

The EDITOR to *Himself.*

Dear S I R,

HOWEVER you came by the excellent *Shamela*, out with it, without Fear or Honour, Dedication and all ; believe me, it will go through many Editions, be tranflated into all Languages, read in all Nations and Ages, and to fay a bold Word, it will do more good than the *C——y* have done harm in the World.

I am, Sir,

Sincerely your Well-wifher,

Yourfelf.

John

John Puff, *Efq; to the* Editor.

S I R,

I HAVE read your *Shamela* through and
through, and a moft inimitable Performance
it is. Who is he, what is he that could write
fo excellent a Book ? he muft be doubtlefs moft
agreeable to the Age, and to *his Honour* himfelf; for he is able to draw every thing to
Perfection but Virtue. Whoever the Author
be, he hath one of the worft and moft fafhionable Hearts in the World, and I would recommend to him, in his next Performance, to un-
dertake the Life of *his Honour.* For he who
drew the Character of Parfon *Williams,* is equal
to the Task ; nay he feems to have little more
to do than to pull off the Parfon's Gown, and
that which makes him fo agreeable to *Shamela,*
and the Cap will fit.

I am, Sir,

Your humble Servant,

John Puff.

Note,

Note, Reader, feveral other COMMENDA-
TORY LETTERS and COPIES of VER-
SES will be prepared againſt the NEXT EDI-
TION.

AN

A N

APOLOGY

For the LIFE of

Mrs. SHAMELA ANDREWS.

Parfon TICKLETEXT *to Parfon* OLIVER.

Rev. S I R,

HEREWITH I tranfmit you a Copy of fweet, dear, pretty *Pamela*, a little Book which this Winter hath produced ; of which, I make no Doubt, you have already heard mention from fome of your Neighbouring Clergy ; for we have made it our common Bufinefs here, not only to cry it up, but to preach it up likewife : The Pulpit, as well as the Coffeehoufe, hath refounded with its Praife, and it is expected fhortly, that his L——p will recommend it in a ——— Letter to our whole Body.

B   And

And this Example, I am confident, will be imitated by all our Cloth in the Country: For besides speaking well of a Brother, in the Character of the Reverend Mr. *Williams,* the useful and truly religious Doctrine of *Grace* is every where inculcated.

This Book is the " Soul of *Religion,* Good-
" Breeding, Discretion, Good-Nature, Wit,
" Fancy, Fine Thought, and Morality. There
" is an Ease, a natural Air, a dignified Simpli-
" city, and MEASURED FULLNESS in it, that
" RESEMBLING LIFE, OUT-GLOWS IT. The
" Author hath reconciled the *pleasing* to the *pro-*
" *per*; the Thought is every where exactly cloath-
" ed by the Expression; and becomes its Dress as
" *roundly* and as close as *Pamela* her Country Ha-
" bit; or *as she doth her no Habit,* when modest
" Beauty seeks to hide itself, by casting off the
" Pride of Ornament, and displays itself without
" any Covering;" which it frequently doth in this admirable Work, and presents Images to the Reader, which the coldest Zealot cannot read without Emotion.

For my own Part (and, I believe, I may say the same of all the Clergy of my Acquaintance)
" I have done nothing but read it to others, and
" hear others again read it to me, ever since it
" came into my Hands; and I find I am like to
" do nothing else, for I know not how long yet
" to come: because if I lay the Book down *it*
" *comes after me.* When it has dwelt all Day
" long upon the Ear, it takes Possession all
" Night of the Fancy. It hath Witchcraft in eve-
" ry Page of it.——Oh! I feel an Emotion even while I am relating this: Methinks I see *Pamela* at this Instant, with all the Pride of Ornament cast off.

" Little

" Little Book, charming *Pamela*, get thee
" gone ; face the World, in which thou wilt
" find nothing like thy felf." Happy would it
be for Mankind, if all other Books were burnt,
that we might do nothing but read thee all Day,
and Dream of thee all Night. Thou alone art
fufficient to teach us as much Morality as we
want. Doft thou not teach us to pray, to fing
Pfalms, and to honour the Clergy ? Are not
thefe the whole Duty of Man ? Forgive me, O
Author of *Pamela*, mentioning the Name of a
Book fo unequal to thine : But, now I think of
it, who is the Author, where is he, what is he,
that hath hitherto been able to hide fuch an en-
circling, all-maftering Spirit, " he poffeffes every
" Quality that Art could have charm'd by : yet
" hath lent it to and concealed it in Nature.
" The Comprehenfivenefs of his Imagination
" muft be truly prodigious! It has ftretched out
" this diminutive mere Grain of Muftard-feed
" (a poor Girl's little, &c.) into a Refemblance
" of that Heaven, which the beft of good Books
" has compared it to. "

To be fhort, this Book will live to the Age of
the Patriarchs, and like them will carry on the
good Work many hundreds of Years hence,
among our Pofterity, who will not HESITATE
their Efteem with Reftraint. If the *Romans*
granted Exemptions to Men who begat a *few*
Children for the Republick, what Diftinction (if
Policy and we fhould ever be reconciled) fhould
we find to reward this Father of Millions, which
are to owe Formation to the future Effect of
his Influence.——I feel another Emotion.

As foon as you have read this your felf five or
fix Times over (which may poffibly happen
within a Week) I defire you would give it to

my little God-Daughter, as a Prefent from me.
This being the only Education we intend henceforth to give our Daughters. And pray let your
Servant-Maids read it over, or read it to them.
Both your felf and the neighbouring Clergy, will
fupply yourfelves for the Pulpit from the Bookfellers, as foon as the fourth Edition is publifhed.
I am,

Sir,

Your moft humble Servant,

Tho. Tickletext.

Parfon Oliver *to Parfon* Tickletext.

Rev. S I R,

I Received the Favour of yours with the inclofed Book, and really muft own myfelf forry, to fee the Report I have heard of an epidemical Phrenzy now raging in Town, confirmed
in the Perfon of my Friend.

If I had not known your Hand, I fhould,
from the Sentiments and Stile of the Letter, have
imagined it to have come from the Author of
the famous Apology, which was fent me laft
Summer; and on my reading the remarkable Paragraph of *meafured Fulnefs, that refembling Life
out-glows it,* to a young Baronet, he cry'd out,
C——ly C——b—r by G——. But I have fince
obferved, that this, as well as many other Expreffions in your Letter, was borrowed from thofe
remarkable Epiftles, which the Author, or the

Editor

Editor hath prefix'd to the fecond Edition which you fend me of his Book.

Is it poffible that you or any of your Function can be in earneft, or think the Caufe of Religion, or Morality, can want fuch flender Support? God forbid they fhould. As for Honour to the Clergy, I am forry to fee them fo folicitous about it; for if worldly Honour be meant, it is what their Predeceffors in the pure and primitive Age, never had or fought. Indeed the fecure Satisfaction of a good Confcience, the Approbation of the Wife and Good, (which never were or will be the Generality of Mankind) and the extatick Pleafure of contemplating, that their Ways are acceptable to the Great Creator of the Univerfe, will always attend thofe, who really deferve thefe Bleffings: But for worldly Honours, they are often the Purchafe of Force and Fraud, we fometimes fee them in an eminent Degree poffeffed by Men, who are notorious for Luxury, Pride, Cruelty, Treachery, and the moft abandoned Proftitution; Wretches who are ready to invent and maintain Schemes repugnant to the Intereft, the Liberty, and the Happinefs of Mankind, not to fupply their Neceffities, or even Conveniencies, but to pamper their Avarice and Ambition. And if this be the Road to worldly Honours, God forbid the Clergy fhould be even fufpected of walking in it.

The Hiftory of *Pamela* I was acquainted with long before I received it from you, from my Neighbourhood to the Scene of Action. Indeed I was in hopes that young Woman would have contented herfelf with the Good-fortune fhe hath attained; and rather fuffered her little Arts to have been forgotten than have revived their Remembrance, and endeavoured by perverting

B 3 and

and mifreprefenting Facts to be thought to deferve what fhe now enjoys: for though we do
not imagine her the Author of the Narrative itfelf, yet we muft fuppofe the Inftructions were
given by her, as well as the Reward, to the Com-
pofer. Who that is, though you fo earneftly require of me, I fhall leave you to guefs from that
Ciceronian Eloquence, with which the Work
abounds; and that excellent Knack of making
every Character amiable, which he lays his hands
on.

But before I fend you fome Papers relating to
this Matter, which will fet *Pamela* and fome o-
thers in a very different Light, than that in
which they appear in the printed Book, I muft
beg leave to make fome few Remarks on the
Book itfelf, and its Tendency, (admitting it to
be a true Relation,) towards improving Morality,
or doing any good, either to the prefent Age, or
Pofterity: which when I have done, I fhall, I
flatter myfelf, ftand excufed from delivering it,
either into the hands of my Daughter, or my Servant-Maid.

The Inftruction which it conveys to Servant-
Maids, is, I think, very plainly this, To look
out for their Mafters as fharp as they can. The
Confequences of which will be, befides Neglect
of their Bufinefs, and the ufing all manner of
Means to come at Ornaments of their Perfons,
that if the Mafter is not a Fool, they will be debauched by him; and if he is a Fool, they will
marry him. Neither of which, I apprehend,
my good Friend, we defire fhould be the Cafe
of our Sons.

And notwithftanding our Author's Profeffions
of Modefty, which in my Youth I have heard at
the

the Beginning of an Epilogue, I cannot agree that my Daughter fhould entertain herfelf with fome of his Pictures ; which I do not expect to be contemplated without Emotion, unlefs by one of my Age and Temper, who can fee the Girl lie lie on her Back, with one Arm round Mrs. *Jervis* and the other round the Squire, naked in Bed, with his Hand on her Breafts, *&c.* with as much Indifference as I read any other Page in the whole Novel. But furely this, and fome other Defcriptions, will not be put in the hands of his Daughter by any wife Man, though I believe it will be difficult for him to keep them from her ; efpecially if the Clergy in Town have cried and preached it up as you fay.

But, my Friend, the whole Narrative is fuch a Mifreprefentation of Facts, fuch a Perverfion of Truth, as you will, I am perfwaded, agree, as foon as you have perufed the Papers I now inclofe to you, that I hope you or fome other welldifpofed Perfon, will communicate thefe Papers to the Publick, that this little Jade may not impofe on the World, as fhe hath on her Mafter.

The true name of this Wench was S H A M E L A, and not *Pamela*, as fhe ftiles herfelf. Her Father had in his Youth the Misfortune to appear in no good Light at the *Old-Baily* ; he afterwards ferved in the Capacity of a Drummer in one of the *Scotch* Regiments in the *Dutch* Service ; where being drummed out, he came over to *England*, and turned Informer againft feveral Perfons on the late Gin-Act ; and becoming acquainted with an Hoftler at an Inn, where a *Scotch* Gentleman's Horfes ftood, he hath at laft by his Intereft obtain'd a pretty fnug Place in the *Cuftom Houfe*. Her Mother fold Oranges in the Play-Houfe ;

and

and whether fhe was married to her Father or
no, I never could learn.

After this fhort Introduction, the reft of her
Hiftory will appear in the following Letters,
which I affure you are authentick.

LETTER

LETTER I.

SHAMELA ANDREWS *to Mrs.* HENRIET-
TA MARIA HONORA ANDREWS *at
her Lodgings at the* Fan *and* Pepper-Box
in Drury-Lane.

Dear Mamma,

THIS comes to acquaint you, that I shall
set out in the Waggon on *Monday*, desir-
ing you to commodate me with a Ludgin, as
near you as possible, in *Coulstin's-Court*, or *Wild-
Street*, or somewhere thereabouts ; pray let it be
handsome, and not above two Stories high : For
Parson *Williams* hath promised to visit me when
he comes to Town, and I have got a good many
fine Cloaths of the Old Put my Mistress's, who
died a wil ago ; and I beleve Mrs. *Jervis* will
come along with me, for she says she would like
to keep a House somewhere about *Short's-Gar-
dens*, or towards *Queen-Street* ; and if there was
convenience for a *Bannio*, she should like it the
better ; but that she will settle herself when she
comes to Town.——*O! How I long to be in the
Balcony at the* Old House —— so no more at
present from

Your affectionate Daughter,

SHAMELA.

LETTER

LETTER II,

SHAMELA ANDREWS *to* HENRIETTA
MARIA HONORA ANDREWS.

Dear Mamma,

O WHAT News, since I writ my last! the
young Squire hath been here, and as sure
as a Gun he hath taken a Fancy to me; *Pamela,*
says he, (for so I am called here) you was a great
Favourite of your late Mistress's; yes, an't please
your Honour, says I; and I believe you deserved
it, says he; thank your Honour for your good
Opinion, says I; and then he took me by the
Hand, and I pretended to be shy: Laud, says
I, Sir, I hope you don't intend to be rude;
no, says he, my Dear, and then he kissed me,
'till he took away my Breath——and I pretended to be Angry, and to get away, and then he
kissed me again, and breathed very short, and
looked very silly; and by Ill-Luck Mrs. *Jervis*
came in, and had like to have spoiled Sport.——
How troublesome is such Interruption! You shall
hear now soon, for I shall not come away yet,
so I rest,

Your affectionate Daughter,

SHAMELA.

LETTER

LETTER III.

HENRIETTA MARIA HONORA AN-
DREWS *to* SHAMELA ANDREWS.

Dear Sham,

YOUR laſt Letter hath put me into a great
hurry of Spirits, for you have a very difficult Part to act. I hope you will remember your
Slip with Parſon *Williams,* and not be guilty of
any more ſuch Folly. Truly, a Girl who hath once
known what is what, is in the higheſt Degree inexcuſable if ſhe reſpects her *Digreſſions* ; but a
Hint of this is ſufficient. When Mrs. *Jervis*
thinks of coming to Town, I believe I can procure her a good Houſe, and fit for the Buſineſs,
ſo I am,

Your affectionate Mother,

HENRIETTA MARIA HONORA ANDREWS.

LETTER IV.

SHAMELA ANDREWS *to* HENRIETTA
MARIA HONORA ANDREWS.

MARRY come up, good Madam, the
Mother had never looked into the Oven
for her Daughter, if ſhe had not been there herſelf.
I ſhall never have done if you upbraid me with
having had a ſmall One by *Arthur Williams,*
when you yourſelf—but I ſay no more. *O! What
fine Times when the Kettle calls the Pot.* Let me
do

do what I will, I ſay my Prayers as often as another, and I read in good Books, as often as I
have Leiſure ; and Parſon *William* ſays, that will
make amends.—So no more, but I reſt

Your afflicted Daughter,

S———.

LETTER V.

HENRIETTA MARIA HONORA AN-
DREWS *to* SHAMELA ANDREWS.

Dear Child,

WHY will you give ſuch way to your Paſſion? How could you imagine I ſhould
be ſuch a Simpleton, as to upbraid thee with being thy Mother's own Daughter! When I ad-
viſed you not to be guilty of Folly, I meant no
more than that you ſhould take care to be well
paid before-hand, and not truſt to Promiſes, which
a Man ſeldom keeps, after he hath had his wicked
Will. And ſeeing you have a rich Fool to deal
with, your not making a good Market will be
the more inexcuſable ; indeed, with ſuch Gentlemen as Parſon *Williams*, there is more to be
ſaid ; for they have nothing to give, and are commonly otherwiſe the beſt Sort of Men. I am
glad to hear you read good Books, pray continue
ſo to do. I have incloſed you one of Mr.
Whitefield's Sermons, and alſo the Dealings with
him, and am

Your affectionate Mother,

HENRIETTA MARIA, &c.

LETTER

LETTER VI.

SHAMELA ANDREWS *to* HENRIETTA MARIA HONORA ANDREWS.

O Madam, I have ftrange Things to tell you! As I was reading in that charming Book about the Dealings, in comes my Mafter—to be fure he is a precious One. *Pamela*, fays he, what Book is that, I warrant you *Rochefter's* Poems.——No, forfooth, fays I, as pertly as I could; why how now Saucy Chops, Boldface, fays he—— Mighty pretty Words, fays I, pert again. —Yes (fays he) you are are a d—d, impudent, ftinking, curfed, confounded Jade, and I have a great Mind to kick your A——.You, kifs—— fays I. A-gad, fays he, and fo I will; with that he caught me in his Arms, and kiffed me till he made my Face all over Fire. Now this ferved purely you know, to put upon the Fool for Anger. O! What precious Fools Men are! And fo I flung from him in a mighty Rage, and pretended as how I would go out at the Door; but when I came to the End of the Room, I ftood ftill, and my Mafter cryed out, Huffy, Slut, Saucebox, Boldface, come hither —— Yes to be fure, fays I; why don't you come, fays he; what fhould I come for fays I; if you don't come to me, I'll come to you, fays he; I fhan't, come to you I affure you, fays I. Upon which he run up, caught me in his Arms, and flung me upon a Chair, and began to offer to touch my Under-Petticoat. Sir, fays I, you had better not offer to be rude; well, fays he, no more I won't then;

and

and away he went out of the Room.   I was fo
mad to be fure I could have cry'd.

Oh what a prodigious Vexation it is to a Wo-
man to be made a Fool of.

Mrs. *Jervis,* who had been without, harkening,
now came to me.   She burft into a violent Laugh
the Moment fhe came in.   Well, fays fhe, as
foon as fhe could fpeak, I have reafon to blefs
myfelf that I am an Old Woman.   Ah Child!
if you had known the Jolly Blades of my Age,
you would not have been left in the Lurch in
this manner.   Dear Mrs. *Jervis,* fays I, don't
laugh at one ; and to be fure I was a little angry
with her.——Come, fays fhe, my dear Honey-
fuckle, I have one Game to play for you; he
fhall fee you in Bed ; he fhall, my little Rofe-
bud, he fhall fee thofe pretty, little, white, round,
panting——and offer'd to pull off my Handkerchief.——Fie, Mrs. *Jervis,* fays I, you make
me blufh, and upon my Fackins, I believe fhe
did : She went on thus.   I know the Squire likes
you, and notwithftanding the Aukwardnefs of
his Proceeding, I am convinced hath fome hot
Blood in his Veins, which will not let him reft,
'till he hath communicated fome of his Warmth
to thee my little Angel ; I heard him laft Night
at our Door, trying if it was open, now to Night
I will take care it fhall be fo ; I warrant that
he makes the fecond Trial ; which if he doth, he
fhall find us ready to receive him.   I will at firft
counterfeit Sleep, and after a Swoon; fo that
he will have you naked in his Poffeffion : and
then if you are difappointed, a Plague of all
young Squires, fay I. —— And fo, Mrs. *Jervis,*
fays I, you would have me yield my felf to him,
would you ; you would have me be a fecond
Time

Time a Fool for nothing. Thank you for that, Mrs. *Jervis.* For nothing! marry forbid fays fhe, you know he hath large Sums of Money, befides abundance of fine Things; and do you think, when you have inflamed him, by giving his Hand a Liberty, with that charming Perfon; and that you know he may eafily think he obtains againft your Will, he will not give any thing to come at all ——. This will not do, Mrs. *Jervis,* anfwered I. I have heard my Mamma fay, (and fo you know, Madam, I have) that in her Youth, Fellows have often taken away in the Morning, what they gave over Night. No, Mrs. *Jervis,* nothing under a regular taking into Keeping, a fettled Settlement, for me, and all my Heirs, all my whole Lifetime, fhall do the Bufinefs —— or elfe crofslegged, is the Word, faith, with *Sham*; and then I fnapt my Fingers.

Thurfday Night, Twelve o'Clock.

Mrs. *Jervis* and I are juft in Bed, and the Door unlocked; if my Mafter fhould come—— Odsbobs! I hear him juft coming in at the Door. You fee I write in the prefent Tenfe, as Parfon *Williams* fays. Well, he is in Bed between us, we both fhamming a Sleep, he fteals his Hand into my Bofom, which I, as if in my Sleep, prefs clofe to me with mine, and then pretend to awake.—I no fooner fee him, but I fcream out to Mrs. *Jervis,* fhe feigns likewife but juft to come to herfelf; we both begin, fhe to becall, and I to befcratch very liberally. After having made a pretty free Ufe of my Fingers, without any great Regard to the Parts I attack'd, I counterfeit a Swoon. Mrs. *Jervis* then cries out, O, Sir,

Sir, what have you done, you have murthered poor *Pamela*: she is gone, she is gone. ——

O what a Difficulty it is to keep one's Countenance, when a violent Laugh desires to burst forth.

The poor Booby frightned out of his Wits, jumped out of Bed, and, in his Shirt, sat down by my Bed-Side, pale and trembling, for the Moon shone, and I kept my Eyes wide open, and pretended to fix them in my Head. Mrs. *Jervis* apply'd Lavender Water, and Hartshorn, and this, for a full half Hour; when thinking I had carried it on long enough, and being likewise unable to continue the Sport any longer, I began by Degrees to come to my self.

The Squire who had sat all this while speechless, and was almost really in that Condition, which I feigned, the Moment he saw me give Symptoms of recovering my Senses, fell down on his Knees; and O *Pamela*, cryed he, can you forgive me, my injured Maid? by Heaven, I know not whether you are a Man or a Woman, unless by your swelling Breasts. Will you promise to forgive me: I forgive you! D—n you (says I) and d—n you says he, if you come to that. I wish I had never seen your bold Face, saucy Sow, and so went out of the Room.

O what a silly Fellow is a bashful young Lover!

He was no sooner out of hearing, as we thought, than we both burst into a violent Laugh. Well, says Mrs. *Jervis*, I never saw any thing better acted than your Part: But I wish you may not have discouraged him from any future Attempt; especially since his Passions are so cool, that you could prevent his Hands going further than your Bosom. Hang him, answered fwer'd I, he is not quite fo cold as that I affure you; our Hands, on neither Side, were idle in the Scuffle, nor have left us any Doubt of each other as to that matter.

Friday Morning.

My Mafter fent for Mrs. *Jervis*, as foon as he was up, and bid her give an Account of the Plate and Linnen in her Care; and told her, he was refolved that both fhe and the little Gipfy (I'll affure him) fhould fet out together. Mrs. *Jervis* made him a faucy Anfwer; which any Servant of Spirit, you know, would, tho' it fhould be one's Ruin; and came immediately in Tears to me, crying, fhe had loft her Place on my Account, and that fhe fhould be forced to take to a Houfe, as I mentioned before; and, that fhe hoped I would, at leaft, make her all the amends in my power, for her Lofs on my Account, and come to her Houfe whenever I was fent for. Never fear, fays I, I'll warrant we are not fo near being turned away, as you imagine; and, i'cod, now it comes into my Head, I have a Fetch for him, and you fhall affift me in it. But it being now late, and my Letter pretty long, no more at prefent from

Your Dutiful Daughter,

SHAMELA.

C LETTER

L E T T E R VII.

Mrs. LUCRETIA JERVIS *to* HENRIETTA
MARIA HONORA ANDREWS.

Madam,

MISS *Sham* being set out in a Hurry for
my Master's House in *Lincolnshire,* desired me to acquaint you with the Success of her
Stratagem, which was to dress herself in the plain
Neatness of a Farmer's Daughter, for she before
wore the Cloaths of my late Mistress, and to be
introduced by me as a Stranger to her Master.
To say the Truth, she became the Dress extremely,
and if I was to keep a House a thousand Years,
I would never desire a prettier Wench in it.

As soon as my Master saw her, he immediately
threw his Arms round her Neck, and smother-
ed her with Kisses (for indeed he hath but very
little to say for himself to a Woman.) He swore
that *Pamela* was an ugly Slut (pardon, dear Madam, the Courseness of the Expression) compared
to such divine Excellence. He added, he would
turn *Pamela* away immediately, and take this new
Girl, whom he thought to be one of his Tenants
Daughters in her room.

Miss *Sham* smiled at these Words, and so did
your humble Servant, which he perceiving looked very earnestly at your fair Daughter, and
discovered the Cheat.

How

How, *Pamela*, fays he, is it you? I thought,
Sir, faid Mifs, after what had happened, you
would have known me in any Drefs. No, Huffy,
fays he, but after what hath happened, I fhould
know thee out of any Drefs from all thy Sex.
He then was what what we Women call rude,
when done in the Prefence of others; but it feems
it is not the firft time, and Mifs defended herfelf
with great Strength and Spirit.

The Squire, who thinks her a pure Virgin,
and who knows nothing of my Character, refolved
to fend her into *Lincolnfhire*, on Pretence of conveying her home; where our old Friend *Nanny
Jewkes* is Houfekeeper, and where Mifs had her
fmall one by Parfon *Williams* about a Year ago:
This is a Piece of News communicated to us by
Robin Coachman, who is intrufted by his Mafter
to carry on this Affair privately for him : But we
hang together, I believe, as well as any Family of
Servants in the Nation.

You will, I believe, Madam, wonder that
the Squire, who doth not want Generofity, fhould
never have mentioned a Settlement all this while,
I believe it flips his Memory : But it will not be
long firft, no Doubt: For, as I am convinced
the young Lady will do nothing unbecoming
your Daughter, nor ever admit him to tafte her
Charms, without fomething fure and handfome
before-hand ; fo, I am certain, the Squire will
never reft till they have danced *Adam* and *Eve's*
kiffing Dance together. Your Daughter fet out
yefterday Morning, and told me, as foon as fhe
arrived, you might depend on hearing from
her.

Be pleased to make my Compliments acceptable to Mrs. *Davis* and Mrs. *Silvester*, and Mrs.
Jolly, and all Friends, and permit me the Honour, Madam, to be with the utmost Sincerity,

Your most Obedient

Humble Servant

LUCRETIA JERVIS.

If the Squire should continue his Displeasure
against me, so as to insist on the Warning he hath
given me, you will see me soon, and I will lodge
in the same House with you, if you have
room, till I can provide for my self to my Liking.

LETTER VIII.

HENRIETTA MARIA HONORA ANDREWS *to* LUCRETIA JERVIS.

Madam,

I Received the Favour of your Letter, and
I find you have not forgot your usual Polute-
ness, which you learned when you was in keeping with a Lord.

I am very much obliged to you for your
Care of my Daughter, am glad to hear she hath
taken such good Resolutions, and hope she will
have sufficient Grace to maintain them.

All

All Friends are well and remember to you. You will excuse the Shortnefs of this Scroll; for I have fprained my right Hand, with boxing three new made Officers. — Tho' to my Comfort, I beat them all. I reft,

Your Friend and Servant,

HENRIETTA, *&c.*

LETTER IX.

SHAMELA ANDREWS *to* HENRIETTA MARIA HONORA ANDREWS.

Dear Mamma,

I Suppofe Mrs. *Jervis* acquainted you with what paft 'till I left *Bedfordſhire*; whence I am after a very pleafant Journey arrived in *Lincolnſhire*, with your old Acquaintance Mrs. *Jewkes*, who formerly helped Parfon *Williams* to me; and now defigns I fee, to fell me to my Mafter; thank her for that; ſhe will find two Words go to that Bargain.

The Day after my Arrival here, I received a Letter from Mr. *Williams*, and as you have often defired to fee one from him, I have inclofed it to you; it is, I think, the fineft I ever received from that charming Man, and full of a great deal of Learning.

O! *What a brave Thing it is to be a Scholard, and to be able to talk Latin.*

C 3 *Par-*

Parſon WILLIAMS to PAMELA ANDREWS.

Mrs. Pamela,

HAVING learnt by means of my Clerk, who Yeſternight viſited the Rev⁴. Mr. *Peters* with my Commands, that you are returned into this County, I purpoſed to have ſaluted your fair Hands this Day towards Even: But am obliged to ſojourn this Night at a neighbouring Clergyman's; where we are to pierce a Virgin Barrel of Ale, in a Cup of which I ſhall not be unmindful to celebrate your Health.

I hope you have remembered your Promiſe, to bring me a Leaden Caniſter of Tobacco (the Saffron Cut) for in Troth, this Country at preſent affords nothing worthy the repleniſhing a Tube with. —— Some I taſted the other Day at an Alehouſe, gave me the Heart-Burn, tho' I filled no oftner than five Times.

I was greatly concerned to learn, that your late Lady left you nothing, tho' I cannot ſay the Tidings much ſurprized me: For I am too intimately acquainted with the Family; (myſelf, Father and Grandfather having been ſucceſſive Incumbents on the ſame Cure, which you know is in their Gift) I ſay, I am too well acquainted with them to expect much from their Generoſity. They are in Verity, as worthleſs a Family as any other whatever. The young Gentleman I am informed, is a perfect Reprobate; that he hath an

Inge-

Ingenium Verfatile to every Species of Vice,
which, indeed, no one can much wonder at, who
animadverts on that want of Refpect to the Clergy, which was obfervable in him when a Child.
I remember when he was at the Age of Eleven
only, he met my Father without either pulling
off his Hat, or riding out of the way. Indeed,
a Contempt of the Clergy is the fafhionable Vice
of the Times; but let fuch Wretches know, they
cannot hate, deteft, and defpife us, half fo much
as we do them.

However, I have prevailed on myfelf to write
a civil Letter to your Mafter, as there is a Probability of his being fhortly in a Capacity of
rendring me a Piece of Service ; my good Friend
and Neighbour the Revᵈ. Mr. *Squeeze-Tithe* being, as I am informed by one whom I have
employed to attend for that Purpofe, very near
his Diffolution.

You fee, fweet Mrs. *Pamela,* the Confidence
with which I dictate thefe Things to you ; whom
after thofe Endearments which have paffed between us, I muft in fome Refpects eftimate as
my Wife: For tho' the Omiffion of the Service
was a Sin ; yet, as I have told you, it was a Ve-
nial One, of which I have truly repented, as I
hope you have ; and alfo that you have continued
the wholefome Office of reading good Books, and
are improved in your Pfalmody, of which I
fhall have a fpeedy Trial: For I purpofe to give
you a Sermon next *Sunday,* and fhall fpend the
Evening with you, in Pleafures which tho' not
ftrictly innocent, are however to be purged

away by frequent and sincere Repentance.
I am,

Sweet Mrs. Pamela,

Your faithful Servant,

ARTHUR WILLIAMS.

You find, Mamma, what a charming way he
hath of Writing, and yet I assure you, that is not
the most charming Thing belonging to him: For,
tho' he doth not put any Dears, and Sweets, and
Loves into his Letters, yet he says a thousand of
them: For he can be as fond of a Woman, as
any Man living.

*Sure Women are great Fools, when they prefer
a laced Coat to the Clergy, whom it is our Duty
to honour and respect.*

Well, on *Sunday* Parson *Williams* came, according to his Promise, and an excellent Sermon
he preached; his Text was, *Be not Righteous
over-much*; and, indeed, he handled it in a very
fine way; he shewed us that the Bible doth not
require too much Goodness of us, and that People
very often call things Goodness that are not so.
That to go to Church, and to pray, and to sing
Psalms, and to honour the Clergy, and to repent, is true Religion; and 'tis not doing good to
one another, for that is one of the greatest Sins
we can commit, when we don't do it for the sake
of Religion. That those People who talk of
Vartue and Morality, are the wickedest of all
Persons. That 'tis not what we do, but what
we believe, that must save us, and a great many
other

other good Things ; I wifh I could remember them all.

As foon as Church was over, he came to the Squire's Houfe, and drank Tea with Mrs. *Jewkes* and me ; after which Mrs. *Jewkes* went, out and left us together for an Hour and half —— Oh! he is a charming Man.

After Supper he went Home, and then Mrs. *Jewkes* began to catechize me, about my Familiarity with him. I fee fhe wants him herfelf. Then fhe proceeded to tell me what an Honour my Mafter did me in liking me, and that it was both an inexcufable Folly and Pride in me, to pretend to refufe him any Favour. Pray, Madam, fays I, confider I am a poor Girl, and have nothing but my Modefty to truft to. If I part with that, what will become of me. Methinks, fays fhe, you are not fo mighty modeft when you are with Parfon *Williams* ; I have obferved you gloat at one another, in a Manner that hath made me blufh. I affure you, I fhall let the Squire know what fort of Man he is ; you may do your Will, fay I, as long as he hath a Vote for Pallamant-Men, the Squire dares do nothing to offend him ; and you will only fhew that you are jealous of him, and that's all. How now, Mynx, fays fhe ; Mynx ! No more Mynx than yourfelf, fays I ; with that fhe hit me a Slap on the Shoulder, and I flew at her and fcratched her Face i'cod, 'till fhe went crying out of the Room ; fo no more at Prefent, from

Your Dutiful Daughter,

SHAMELA.
LETTER

LETTER X.

SHAMELA ANDREWS *to* HENRIETTA
MARIA HONORA ANDREWS.

O Mamma! Rare News! As foon as I was
up this Morning, a Letter was brought
me from the Squire, of which I fend you a Copy.

Squire BOOBY *to* PAMELA.

Dear Creature,

I HOPE you are not angry with me for the Deceit put upon you, in conveying you to *Lincolnſhire,* when you imagined yourſelf going to
London. Indeed, my dear *Pamela,* I cannot live
without you; and will very ſhortly come down
and convince you, that my Deſigns are better
than you imagine, and ſuch as you may with
Honour comply with. I am,

My Dear Creature,

Your doting Lover,

BOOBY.

Now, Mamma, what think you?——For my
own Part, I am convinced he will marry me,
and faith ſo he ſhall. O! Bleſs me! I ſhall be
Mrs. *Booby,* and be Miſtreſs of a great Eſtate,
and have a dozen Coaches. and Six, and a fine
Houſe at *London,* and another at *Bath,* and Servants, and Jewels, and Plate, and go to Plays,
and

and Opera's, and Court; and do what I will, and
spend what I will. But, poor Parson *Williams* !
Well ; and can't I see Parson *Williams*, as
well after Marriage as before: For I shall never
care a Farthing for my Husband. No, I hate
and despise him of all Things.

Well, as soon as I had read my Letter, in came
Mrs. *Jewkes*. You see, Madam, says she, I carry the
Marks of your Passion about me; but I have received Order from my Master to be civil to you, and I
must obey him: For he is the best Man in the
World, notwithstanding your Treatment of him.
My Treatment of him; Madam, says I? Yes,
says she, your Insensibility to the Honour he intends you, of making you his Mistress. I would
have you to know, Madam, I would not be Mistress to the greatest King, no nor Lord in the
Universe. I value my Vartue more than I do any
thing my Master can give me ; and so we talked
a full Hour and a half, about my Vartue ; and I
was afraid at first, she had heard something about
the Bantling, but I find she hath not ; tho' she is
as jealous, and suspicious, as old Scratch.

In the Afternoon, I stole into the Garden to
meet Mr. *Williams* ; I found him at the Place of
his Appointment, and we staid in a kind of
Arbour, till it was quite dark. He was very
angry when I told him what Mrs. *Jewkes* had
threatned ——— Let him refuse me the Living,
says he, if he dares, I will vote for the other
Party ; and not only so, but will expose him all
over the Country. I owe him 150*l*. indeed,
but I don't care for that, by that Time the
Election

Election is paft, I fhall be able to plead the
the *Statue* of *Lamentations.*

I could have ftayed with the dear Man for ever,
but when it grew dark, he told me, he was to
meet the neighbouring Clergy, to finifh the Barrel of Ale they had tapped the other Day, and
believed they fhould not part till three or four in
the Morning —— So he left me, and I promifed
to be penitent, and go on with my reading in
good Books.

As foon as he was gone, I bethought myfelf,
what Excufe I fhould make to Mrs. *Jewkes,* and
it came into my Head to pretend as how I intended
to drown myfelf; fo I ftript off one of my Pet-
ticoats, and threw it into the Canal; and then I
went and hid myfelf in the Coal-hole, where I
lay all Night; and comforted myfelf with repeating over fome Pfalms, and other good things,
which I had got by heart.

In the Morning Mrs. *Jewkes* and all the Servants were frighted out of their Wits, thinking
I had run away; and not devifing how they
fhould anfwer it to their Mafter. They fearched
all the likelieft Places they could think of for me,
and at laft faw my Petticoat floating in the Pond.
Then they got a Drag-Net, imagining I was
drowned, and intending to drag me out; but at
laft *Moll* Cook coming for fome Coals, difcovered me lying all along in no very good Pickle.
Blefs me! Mrs. *Pamela,* fays fhe, what can be
the Meaning of this? I don't know, fays I,
help me up, and I will go in to Breakfaft, for
indeed I am very hungty. Mrs. *Jewkes* came in
imme-

immediately, and was so rejoyced to find me alive, that she asked with great good Humour, where I had been? and how my Petticoat came into the Pond. I answered, I believed the Devil had put it into my Head to drown my self; but it was a Fib; for I never saw the Devil in my Life, nor I don't believe he hath any thing to do with me.

So much for this Matter. As soon as I had breakfasted, a Coach and Six came to the Door, and who should be in it but my Master.

I immediately run up into my Room, and stript, and washed, and drest my self as well as I could, and put on my prettiest round-ear'd Cap, and pulled down my Stays, to shew as much as I could of my Bosom, (for Parson *Williams* says, that is the most beautiful part of a Woman) and then I practised over all my Airs before the Glass, and then I sat down and read a Chapter in the whole Duty of Man.

Then Mrs. *Jewkes* came to me and told me, my Master wanted me below, and says she, Don't behave like a Fool; No, thinks I to my self, I believe I shall find Wit enough for my Master and you too.

So down goes me I into the Parlour to him. *Pamela*, says he, the Moment I came in, you see I cannot stay long from you, which I think is a sufficient Proof of the Violence of my Passion. Yes, Sir, says I, I see your Honour intends to ruin me, that nothing but the Destruction of my Vartue will content you.

O what a charming Word that is, reſt his Soul who firſt invented it.

How can you ſay I would ruin you, anſwered the Squire, when you ſhall not aſk any thing which I will not grant you. If that be true, ſays I, good your Honour let me go Home to my poor but honeſt Parents ; that is all I have to aſk, and do not ruin a poor Maiden, who is reſolved to carry her Vartue to the Grave with her.

Huſſy, ſays he, don't provoke me, don't provoke me, I ſay. You are abſolutely in my power, and if you won't let me lie with you by fair Means, I will by Force. O La, Sir, ſays I, I don't underſtand your paw Words. —— Very pretty Treatment indeed, ſays he, to ſay I uſe paw Words; Huſſy, Gipſie, Hypocrite, Saucebox, Boldface, get out of my Sight, or I will lend you ſuch a Kick in the ——I don't care to repeat the Word, but he meant my hinder part. I was offering to go away, for I was half afraid, when he called me back, and took me round the Neck and kiſſed me, and then bid me go about my Buſineſs.

I went directly into my Room, where Mrs. *Jewkes* came to me ſoon afterwards. So Madam, ſays ſhe, you have left my Maſter below in a fine Pet, he hath threſhed two or three of his Men already : It is mighty pretty that all his Servants are to be puniſhed for your Impertinence.

Harkee, Madam, ſays I, don't you affront me, for if you do, d——n me (I am ſure I have
repented

repented for uſing ſuch a Word) if I am not re-
venged.

*How ſweet is Revenge : Sure the Sermon Book
is in the Right, in calling it the ſweeteſt Morſel
the Devil ever dropped into the Mouth of a Sinner.*

Mrs. *Jewkes* remembered the Smart of my Nails
too well to go farther, and and ſo we ſat down
and talked about my Vartue till Dinner-time, and
then I was ſent for to wait on my Maſter. I took
care to be often caught looking at him, and then
I always turn'd away my Eyes and pretended to
be aſhamed. As ſoon as the Cloth was removed,
he put a Bumper of Champagne into my Hand,
and bid me drink——O la I can't name the
Health. Parſon *Williams* may well ſay he is a
wicked Man.

Mrs. *Jewkes* took a Glaſs and drank the dear
Monyſyllable; I don't underſtand that Word but
I believe it is baudy. I then drank towards his
Honour's good Pleaſure. Ay, Huſſy, ſays he,
you can give me Pleaſure if you will; Sir, ſays
I, I ſhall be always glad to do what is in my
power, and ſo I pretended not to know what he
meant. Then he took me into his Lap.—O
Mamma, I could tell you ſomething if I would—
and he kiſſed me—and I ſaid I won't be ſlobber'd
about ſo, ſo I won't, and he bid me get out of
the Room for a ſaucy Baggage, and ſaid he had
a good mind to ſpit in my Face.

*Sure no Man ever took ſuch a Method to gain a
Woman's Heart.*

I

I had not been long in my Chamber before Mrs. *Jewkes* came to me and told me, my Mafter would not fee me any more that Evening, that is, if he can help it ; for, added fhe, I eafily perceive the great Afcendant you have over him ; and to confefs the Truth, I don't doubt but you will fhortly be my Miftrefs.

What fays I, dear Mrs. *Jewkes*, what do you fay ? Don't flatter a poor Girl, it is impoffible his Honour can have any honourable Defign upon me. And fo we talked of honourable Defigns till Supper-time. And Mrs. *Jewkes* and I fupped together upon a hot buttered Apple-Pie ; and about ten o' Clock we went to Bed.

We had not been a Bed half an Hour, when my Mafter came pit a pat into the Room in his Shirt as before, I pretended not to hear him, and Mrs. *Jewkes* laid hold of one Arm, and he pulled down the Bed-cloaths and came into Bed on the other Side, and took my other Arm and laid it under him, and fell a kiffing one of my Breafts as if he would have devoured it ; I was then forced to awake, and began to ftruggle with him, Mrs. *Jewkes* crying why don't you do it ? I have one Arm fecure, if you can't deal with the reft I am forry for you. He was as rude as poffible to me ; but I remembered, Mamma, the Inftructions you gave me to avoid being ravifhed, and followed them, which foon brought him to Terms, and he promifed me on quitting my hold, that he would leave the Bed.

O Parfon Williams, *how little are all the Men in the World compared to thee.*

My

My Mafter was as good as his Word; upon which Mrs. *Jewkes* faid, O Sir, I fee you know very little of our *Sect*, by parting fo eafily from the Bleffing when you was fo near it. No, Mrs. *Jewkes*, anfwered he, I am very glad no more hath happened, I would not have injured *Pamela* for the World. And to-morrow Morning perhaps fhe may hear of fomething to her Advantage. This fhe may be certain of, that I will never take her by Force, and then he left the Room.

What think you now, Mrs. *Pamela*, fays Mrs. *Jewkes*, Are you not yet perfuaded my Mafter hath honourable Defigns? I think he hath given no great Proof of them to-night, faid I. Your Experience I find is not great, fays fhe, but I am convinced you will fhortly be my Miftrefs, and then what will become of poor me.

With fuch Sort of Difcourfe we both fell afleep. Next Morning early my Mafter fent for me, and after kiffing me, gave a Paper into my Hand which he bid me read; I did fo, and found it to be a Propofal for fettling 250*l.* a Year on me, befides feveral other advantagious Offers, as Prefents of Money and other Things. Well, *Pamela*, faid he, what Anfwer do you make me to this. Sir, faid I, I value my Vartue more than all the World, and I had rather be the pooreft Man's Wife, than the richeft Man's Whore. You are a Simpleton, faid he; That may be, and yet I may have as much Wit as fome Folks, cry'd I; meaning me, I fuppofe, faid he; every Man knows himfelf beft, fays I. Huffy fays

D he,

he, get out of the Room, and let me fee your faucy Face no more, for I find I am in more Danger than you are, and therefore it fhall be my Bufinefs to avoid you as much as I can ; and it fhall be mine, thinks I, at every turn to throw my felf in your Way. So I went out, and as I parted, I heard him figh and fay he was be-witched.

Mrs. *Jewkes* hath been with me fince, and fhe affures me fhe is convinced I fhall fhortly be Miftrefs of the Family, and fhe really behaves to me, as if fhe already thought me fo. I am refolved now to aim at it. I thought once of making a little Fortune by my Perfon. I now intend to make a great one by my Vartue. So asking Pardon for this long Scroll, I am,

Your dutiful Daughter,

SHAMELA,

LETTER

L E T T E R, XI.

HENRIETEA MARIA HONORA AN-
DREWS *to* SHAMELA ANDREWS.

Dear Sham,

I RECEIVED your laſt Letter with infinite
Pleaſure, and am convinced it will be your
own Fault if you are not married to your Maſter, and I would adviſe you now to take no
leſs Terms. But, my dear Child, I am afraid
of one Rock only, That Parſon *Williams,* I
wiſh he was out of the Way. A Woman never
commits Folly but with ſuch Sort of Men, as by
many Hints in the Letters I collect him to be:
but, conſider, my dear Child, you will hereafter have Opportunities ſufficient to indulge
yourſelf with Parſon *Williams,* or any other you
like. My Advice therefore to you is, that you
would avoid ſeeing him any more till the Knot
is tied. Remember the firſt Leſſon I taught
you, that a Married Woman injures only her
Huſband, but a Single Woman herſelf. I am,
in hopes of ſeeing you a great Lady,

Your affectionate Mother,

HENRIETTA MARIA, *&c.*

The

The following Letter feems to have been written before *Shamela* received the laft from her
Mother.

LETTER XII.

SHAMELA ANDREWS *to* HENRIETTA
MARIA HONORA ANDREWS.

Dear Mamma,

I LITTLE feared when I fent away my laft,
that all my Hopes would be fo foon fruftrated; but I am certain you will blame Fortune and
not me. To proceed then. About two Hours
after I had left the Squire, he fent for me into the
Parlour. *Pamela,* faid he, and takes me gently by the Hand, will you walk with me in the
Garden; yes, Sir, fays I, and pretended to trem-
ble; but I hope your Honour will not be rude.
Indeed, fays he, you have nothing to fear from
me, and I have fomething to tell you, which if
it doth not pleafe you, cannot offend. We walked out together, and he began thus, *Pamela,*
will you tell me Truth? Doth the Refiftance you
make to my Attempts proceed from Vartue only, or have I not fome Rival in thy dear Bofom
who might be more fuccefsful? Sir, fays I, I
do affure you I never had a thought of any Man
in the World. How fays he, not of Parfon
Williams! Parfon *Williams,* fays I, is the laft
Man upon Earth, and if I was a Dutchefs, and
your Honour was to make your Addreffes to
me, you would have no Reafon to be jealous of
any

any Rival, especially such a Fellow as Parson *Williams.* If ever I had a Liking, I am sure— but I am not worthy of you one Way, and no Riches should ever bribe me the other. My Dear, says he, you are worthy of every Thing, and suppose I should lay aside all Considerations of Fortune, and disregard the Censure of the World, and marry you. O Sir, says I, I am sure you can have no such Thoughts, you cannot demean your self so low. Upon my Soul, I am in earnest, says he,——O Pardon me, Sir, says I, you can't persuade me of this. How Mrs. says he in a violent Rage, do you give me the Lie? Huffy, I have a great mind to box your saucy Ears, but I am resolved I will never put it in your power to affront me again, and therefore I desire you to prepare your self for your Journey this Instant. You deserve no better Vehicle than a Cart; however, for once you shall have a Chariot, and it shall be ready for you within this half Hour; and so he flung from me in a Fury.

What a foolish Thing it is for a Woman to dally too long with her Lover's Desires; how many have owed their being old Maids to their holding out too long.

Mrs. *Jewkes* came to me presently, and told me, I must make ready with all the Expedition imaginable, for that my Master had ordered the Chariot, and that if I was not prepared to go in it, I should be turned out of Doors and left to find my way Home on Foot. This startled me a little, yet I resolved, whether in the right or wrong, not to submit nor ask Pardon: For that

you

you know, Mamma, you never could your felf
bring me to from my Childhood: Befides, I
thought he would be no more able to mafter his
Paffion for me now, than he had been hitherto;
and if he fent two Horfes away with me, I concluded he would fend four to fetch me back. So,
truly, I refolved to brazen it out, and with all
the Spirit I could mufter up, I told Mrs. *Jewkes*
I was vaftly pleafed with the News fhe brought
me; that no one ever went more readily than I
fhould, from a Place where my Vartue had been
in continual Danger. That as for my Mafter,
he might eafily get thofe who were fit for his
Purpofe; but, for my Part, I preferred my
Vartue to all Rakes whatever——And for his
Promifes, and his Offers to me, I don't value them
of a Fig——Not of a Fig, Mrs. *Jewkes*; and
then I fnapt my Fingers.

Mrs. *Jewkes* went in with me, and helped me to
pack up my little All, which was foon done;
being no more than two Day-Caps, two Night-
Caps, five Shifts, one Sham, a Hoop, a Quilted-
Petticoat, two Flannel-Petticoats, two pair of
Stockings, one odd one, a pair of lac'd Shoes, a
fhort flowered Apron, a lac'd Neck-Handker-
chief, one Clog, and almoft another, and fome
few Books: as, *a full Anfwer to a plain and
true Account*, &c. *The Whole Duty of Man*, with
only the Duty to one's Neighbour, torn out.
The Third Volume of the *Atalantis*. *Venus in
the Cloyfter: Or, the Nun in her Smock. God's
Dealings with Mr. Whitefield. Orfus and Eury-
dice.* Some Sermon-Books; and two or three
Plays, with their Titles, and Part of the firft
Act torn off.

So

So as foon as we had put all this into a Bundle, the Chariot was ready, and I took leave of all the Servants, and particularly Mrs. *Jewkes,* who pretended, I believe, to be more forry to part with me than fhe was; and then crying out with an Air of Indifference, my Service to my Mafter, when he condefcends to enquire after me, I flung my felf into the Chariot, and bid *Robin* drive on.

We had not gone far, before a Man on Horfe-back, riding full Speed, overtook us, and coming up to the Side of the Chariot, threw a Letter in-to the Window, and then departed without ut-tering a fingle Syllable.

I immediately knew the Hand of my dear *Williams,* and was fomewhat furprized, tho' I did not apprehend the Contents to be fo terrible, as by the following exact Copy you will find them.

Parfon WILLIAMS *to* PAMELA.

Dear Mrs. PAMELA,

THAT Difrefpect for the Clergy which I have formerly noted to you in that Villain your Mafter, hath now broke forth in a manifeft Fact. I was proceeding to my Neighbour *Spruce's* Church, where I purpofed to preach a Funeral Sermon, on the Death of Mr. *John Gage,* the Excifeman; when I was met by two Perfons who are, it feems, Sheriffs Officers, and arrefted for the 150 *l.* which your Mafter had lent me;

and

and unlefs I can find Bail within thefe few Days, of which I fee no likelihood, I fhall be carried to Goal. This accounts for my not having vifited you thefe two Days; which you might affure your felf, I fhould not have fail'd, if the *Poteftas* had not been wanting. If you can by any means prevail on your Mafter to releafe me, I befeech you fo to do, not fcrupling any thing for Righteoufnefs fake. I hear he is juft arrived in this Country, I have herewith fent him a Letter, of which I tranfmit you a Copy. So with Prayers for your Succefs, I fubfcribe my felf

Your affectionate Friend

ARTHUR WILLIAMS.

Parfon WILLIAMS *to Squire* BOOBY.

Honoured Sir,

I Am juftly furprized to feel fo heavy a Weight of your Difpleafure, without being confcious of the leaft Demerit towards fo good and generous a Patron, as I have ever found you: For my own Part, I can truly fay,

Nil confcire fibi nullæ pallefcere culpæ.

And therefore, as this Proceeding is fo contrary to your ufual Goodnefs, which I have often experienced, and more efpecially in the Loan of this Money for which I am now arrefted; I cannot avoid thinking fome malicious Perfons have infinuated falfe Suggeftions againft me; intending thereby, to eradicate thofe Seeds of Affection
which

which I have hardly travailed to fowe in your Heart, and which promifed to produce fuch excellent Fruit. If I have any ways offended you, Sir, be gracioufly pleafed to let me know it, and likewife to point out to me, the Means whereby I may reinftate myfelf in your Favour : For next to him whom the great themfelves muft bow down before, I know none to whom I fhall bend with more Lowlinefs than your Honour. Permit me to fubfcribe my felf,

Honoured Sir,

Your moft obedient, and moft obliged,

And moft dutiful humble Servant,

ARTHUR WILLIAMS.

The Fate of poor Mr. *Williams* fhocked me more than my own : For, as the *Beggar's Opera* fays, *Nothing moves one fo much as a great Man in Diftrefs.* And to fee a Man of his Learning forced to fubmit fo low, to one whom I have often heard him fay, he defpifes, is, I think, a moft affecting Circumftance. I write all this to you, Dear Mamma, at the Inn where I lie this firft Night, and as I fhall fend it immediately, by the Poft, it will be in Town a little before me. ——Don't let my coming away vex you : For, as my Mafter will be in Town in a few Days, I fhall have an Opportunity of feeing him ; and let the worft come to the worft, I fhall be fure of my Settlement at laft. Which is all, from

Your Dutiful Daughter,

SHAMELA.

P. S.

P. S. Juft as I was going to fend this away a Letter is come from my Mafter, defiring me to return, with a large Number of Promifes.—— I have him now as fure as a Gun, as you will perceive by the Letter itfelf, which I have inclofed to you.

This Letter is unhappily loft, as well as the next which *Shamela* wrote, and which contained an Account of all the Proceedings previous to her Marriage. The only remaining one which I could preferve, feems to have been written about a Week after the Ceremony was perform'd, and is as follows:

SHAMELA BOOBY *to* HENRIETTA
MARIA HONORA ANDREWS.

Madam,

IN my laft I left off at our fitting down to Supper on our Wedding Night, * where I behaved with as much Bafhfulnefs as the pureft Virgin in the World could have done. The moft difficult Tafk for me was to blufh ; however, by holding my Breath, and fqueezing my Cheeks with my Handkerchief, I did pretty well. My Husband was extreamly eager and impatient to have Supper removed, after which he gave me leave to retire into my Clofet for a Quarter of an Hour, which was very agreeable to me ; for I employed that time in writing to Mr. *Williams,*

* This was the Letter which is loft.

who

who, as I informed you in my laft, is releafed, and prefented to the Living, upon the Death of the laft Parfon. Well, at laft I went to Bed, and my Husband foon leapt in after me; where I fhall only affure you, I acted my Part in fuch a manner, that no Bridegroom was ever better fatisfied with his Bride's Virginity. And to confefs the Truth, I might have been well enough fatisfied too, if I had never been acquainted with Parfon *Williams*.

O what regard Men who marry Widows fhould have to the Qualifications of their former Hufbands.

We did not rife the next Morning till eleven, and then we fat down to Breakfaft; I eat two Slices of Bread and Butter, and drank three Difhes of Tea, with a good deal of Sugar, and we both look'd very filly. After Breakfaft we dreft our felves, he in a blue Camlet Coat, very richly lac'd, and Breeches of the fame; with a Paduofoy Waftecoat, laced with Silver; and I, in one of my Miftrefs's Gowns. I will have finer when I come to Town. We then took a Walk in the Garden, and he kiffed me feveral Times, and made me a Prefent of 100 Guineas, which I gave away before Night to the Servants, twenty to one, and ten to another, and fo on.

We eat a very hearty Dinner, and about eight in the Evening went to Bed again. He is prodigioufly fond of me; but I don't like him half fo well as my dear *Williams*. The next Morning we rofe earlier, and I asked him for another hundred Guineas, and he gave them me. I fent
fifty

fifty to Parſon *Williams*, and the reſt I gave a-
way, two Guineas to a Beggar, and three to a
Man riding along the Road, and the reſt to other
People. I long to be in *London* that I may have
an Opportunity of laying ſome out, as well as
giving away. I believe I ſhall buy every Thing
I ſee. What ſignifies having Money if one doth
not ſpend it.

The next Day, as ſoon as I was up, I asked
him for another Hundred. Why my Dear, ſays
he, I don't grudge you any thing, but how was
it poſſible for you to lay out the other two Hundred here. La! Sir, ſays I, I hope I am not
obliged to give you an Account of every Shilling ; Troth, that will be being your Servant
ſtill. I aſſure you, I married you with no ſuch
view, beſides did not you tell me I ſhould be
Miſtreſs of your Eſtate ? And I will be too. For
tho' I brought no Fortune, I am as much your
Wife as if I had brought a Million——yes but,
my Dear, ſays he, if you had brought a Million,
you would ſpend it all at this rate ; beſides, what
will your Expences be in *London*, if they are ſo
great here. Truly, ſays I, Sir, I ſhall live like
other Ladies of my Faſhion ; and if you think,
becauſe I was a Servant, that I ſhall be contented
to be governed as you pleaſe, I will ſhew you,
you are miſtaken. If you had not cared to marry me, you might have let it alone. I did not
ask you, nor I did not court you. Madam, ſays
he, I don't value a Hundred Guineas to oblige
you ; but this is a Spirit which I did not expect
in you, nor did I ever ſee any Symptoms of it before. O but Times are altered now, I am your
Lady, Sir ; yes to my Sorrow, ſays he, I am
afraid——

afraid—and I am afraid to my Sorrow too : For
if you begin to ufe me in this manner already,
I reckon you will beat me before a Month's at an
End. I am fure if you did, it would injure me
lefs than this barbarous Treatment ; upon which
I burft into Tears, and pretended to fall into a
Fit. This frighted him out of his wits, and he
called up the Servants. Mrs. *Jewkes* immediately came in, and fhe and another of the Maids
fell heartily to rubbing my Temples, and holding Smelling-Bottles to my Nofe. Mrs. *Jewkes*
told him fhe fear'd I fhould never recover, upon
which he began to beat his Breafts, and cried out,
O my deareft Angel, curfe on my paffionate
Temper, I have deftroy'd her, I have deftroy'd
her,——would fhe had fpent my whole Eftate rather than this had happened. Speak to me, my
Love, I will melt my felf into Gold for thy
Pleafure. At laft having pretty well tired my
felf with counterfeiting, and imagining I had
continu'd long enough for my purpofe in the
fham Fit, I began to move my Eyes, to loofen
my Teeth, and to open my Hands, which Mr.
Booby no fooner perceived then he embraced and
kiffed me with the eagereft Extacy, asked my
Pardon on his Knees for what I had fuffered
through his Folly and Perverfenefs, and without
more Queftions fetched me the Money. I fancy
I have effectually prevented any farther Refufals
or Inquiry into my Expences. It would be hard
indeed that a Woman who marries a Man only
for his Money fhould be debarred from fpending
it.

Well, after all Things were quiet, we fat down
to Breakfaft, yet I refolved not to fmile once,

nor

nor to fay one good-natured, or good-humoured
Word on any Account.

*Nothing can be more prudent in a Wife, than
a fullen Backwardnefs to Reconciliation; it makes
a Husband fearful of offending by the Length of
his Punifhment.*

When we were dreft, the Coach was by my
Defire ordered for an Airing, which we took in
it. A long Silence prevailed on both Sides, tho'
he conftantly fqueezed my Hand, and kiffed me,
and ufed other Familiarities, which I peevifhly
permitted. At laft, I opened my Mouth firft.—
And fo, fays I, you are forry you are married?
—Pray, my Dear, fays he, forget what I faid
in a Paffion. Paffion, fays I, is apter to difcover our Thoughts than to teach us to counterfeit.
Well, fays he, whether you will believe me or
no, I folemnly vow, I would not change thee for
the richeft Woman in the Univerfe. No, I
warrant you, fays I; and yet you could refufe
me a nafty hundred Pound. At thefe very Words,
I faw Mr. *Williams* riding as faft as he could a-
crofs a Field; and I looked out, and faw a Leafe
of Greyhounds courfing a Hare, which they prefently killed, and I faw him alight, and take it
from them.

My Husband ordered *Robin* to drive towards
him, and looked horribly out of Humour, which
I prefently imputed to Jealoufy. So I began with
him firft; for that is the wifeft way. La, Sir,
fays I; what makes you look fo Angry and
Grim? Doth the Sight of Mr. *Williams* give you
all this Uneafinefs? I am fure, I would never
                                                    have

have married a Woman of whom I had so bad an Opinion, that I must be uneasy at every Fellow she looks at. My Dear, answered he, you injure me extremely, you was not in my Thoughts, nor, indeed, could be while they were covered by so morose a Countenance; I am justly angry with that Parson, whose Family hath been raised from the Dunghill by ours; and who hath received from me twenty Kindnesses, and yet is not contented to destroy the Game in all other Places, which I freely give him leave to do; but hath the Impudence to pursue a few Hares, which I am desirous to preserve, round about this little Coppice. Look, my Dear, pray look, says he; I believe he is going to turn Higler. To confess the Truth, he had no less than three ty'd up behind his Horse, and a fourth he held in his Hand.

Pshaw, says I, I wish all the Hares in the Country were d————d (the Parson himself chid me afterwards for using the Word, tho' it was in his Service.) Here's a Fuss, indeed, about a nasty little pitiful Creature, that is not half so useful as a Cat. You shall not persuade me, that a Man of your Understanding, would quarrel with a Clergyman for such a Trifle. No, no, I am the Hare, for whom poor Parson *Williams* is persecuted; and Jealousy is the Motive. If you had married one of your Quality Ladies, she would have had Lovers by dozens, she would so; but because you have taken a Servant-Maid, forsooth! You are jealous if she but looks (and then I began to Water) at a poor P——a——a——rson in his Pu——u——u——lpit, and then out burst a Flood of Tears.

My

My Dear, faid he, for Heaven's fake dry your
Eyes, and don't let him be a Witnefs of your
Tears, which I fhould be forry to think might be
imputed to my Unkindnefs; I have already gi-
ven you fome Proofs that I am not jealous of this
Parfon; I will now give you a very ftrong One:
For I will mount my Horfe, and you fhall take
Williams into the Coach. You may be fure, this
Motion pleafed me, yet I pretended to make as
light of it as poffible, and told him, I was forry his
Behaviour had made fome fuch glaring Inftance,
neceffary to the perfect clearing my Character.

He foon came up to Mr. *Williams*, who had
attempted to ride off, but was prevented by one of
our Horfemen, whom my Husband fent to ftop
him. When we met, my Husband asked him
how he did with a very good humoured Air, and
told him he perceived he had found good Sport
that Morning. He anfwered pretty moderate, Sir;
for that he had found the three Hares tied on to
the Saddle dead in a Ditch (winking on me at
the fame Time) and added he was forry there
was fuch a Rot among them.

Well, fays Mr. *Booby*, if you pleafe, Mr.
Williams, you fhall come in and ride with my
Wife. For my own part, I will mount on
Horfeback; for it is fine Weather, and befides
it doth not become me to loll in a Chariot, whilft
a Clergyman rides on Horfeback.

At which Words, Mr. *Booby* leapt out, and
Mr. *Williams* leapt in, in an inftant, telling my
Hufband as he mounted, he was glad to fee fuch

a

a Reformation, and that if he continued his Refpect to the Clergy, he might aſſure himſelf of Bleſ- ſings from above.

It was now that the Airing began to grow plea- ſant to me. Mr. *Williams,* who never had but one Fault, *viz.* that he generally ſmells, of Tobacco, was now perfectly ſweet ; for he had for two Days together enjoined himſelf as a Penance not to ſmoke till he had kiſſed my Lips. I will looſen you from that Obligation, ſays I, and ob- ſerving my Huſband looking another way, I gave him a charming Kiſs, and then he asked me Queſtions concerning my Wedding-night ; this actually made me bluſh: I vow I did not think it had been in him.

As he went along, he began to diſcourſe very learnedly, and told me the Fleſh and the Spirit were too diſtinct Matters, which had not the leaſt relation to each other. That all immaterial Subſtances (thoſe were his very Words) ſuch as Love, Deſire, and ſo forth, were guided by the Spirit : But fine Houſes, large Eſtates, Coaches, and dainty Entertainments were the Product of the Fleſh. Therefore, ſays he, my Dear, you have two Husbands, one the Object of your Love, and to ſatisfy your Deſire ; the other the Object of your Neceſſity, and to furniſh you with thoſe other Conveniencies. (I am ſure I remember every Word, for he repeated it three Times ; O he is very good whenever I deſire him to repeat a thing to me three times he always doth it!) as then the Spirit is preferable to the Fleſh, ſo am I preferable to your other Huſband, to whom I am antecedent in Time likewiſe. I

E ſay

say these things, my Dear, (said he) to satisfie your Conscience. A Fig for my Conscience, said I, when shall I meet you again in the Garden?.

My Husband now rode up to the Chariot, and asked us how we did I hate the Sight of him. Mr. *Williams* answered very well, at your Service. They then talked of the Weather, and other things, I wished him gone again, every Minute; but all in vain I had no more Opportunity of conversing with Mr. *Williams.*

Well; at Dinner Mr. *Booby* was very civil to Mr. *Williams,* and told him he was sorry for what had happened, and would make him sufficient Amends, if in his power, and desired him to accept of a Note for fifty Pounds; which he was so *good* to receive, notwithstanding all that had past, and told Mr. *Booby,* he hop'd he would be forgiven, and that he would pray for him.

We make a charming Fool of him, i'fackins Times are finely altered, I have entirely got the better of him, and am resolved never to give him his Humour.

O how foolish it is in a Woman, who hath once got the Reins into her own Hand, ever to quit them again.

After Dinner Mr. *Williams* drank the Church *et cætera*; and smiled on me; when my Husband's Turn came, he drank *et cætera* and the Church; for which he was very severely rebuked

by

by Mr. *Williams,* it being a high Crime, it seems, to name any thing before the Church. I do not know what *Et cetera* is, but I believe it is something concerning chusing Pallament Men; for I asked if it was not a Health to Mr. *Booby's* Borough, and Mr. *Williams* with a hearty Laugh answered, Yes, Yes, it is his Borough we mean.

I slipt out as soon as I could, hoping Mr. *Williams* would finish the Squire, as I have heard him say he could easily do, and come to me; but it happened quite otherwise, for in about half an Hour, *Booby* came to me, and told me he had left Mr. *Williams,* the Mayor of his Borough, and two or three Alderman heartily at it, and asked me if I would go hear *Williams* sing a Catch, which, added he, he doth to a Miracle.

Every Opportunity of seeing my dear *Williams,* was agreeable to me, which indeed I scarce had at this Time; for when we returned, the whole Corporation were got together, and the Room was in a Cloud of Tobacco; Parson *Williams* was at the upper End of the Table, and he hath pure round cherry Cheeks, and his Face look'd all the World to nothing like the Sun in a Fog. If the Sun had a Pipe in his Mouth, there would be no Difference.

I began now to grow uneasy, apprehending I should have no more of Mr. *Williams's* Company that Evening, and not at all caring for my Husband, I advised him to sit down and drink for his Country with the rest of the Company; but he refused, and desired me to give him some Tea; swearing nothing made him so sick as to

hear

hear a Parcel of Scoundrels roaring forth the Principles of honeft Men over their Cups, when, fays he, I know moft of them are fuch empty Blockheads, that they don't know their right Hand from their left, and that Fellow there, who hath talked fo much of *Shipping*, at the left Side of the Parfon, in whom they all place a Confidence, if I don't take care, will fell them to my Adverfary.

I don't know why I mention this Stuff to you ; for I am fure I know nothing about *Pollitricks*, more than Parfon *Williams* tells me, who fays that the Court-fide are in the right on't, and that every Chriftian ought to be on the fame with the Bifhops.

When we had finifhed our Tea, we walked in the Garden till it was dark, and then my Hufband propofed, inftead of returning to the Company, (which I defired, that I might fee Parfon *Williams* again,) to fup in another Room by our felves, which, for fear of making him jealous, and confidering too, that Parfon *Williams* would be pretty far gone, I was obliged to confent to.

O! what a devilifh Thing it is, for a Woman to be obliged to go to Bed to a fpindle-fhanked young Squire, fhe doth not like, when there is a jolly Parfon in the fame Houfe fhe is fond of.

In the Morning I grew very peevifh, and in the Dumps, notwithftanding all he could fay or do to pleafe me. I exclaimed againft the Priviledge of Hufbands, and vowed I would not be pulled and tumbled about. At laft he hit on the only Method, which could have brought me into Humour, **and**

and propofed to me a Journey to *London,* within a few Days. This you may eafily guefs pleafed me; for befides the Defire which I have of fhewing my felf forth, of buying fine Cloaths, Jewels, Coaches, Houfes, and ten thoufand other fine Things, Parfon *Williams* is, it feems, going thither too, to be *inftuted.*

O! what a charming Journey I fhall have; for I hope to keep the dear Man in the Chariot with me all the way; and that foolifh Booby (for that is the Name Mr. Williams *hath fet him) will ride on Horfeback.*

So as I fhall have an Opportunity of feeing you fo fhortly, I think I will mention no more Matters to you now. O I had like to have forgot one very material Thing; which is that it will look horribly, for a Lady of my Quality and Fafhion, to own fuch a Woman as you for my Mother. Therefore we muft meet in private only, and if you will never claim me, nor mention me to any one, I will always allow you what is very handfome. Parfon *Williams* hath greatly advifed me in this, and fays, he thinks I fhould do very well to lay out twenty Pounds, and fet you up in a little Chandler's Shop: but you muft remembr all my Favours to you will depend on your Secrecy; for I am pofitively refolved, I will not be known to be your Daughter; and if you tell any one fo, I fhall deny it with all my Might, which Parfon *Williams* fays, I may do with a fafe Confcience, being now a married Woman. So I reft

Yonr humble Servant

SHAMELA.
P.

P. S. The ftrangeft Fancy hath enter'd into my Booby's Head, that can be imagined. He is refolved to have a Book made about him and me, he propofed it to Mr. *Williams*; and offered him a Reward for his Pains; but he fays he never writ any thing of that kind, but will recommend my Hufband, when he comes to Town, to a Parfon *who does that Sort of Bufinefs for Folks*, one who can make my Hufband, and me, and Parfon *Williams*, to be all great People; for he *can make black white*, it feems. Well, but they fay my Name is to be altered, Mr. *Williams*, fays the firft Syllabub hath too comical a Sound, fo it is to be changed into *Pamela*; I own I can't imagine what can be faid ; for to be fure I fhan't confefs any of my Secrets to them, and fo I whifpered Parfon *Williams* about that, who anfwered me, I need not give my felf any Trouble: for the Gentleman *who writes Lives*, never afked more than a few Names of his Cuftomers, and that he made all the reft out of his own Head; you miftake, Child, faid he, if you apprehend any Truths are to be delivered. So far on the contrary, if you had not been acquainted with the Name, you would not have known it to be your own Hiftory. I have feen a *Piece of his Performance*, where the Perfon, whofe Life was written, could he have rifen from the Dead again, would not have even fufpected he had been aimed at, unlefs by the Title of the Book, which was fuperfcribed with his Name. Well, all thefe Matters are ftrange to me, yet I can't help laughing, to think I fhall fee my felf in a printed Book.

So

SHAMELA. 55

So much for Mrs. *Shamela*, or *Pamela*, which
I have taken Pains to tranfcribe from the Originals, fent down by her Mother in a Rage, at the
Propofal in her laft Letter. The Originals themfelves are in my Hands, and fhall be communicated to you, if you think proper to make them
publick ; and certainly they will have their Ufe.
The Character of *Shamela*, will make young
Gentlemen wary how they take the moft fatal
Step both to themfelves and Families, by youthful, hafty and improper Matches; indeed, they
may affure themfelves, that all fuch Profpects of
Happinefs are vain and delufive, and that they
facrifice all the folid Comforts of their Lives, to
a very tranfient Satisfaction of a Paffion, which
how hot fo ever it be, will be foon cooled; and
when cooled, will afford them nothing but
Repentance.

Can any thing be more miferable, than to be
defpifed by the whole World, and that muft certainly be the Confequence ; to be defpifed by the
Perfon obliged, which it is more than probable
will be the Confequence, and of which, we fee
an Inftance in *Shamela*; and laftly to defpife one's
felf, which muft be the Refult of any Reflection
on fo weak and unworthy a Choice.

As to the Character of Parfon *Williams*, I am
forry it is a true one. Indeed thofe who do not
know him, will hardly believe it fo; but what
Scandal doth it throw on the Order to have one
bad Member, unlefs they endeavour to fcreen
and protect him? In him you fee a Picture of
almoft every Vice expofed in naufeous and odious
Colours, and if a Clergyman would afk me by
what

what Pattern he fhould form himfelf, I would
fay, Be the reverfe of *Williams*: So far therefore
he may be of ufe to the Clergy themfelves,
and though God forbid there fhould be many
Williams's amongft them, you and I are too
honeft to pretend, that the Body wants no Reformation.

To fay the Truth, I think no greater Inftance
of the contrary can be given than that which appears in your Letter. The confederating to cry
up a nonfenfical ridiculous Book, (I believe the
moft extenfively fo of any ever yet publifhed,)
and to be fo weak and fo wicked as to pretend
to make it a Matter of Religion ; whereas fo far
from having any moral Tendency, the Book is
by no means innocent : For,

Firft, There are many lafcivious Images in it,
very improper to be laid before the Youth of
either Sex.

2*dly*, Young Gentlemen are here taught, that
to marry their Mother's Chambermaids, and to
indulge the Paffion of Luft, at the Expence of
Reafon and Common Senfe, is an Act of Religion, Virtue, and Honour ; and, indeed the fureft
Road to Happinefs.

3*dly*, All Chambermaids are ftrictly enjoyned
to look out after their Mafters; they are taught
to ufe little Arts to that purpofe : And laftly, are
countenanced in Impertinence to their Superiours,
and in betraying the Secrets of Families.

4*thly,*

4*thly,* In the Character of Mrs. *Jewkes* Vice is rewarded; whence every Housekeeper may learn the Usefulness of pimping and bawding for her Master.

5*thly,* In Parson *Williams,* who is represented as a faultless Character, we see a busy Fellow, intermeddling with the private Affairs of his Patron, whom he is very ungratefully forward to expose and condemn on every Occasion.

Many more Objections might, if I had Time or Inclination, be made to this Book; but I apprehend, what hath been said is sufficient to perswade you of the use which may arise from publishing an Antidote to this Poison. I have therefore sent you the Copies of these Papers, and if you have Leisure to communicate them to the Press, I will transmit you the Originals, tho' I assure you, the Copies are exact.

I shall only add, that there is not the least Foundation for any thing which is said of Lady *Davers,* or any of the other Ladies; all that is merely to be imputed to the Invention of the Biographer. I have particularly enquired after Lady *Davers,* and don't hear Mr. *Booby* hath such a Relation, or that there is indeed any such Person existing. I am,

Dear Sir,

Most faithfully and respectfully,

Your humble Servant,

J. OLIVER.

F   *Parson*

Parſon TICKLETEXT *to Parſon* OLIVER.

Dear *S I R,*

I Have read over the Hiſtory of *Shamela,* as it
appears in thoſe authentick Copies you favour
me with, and am very much aſhamed of the
Character, which I was haſtily prevailed on to
give that Book. I am equally angry with the
pert Jade herſelf, and with the Author of her
Life: For I ſcarce know yet to whom I chiefly
owe an Impoſition, which hath been ſo general,
that if Numbers could defend me from Shame, I
ſhould have no Reaſon to apprehend it.

As I have your implied Leave to publiſh,
what you ſo kindly ſent me, I ſhall not wait for
the Originals, as you aſſure me the Copies are
exact, and as i am really impatient to do what
I think a ſerviceable Act of Juſtice to the
World.

Finding by the End of her laſt Letter, that
the little Huſſy was in Town, I made it pretty
much my Buſineſs to enquire after her, but with
no effect hitherto: As ſoon as I ſucceed in this
Enquiry, you ſhall hear what Diſcoveries I can
learn. You will pardon the Shortneſs of this
Letter, as you ſhall be troubled with a much
longer very ſoon: And believe me,

Dear Sir,

Your moſt faithful Servant,

THO. TICKLETEXT.

P. S.

P. S. Since I writ, I have a certain Account, that Mr. *Booby* hath caught his Wife in bed with *Williams*; hath turned her off, and is profecuting him in the fpiritual Court.

F I N I S.